Praise for Curiosity House:
The Shrunken Head and Lauren Oliver's Liesl & Po

'Stupendous and stupefying! A riddle wrapped in a mystery inside a Shrunken Head. If you aren't curious about *Curiosity House* somebody must have pickled your brain and put it in a jar. Read this book immediately.'

Pseudonymous Bosch, *New York Times*
bestselling author of the Secret Series and *Bad Magic*

'Step right up! Step right up! Mystery, murder, curses, and sideshow freaks! Or are they superheroes? There's only one way to find out . . . Read *Curiosity House*! You'll be glad you did!'

Adam Gidwitz, *New York Times* bestselling
author of the A Tale Dark and Grimm series

'An absolute delight . . . The story is packed with mystery, murder, adventure, humour and magic, but above all it is a beautiful evocation of loss, tempered by the gradual blossoming of friendship, trust and hope. Although aimed at younger readers, the lightness of touch and the tenderness of the message could make grown men weep.'

Daily Mail on *Liesl & Po*

'A gorgeous story – timeless and magical.'

Rebecca Stead, Newbery winner
for *When You Reach Me*

'*Liesl & Po* by Lauren Oliver brings much-needed magic to an increasingly neglected age group . . . there are some exquisitely drawn characters . . . it's books like this, with its classic quest plot, intertwined with lyrical metaphysics, that can set a child up for life.'

Sunday Telegraph on *Liesl & Po*

CURIOSITY HOUSE

~THE~
SCREAMING STATUE

LAUREN OLIVER
& H.C. CHESTER

HODDER

First published in the United States in 2016 by HarperCollins Children's Books,
a division of HarperCollins Publishers.

First published in Great Britain in 2016 by Hodder & Stoughton
An Hachette UK company

First published in paperback in 2017

I

A CIP catalogue record for this title is available from the British Library

ISBN 978 1 444 77725 3

Typeset in Mrs Eaves

Printed and bound in Great Britain by Clays Ltd, St Ives plc

Hodder & Stoughton policy is to use papers that are
natural, renewable and recyclable products and made from
wood grown in sustainable forests. The logging and manufacturing
processes are expected to conform to the environmental
regulations of the country of origin.

Hodder & Stoughton Ltd
Carmelite House
50 Victoria Embankment
London EC4Y 0DZ

www.hodder.co.uk

Lauren Oliver dedicates this book to her amazing aunt Sandy, for her support—and copyediting skills!

Once again, H. C. Chester wishes to dedicate the following volume to his faithful companion (and most appreciative reader!), Trudy.

1

"Nothing," Max said disgustedly, peeling away from the window. Her palms had left prints on the glass. "Not a single stupid visitor."

Pippa groaned. "It's too hot for a show," she said. She was sprawled out on the cool linoleum floor, fanning herself with one of the brochures from the information table, which advertised the museum's newest exhibit: a pair of ancient scissors said to be the ones used by Delilah to cut off Samson's hair.

It was only eleven o'clock in the morning and already topping ninety degrees in New York City. The street outside of Dumfrey's Dime Museum of Freaks, Oddities, and Wonders was as still as a painting. Max, Sam,

Thomas, and Pippa had camped out in the lobby overnight, since the attic where they slept with the other performers felt like a steam bath.

"Pip's right," Sam said, glancing up temporarily from the steel pipe in his hands, which he was twisting and bending into a circle. "Anyone with a brain is at home in front of a fan."

"Or swimming in an ice bath," Pippa said. "Or moving to the North Pole."

Max sighed. What was the point of perfecting her knife act—what was the point of doing *anything*?—if there was never an audience to applaud her? Nonetheless, she removed an apple from the basket at her feet and balanced it carefully on the mounted head of a grizzly bear. Then she backed up a dozen feet, wrestled a blindfold over her eyes, lifted the knife, and threw.

She imagined, as she did, that the apple was the face of Professor Nicholas Rattigan: scientist, madman, fugitive.

Maker.

There was a loud thunk.

"Yikes," Pippa said. "Remind me not to volunteer for your act."

Max whipped off the blindfold and saw the knife buried deep in the fur between the bear's glass eyes.

2 ☞

She scowled. "There must be a draft in here," she said.

"I wish." Pippa began fanning more vigorously.

"What do you think?" Sam held out the metal pipe he had been shaping, which was now a complicated pattern of loops and twists. "Does this look like a rabbit to you?"

"Is it upside down?" Pippa said, squinting.

"It looks like a rabbit that got run over by a garbage truck," Max said. The heat made her very moody.

Sam sighed and began straightening out the pipe again. "If Mr. Dumfrey would only let me have a *real* rabbit to model from . . ."

Pippa reached over to pat his foot consolingly. Sam was absolutely desperate for a pet, and was always pushing crackers through the bars of Mr. Dumfrey's pet cockatoo's cage and trying to make friends with the mice that lived in the walls. But Mr. Dumfrey wouldn't let him have an animal of his own, for fear that Sam would accidentally crush, squeeze, or pulverize it, as he often did to doorknobs, railings, and chairbacks. It wasn't Sam's fault. As Mr. Dumfrey was fond of reminding him, he was the strongest twelve-and-three-quarters-year-old in the country—possibly in the whole world.

"Listen to this," Thomas said, smoothing down his

hair, which as usual was coated with plaster and dust and refused to lie down flat. Thomas used the stairs only when he couldn't help it. He mostly preferred to travel the museum's walls, squeezing himself into the pipes and air ducts, shimmying through narrow spaces hardly wider than a flowerpot, and popping out of metal grates when you least expected it. "What do you call a woman who doesn't have all her fingers on one hand?"

Pippa groaned again. "Come on, Thomas. Lay off. It's too hot for riddles."

"Just try," he urged. Thomas always had his nose stuck in a book. Lately, it was *Brain Puzzles & Teasers*. He read even when he was eating; the pages were splattered with tomato sauce and bacon grease.

"Unlucky," Max said.

"I'd call her normal." The new janitor, William "Lash" Langtry, sauntered into the lobby, carrying a bucket and a mop. He wiggled the fingers of his left hand. "I'd hate to have all ten fingers on one hand."

Thomas grinned and shut the book. "Lash wins."

Max rebalanced the apple on the grizzly's head, backed up, and took aim again. This time the knife went straight through the core, and the apple, now sliced neatly in two, thudded to the floor.

"Now there's a pretty trick." Lash leaned on his broom. "Reminds me of my old bullwhip routine. 'Course I was particular to strawberries . . . Make a nice kind of mess when they explode."

"Show us," Max said.

"Yeah, show us," Pippa said, munching on one of the apple halves.

"Just one trick," Sam said.

Lash colored a deep red. He turned his attention to the floor and began furiously sweeping the same six-inch patch of linoleum. "I reckon those days are behind me," he said. "My hands ain't what they used to be. Eyes, neither."

The kids exchanged a look. William "Lash" Langtry had known Mr. Dumfrey years and years earlier, when Lash was a world-famous circus performer. He was an ace with a whip: he could snuff out a candle from a distance of forty yards, and knock a stick of gum off the tongue of a volunteer.

But the years had taken their toll. He was as thin as a fence pole and his skin was red and deeply wrinkled, like a sun-dried tomato. And nobody could miss the flask tucked in his waistband, the redness of his eyes, or the way his hands shook, especially in the morning. When he had turned up at the museum only a few weeks earlier, Mr. Dumfrey had given him the only available position.

The once world-famous Lash Langtry was the museum's new janitor, replacing the late—and not especially lamented—Potts.

Miss Fitch bustled in from the Hall of Worldwide Wonders. "There you are," she said to Lash in a curiously high-pitched voice. "I've been looking all over for you."

Max swallowed back a snort. Sam rapidly transformed a laugh into a cough. And Thomas opened his book and once again plastered his nose to the page.

Typically, Miss Fitch wore a variation of the same shapeless black dress, black stockings, and black shoes, as if she were always prepared to attend someone's funeral. But today, she had on a dress in a hideous yellow that made her look like an overgrown banana. Her cheeks were streaked with rouge, applied so recklessly it looked as though a child had been finger painting on her face. Her lashes were thickly clumped with mascara, and her lips were the color of a fire truck.

"Are . . . you all right?" Pippa asked.

"Why wouldn't I be?" Miss Fitch snapped in her usual voice. She smoothed her hair down anxiously. "The twins insisted on making me up . . . I daresay it's very silly." She batted her eyelashes furiously at Lash. Flakes of mascara swirled to the floor.

Sam's coughing fit got even louder.

Lash tipped his hat. "I think you look mighty pretty, Miss Fitch," he said.

"Oh, Lash!" Miss Fitch turned nearly as red as her lipstick. "You're too much." She let out a series of tittering squeaks. Max felt like she had swallowed a balloon. Was Miss Fitch *giggling*? "I need your help in the, erm, Hall of Wax. We're rearranging the French Revolution exhibit and I'm simply not *strong* enough to move the guillotine by myself."

"Anything for you, lil lady," Lash said, offering his arm to Miss Fitch. She squeaked with pleasure again. She was fluttering her eyelashes so fast, it was a miracle she didn't begin to levitate.

Sam was now coughing so much, his face had turned purple.

"For heaven's sake, drink some water, Sam," Miss Fitch hissed, before turning back to Lash and plastering a smile on her face.

As Lash and Miss Fitch proceeded up the stairs to the second floor, Lash's voice floated back to them.

"Did I ever tell you about the time a lion busted out of its cage and my bullwhip saved a whole passel of people from getting chewed to splinters? No? Why, it must have been twenty years ago now . . ."

Max sighed. She was all out of apples, and she doubted whether Danny, the dwarf, who was doing the cooking today, would spare her any more. Time seemed to be moving at a crawl. She returned to the window, hoping the view might have changed. But Forty-Third Street was as empty as ever. Sergio was trudging slowly down the street from Ninth Avenue, pushing his pretzel cart. Henry, the day porter at the St. Edna Hotel, was sleeping, chin-to-chest, on his stool. Little Jack McDonnell, who lived across the street, was playing jacks on his stoop.

She looked the other way and saw a large red blob carrying a vast handkerchief barreling toward the museum. Then she realized it was not a blob carrying a handkerchief, but Mr. Dumfrey carrying a newspaper. He was red in the face and wearing a typically outlandish outfit: this time, a red silken kimono and matching slippers.

"Mr. Dumfrey's—" she began. Before she could say *back*, the front door flew open and Mr. Dumfrey burst into the lobby, waving the paper triumphantly above his head. Max recognized it as *The Daily Screamer*, the tabloid that had only a few months ago featured several articles, most of them insulting, about the children and their abilities.

"I've got it!" he cried. "A guaranteed crowd-pleaser! A surefire showstopper! A bona fide blockbuster! They'll come running like bees to a flame, like moths to honey!"

"I think you mean like *moths* to a flame and *bees* to honey," Pippa said.

Mr. Dumfrey evidently didn't hear her. "We'll be rich!" he said, beaming. "Nothing to drum up business like an execution."

And he shook out the newspaper so that the headline was visible:

RICHSTONE TO FRY FOR WIFE'S MURDER!

"I don't get it," Max said. "What's so special about this Richbone—Witchstone—*whatever* his name is?"

"My dear child." Mr. Dumfrey snatched off his glasses and peered at Max as if to verify that she wasn't an impostor. "The murder of Mrs. Richstone is an absolute sensation! It's the crime of the century!"

Six months earlier, heiress Rachel Richstone had been found dead in the bedroom of her Park Avenue apartment, killed by a blow to her head from a golf club belonging to her husband. Rumor was that she had recently become involved with a young Australian fortune hunter, Mr. Edmund Snyder, and that Manfred Richstone was mad with jealousy. Though Manfred protested his innocence, he was arrested and quickly found guilty of murder.

"I think what Max *means*, Mr. Dumfrey," Pippa interjected softly, "is what's Mrs. Richstone's murder got to do with us?"

"Everything!" he answered gaily. "People are clamoring for every last detail about the case—and we'll give it to them. Oh, yes. We'll *show* them! Just imagine: A new wax installation. A diorama of the whole grisly, gruesome scene, from the bed frame down to the bloodstains. It has the makings of a classic piece: the beautiful heiress, Rachel, clubbed to death by her dashing husband! We'll be flooded with business! We'll be drowning in it!"

Thomas had at last abandoned his book and was reading the paper instead. "Mr. Richstone says he's innocent," he said, looking up from the article.

Dumfrey waved a hand. "You can't expect him to say anything else, can you?" he said dismissively. "He's facing the chair."

"I don't know." Pippa had never liked the Hall of Wax, and Murderers' Row was her least favorite place in the museum. The small and dusty room on the second floor contained a vast selection of life-sized wax figures and dummy models, depicting famous crime scenes and grisly murders. She avoided Murderers' Row whenever she could; when she couldn't, she walked as quickly as possible past the exhibits, holding her breath, as she did when she passed a graveyard. "It seems kind of . . . wrong."

Dumfrey patted her shoulder affectionately. "Dear, sweet Pippa," he said, as if she were five years old and not twelve. "Nothing could be more *right*. We'll be preserving dear Mrs. Richstone's memory. We'll be keeping her spirit alive!"

Pippa shivered. That's exactly what she was worried about: that somewhere, trapped in those wax bodies, was a live spirit.

"Now let me see. . . ." Mr. Dumfrey tapped a finger on his chin, as he often did when he was thinking. "We'll take two dummies from the costume room—I'm sure Miss Fitch can spare them. We'll need new heads, of course. . . ."

Thomas groaned. "I thought we agreed. No more heads."

In the spring, Mr. Dumfrey's Dime Museum had suffered a series of misfortunes, beginning with the theft of a prized shrunken head, supposedly a relic from an ancient Amazonian tribe. *The Curse of the Shrunken Head* had become a citywide sensation, especially when several people turned up dead. The children had been forced to try to clear Mr. Dumfrey's name when he was accused of murder.

Mr. Dumfrey had been released. But the search for the real murderer had led the children directly into the arms of Professor Rattigan. Brilliant, ruthless, and recently a fugitive from prison, Professor Rattigan had stolen the kids when they were young for his twisted experiments. Now he wanted to use the children to help rebuild his empire. They had barely escaped him, and for two months had lived in fear of his return. But it had been more than sixty days and still no sign of him, so they were at last starting to relax.

"No more *shrunken* heads," Mr. Dumfrey corrected him, wagging a finger in Thomas's face. "This is altogether different. I'll need to pay a visit to our old friend Eckleberger right away."

"Freckles!" Pippa exclaimed. She had known Herr Eckleberger since she was little more than a toddler and had invented his nickname then, when she was unable to string together the long series of syllables that made up his name and had instead shortened them into a word her tongue could find its way around. "We haven't seen him in ages."

"I never thanked him for the present he sent me,"

Sam said. For Christmas, Herr Eckleberger had sent him an impressively realistic bust of Sam's head, crafted entirely out of candy. Much of the head had been cannibalized by now, so that only one half of Sam's candy face remained, along with a single jelly bean where his left ear had once been.

"And I never returned the book he lent me," Thomas said. "*The Hidden World of Mathematical Proportions*."

"*Please*, Mr. Dumfrey," Pippa said, "can we come?"

Mr. Dumfrey consulted his pocket watch. "All right, then," he said. "Run along and get your shoes on. Our dear old Freckles is a very busy man."

Siegfried Eckleberger, nicknamed Freckles, was the closest thing to a grandparent Thomas, Pippa, and Sam had ever known, and Pippa found that even the thought of visiting him lifted her spirits enormously.

For weeks she had been dogged by a nasty, lingering feeling of unease, a feeling kind of like turning a corner and realizing you were lost. More than ever she found herself thinking of the parents she had never known, obsessing about them, wondering whether they were still out there and still looking for her.

She knew why, of course. Until a few months ago she'd always believed that her parents had abandoned her because she was different. But she knew the truth now. She'd been taken from her parents, stolen as a child by Nicholas Rattigan, deranged scientist, to be the guinea pig in one of his terrible experiments. She hadn't been born different; she'd been *made* different. Her parents hadn't gotten rid of her.

Which maybe, just maybe, meant they might want her back.

As they walked, Mr. Dumfrey told Max all about Eckleberger as they left the museum and ventured into the heat, which was as wet and heavy as the slap of a dog's tongue. A famous sculptor, Eckleberger had once traveled the whole world, molding portraits of queens and dictators, business tycoons and baseball players, out of plaster and wax. He had shaken hands with Al Capone and once, famously, lost a game of bridge to Winston Churchill. He also did work for the police department, creating sculpted busts of wanted men based on the descriptions of their victims; one such model had been used to capture the notorious "Necktie Strangler of Staten Island," Sergio Voss.

One of Pippa's favorite stories involved Freckles's involvement in a government plot in Belgium. Freckles had saved the day by smuggling a critical document from one person to another inside the wax head of

Thomas Jefferson, thus saving the country from ruin. To this day, Monsieur Cabillaud, the children's pinhead tutor and a Belgian, could not see Herr Eckleberger without saluting.

But now he was nearly eighty-five years old, and though he was as smart as ever, and as capable with his hands, he hardly ever left his studio anymore.

"You'll see, Max," Sam said reassuringly as they made their way with Dumfrey through the bustle of Times Square. "You're going to love him."

"He sounds like a dingbat to me," Max said.

"Now, now, Max." Using his large stomach to clear a path for himself, Mr. Dumfrey pushed his way through a knot of people gathered outside of the Metropole Radio Store. "It isn't fair to judge. Some of my very best friends are dingbats! Smalls the giant was once declared insane in the state of Florida . . . all a terrible misunderstanding . . . apparently a newspaper mistook one of his poems for a bomb threat . . . really it was about the lily flower but, well, with a title like 'The Explosion,' I suppose you can understand—"

"Mr. Dumfrey, *wait*." Pippa seized Mr. Dumfrey's arm. Despite the heat, she suddenly felt very cold.

A newscaster's voice was blaring from one of the

radios on display in the window of the Metropole.

". . . reliable reports say that Professor Nicholas Rattigan, the FBI's public enemy number one, has been spotted in the Chicago area . . ."

Just the name, *Nicholas Rattigan*, was like something unpleasant snaking down one's back. Pippa shivered.

"Oh, dear," Mr. Dumfrey murmured. His lips tightened to a fine white line. For the thousandth time since Pippa and the others had first confronted Nicholas Rattigan—and then learned, to their utter shock, that Rattigan and Dumfrey were actually related—she searched Mr. Dumfrey's face for some resemblance to his half brother. But she could find none. Mr. Dumfrey was round everywhere that Rattigan was angular. His face was pink where Rattigan's face was the sallow color of a dirty yellow waistband. The only similarity was in their eyes, which were blue. But where Mr. Dumfrey's eyes reminded Pippa of a summer sky, Rattigan's eyes were the pale blue color of an ice-covered lake. Sometimes now, when the old nightmare visited of long, dim hallways and cage bars and the sound of crying, she thought she heard also the echo of his laugh, cold and mirthless, like the howl of wind across snow.

"Rattigan!" Thomas cried. "What's he doing all the way out in Chicago?"

"Good riddance," Max said. "I hope he keeps going all the way to China."

"I hope he gets caught and thrown into a cage, where he belongs," Sam said with uncharacteristic anger.

Mr. Dumfrey patted Sam's shoulder. "I'm sure the police will close in on him soon," he said. But Pippa saw his left eyelid give a little flutter, as it did whenever he was telling a lie: declaring that a shriveled mermaid was absolutely authentic, when it was actually made of plaster, assorted doll parts, and a dried fishtail; or claiming that an old turkey feather was the actual quill used by Thomas Jefferson to sign the Declaration of Independence.

The newscaster on the radio had passed on to another story. A tiger had escaped from the Bronx Zoo and had been spotted prowling down Pelham Parkway. The crowd around the Metropole store began to disperse.

"Sam's right," Thomas said. "I won't feel safe until Rattigan's behind bars again."

"Don't worry, Thomas," Mr. Dumfrey said as they continued on their way. "I won't let him get to you again. You can count on me."

That time, Pippa was *sure* his eyelid fluttered.

3

Freckles lived in a narrow three-story brownstone with a dingy facade and a half dozen brown plants withering on the front stoop. The shades were drawn in every window, but Max yelped when she thought she saw a terrible face leering out at her from the second floor: straggly black hair, crooked yellow teeth, mouth open as though in an animal roar.

Mr. Dumfrey followed her gaze.

"Don't be afraid, Max," he said. "That's just one of Herr Eckleberger's little jokes. It's a statue, you see? Designed to keep the children away on Halloween, I daresay."

Max blinked. Mr. Dumfrey was right, of course. When she looked a little longer, she saw that the man in the window didn't move or blink. "Nuttier than an almond factory," she muttered. Embarrassed to have been so easily fooled, she hung back while the others gathered in front of the door. On it, a small brass plaque read: *Go Away*.

The words were repeated when Mr. Dumfrey raised his fist to knock. "Go away!" cried a gravelly and heavily accented voice, so it sounded like *Go avay*.

"My dear Siegfried," said Mr. Dumfrey, raising his voice to be heard through the door. "It's Horatio Dumfrey. I've brought the children, too."

A rectangular peephole slid open. A pair of dark eyes appeared, surrounded by so many wrinkles and folds they looked like raisins set in the middle of a collapsing soufflé.

"Hello, Freckles," Sam said cheerfully. Other than Dumfrey, he was the only one tall enough to be visible to the man behind the door.

"Dumfrey, eh?" the man croaked out, his eyes ticking from Dumfrey to Sam and back again.

"The very same," Dumfrey said pleasantly.

"Prove it!" he trumpeted. "What's the secret password?" It sounded like: *Vat iss der zeegret passvort?*

Mr. Dumfrey frowned. "Surely, Siegfried. After all these years . . ."

"Der passvort!"

"For heaven's sake." Mr. Dumfrey began patting his checkered vest front. "I always mean to write it down . . ."

"Try the date book in your left pants pocket," Pippa suggested.

"What have I told you, Pippa, about reading the contents of people's pockets without their permission? Although I suppose in this case . . ." Mr. Dumfrey withdrew a small leather-bound book from his tailcoat pocket, so stuffed with extra papers, crumpled receipts, and miscellaneous scribbled notes, it looked as though the leather binding had tried to swallow the contents of a paper factory. No sooner had he cracked open the cover than dozens of scraps of paper swirled onto the stoop. "Oh, dear, oh, dear," Mr. Dumfrey said, flipping forward a few pages, and shedding more notes and business cards as he went. "Let me think. I'm sure I did write it down somewhere. Is it 'A quart of milk, two cans of tuna, and a dozen eggs'? No, wait. That's a grocery list for Miss Fitch. What about 'notice of overdrawn account'? No. That can't be right. That's a letter from my bank. How about"—he squinted at the slip of the paper in his hand—"'two-headed mongoose?'"

"Not even close!" howled Herr Eckleberger.

Mr. Dumfrey scratched his head, frowning. "Hmm. That must have been part of my Christmas wish list. Now let me think . . ."

"I'm losing patience," said Herr Eckleberger. His eyebrows—huge and knitted as fleece socks—were drawn tightly over his glittering dark eyes.

"A moment, my friend, a moment," Mr. Dumfrey said, still flipping through his date book. "It isn't 'Mexican python' or 'Chinese funeral urn' or 'stuffed cabbage' . . . ?"

"No, no, and no."

"Here, Mr. Dumfrey." Pippa had kneeled to sweep up the mass of fallen papers on the stoop. Dumfrey shoved them carelessly into his pocket.

"You missed one," Max said, and plucked a small printed receipt from the straggly arms of a dying azalea bush.

"Thank you, Mackenzie," Mr. Dumfrey said, glancing absentmindedly at the receipt. Then he let out a triumphant cry. "Aha! I knew I had marked it down somewhere." He held out the receipt so that Max could see the letters scribbled across the top. "The password is . . . *Schokoladeveinetzmann!*" The eyes vanished from the peephole. Max counted the sound of four locks opening, one after the other.

"*Schokolade*what?" Thomas whispered to Dumfrey.

"It's a kind of Christmas chocolate," Dumfrey responded, also in a whisper. "German, of course. One of his harder passwords to remember. Dear old Siegfried has an absolute passion for chocolate. Ah, but here he is. Siegfried, my fine fellow!"

The door swung open. Max didn't know what to expect after their rude treatment. Even Herr Eckleberger's bushy gray eyebrows had looked threatening through the peephole, as if they might jump off his face and tickle a person to death. Dumfrey said Eckleberger hardly left the house anymore. Maybe he'd finally cracked, like an egg, and all his brains had been scrambled.

But the man standing before them, arms open, was smiling widely, so that all his wrinkles melted toward his ears and he suddenly looked much younger.

"Horatio, *mein* old friend!" he said warmly, stepping forward to pump Mr. Dumfrey's hand vigorously. "Thomas! Pippa! Samson! Come in, come in. It has been too long." He turned his twinkling black eyes on Max. "And who is this?"

"That's Mackenzie," Mr. Dumfrey said. "Say hello, Max."

Something in Eckleberger's kind expression made

Max feel shy. "Hullo," she muttered.

"Mackenzie's incredible with a knife," Sam piped up, and then blushed.

"Is she? How wonderful!" It came out: *Hovunderful.* "Now come in, come in! You're just in time. I vas just making some *Plätzchen.*"

"Some what?" Max said as they all shuffled forward into the darkness of the hall.

"Cookies, child!" Eckleberger said, beaming, and closed the door behind them, carefully locking all four locks.

Eckleberger's studio was large, high-ceilinged, and full of light. Every possible surface was cluttered with statues in varying degrees of completion: a plaster head sat next to several clay noses, drying on a tray; an enormous wax torso shouldered up next to a wire frame, roughly human-shaped, covered with papier-mâché and strips of newspaper. The bed—the only indication Max could see that Eckleberger used the space for living as well as for work—was strewn with sketchbooks, cardboard boxes, and colored pencils. Sketches were tacked to every wall, and when the breeze came in through one of the open windows, they rustled like autumn leaves. The air smelled equally of paper and clay, cinnamon and butter.

While Thomas peppered Eckleberger with various riddles from his new book, Max wandered the room, careful not to knock into anything. She was immediately drawn to a beautiful silver scalpel, with a teardrop-shaped blade, which was sitting out next to a lump of unformed clay. Unconsciously, she reached out to touch it, but Eckleberger stopped her.

"Careful, fräulein," he said. He waggled a finger—which was as knotted as an old piece of oak—in her direction. "It's very sharp."

"It'd be perfect for my act," Max said wistfully.

"Watch out, Freckles. She might *steal* it," Pippa said. Pippa had obviously not forgiven Max for her habit of pocketing whatever items happened to be conveniently lying around.

Max glared. "I never stole nothing."

"For heaven's sake, Max," cried Pippa, exhaling so hard that her long, straight bangs lifted off her forehead. "It's 'I never stole *anything*.' How many times do I have to tell you?"

Eckleberger just laughed. "Perhaps I vill leaf you ze little knife in my vill, if you are a very goot girl, Max."

Thomas grinned. "Fat chance of that." Max stuck her tongue out at him when Eckleberger wasn't looking.

"Now, my dear friends," Eckleberger said as he

bustled over to a worktable, shoving aside a wax head bearing an uncanny resemblance to the King of England, and gestured for the children and Dumfrey to sit, "to vat do I owe the pleasure?"

"I have a job for you, old friend," Mr. Dumfrey said as Eckleberger bent over an oven in the corner, almost entirely obscured from view by a large coatrack filled with hanging wigs, and produced a large tray filled with lacy, golden-brown cookies. That must be where the smell of butter came from, Max realized.

"It'll be your best—your most astounding—your most momentous work yet!" Mr. Dumfrey kept talking, even as he fed a large cookie into his mouth. "Surely you've been following the case of poor Mrs. Richstone and her husband, Manfred?"

"I have seen it mentioned, yes," Eckleberger said. Then: "Be careful, children. Zey are very hot."

It was too late: Max had already burned her tongue. It was worth it. The cookie tasted like hot cocoa and spiced milk and snuggling under a blanket by a warm fire.

"Seen it mentioned?" Mr. Dumfrey repeated. His eyes went wide behind his glasses. "My dear Freckles"— agitatedly, he brushed the crumbs off his shirtfront, leaving buttery streaks in their place—"it's the crime of the century. *Seen it mentioned?* It's been everywhere! People can talk of nothing else!"

"Manfred Richstone will get the chair for it," Thomas said in between mouthfuls of cookie.

Eckleberger looked at him sharply. "Vill he now?" He stroked the half dozen gray whiskers sprouting from the end of his chin, which reminded Max very much of the straggly plants outside on his doorstep. After a moment, he roused himself. "Let me guess, Horatio. You vant me to re-create the scene—the beautiful young woman in her bedroom—the jealous husband—the last horrible moment!"

"So you *do* know all about it," Pippa said reproachfully.

"I know all about everything," Eckleberger said with a wave of his hand. "You see, children, inspiration is everywhere. It is in everything! Even in zese awful modern newspapers." He stubbed a crooked finger down onto a stack of folded-up papers, which Max recognized as *The Daily Screamer*.

"Does that mean you'll do it?" Sam was crouching several feet away, attempting to coax an enormous fluffy white cat, which Max had originally mistaken for a giant ball of yarn, from underneath a bureau. Eckleberger, Mr. Dumfrey had told her, was always taking in stray cats and dogs. He treated them like artistic projects, nursing them back to health before placing them in families that could care for them.

"Come on, Freckles," Thomas said. "The museum needs you."

Max would have added that so far that week they had had only three visitors, one of whom merely wanted to use the toilets, but she was already on her third cookie and her mouth was full.

Just then, a tremendous yowl split the air. Sam had at last succeeded in luring the cat out into the open. But no sooner had he made his first tentative attempt to pet it than the cat streaked away, shooting Sam an injured look.

"It's no use." Sam seemed to be on the verge of tears. Even when he was trying to be gentle, he ended up smashing or squeezing things to splinters. Max had once seen him accidentally topple a stone pillar when he had done nothing more than lean against it. "Animals never like me."

"Maybe you should get an armadillo," Pippa suggested. "They have lots of natural armor."

Eckleberger was still lost in thought. "I see . . . perhaps . . . zer might be a vay . . . But it vill be difficult . . . very difficult."

"Come on, Freckles," Thomas said. "Be a sport."

Eckleberger slammed his gnarled fist down on the worktable. "I'll do it!" he said, and everyone cheered. Pippa had obviously forgotten that she had been initially against the idea; she applauded louder than anyone. But Eckleberger quickly silenced them. "But first, I vill need photographs. Photographs of everyone and everything—the wife, the jealous husband, the bedroom ver she vas killed. I can do nothing without photographs."

"That's easy enough," Dumfrey said. "Mr. and Mrs. Richstone have been on the front page every day for the last week."

"Bah." When Eckleberger frowned, he resembled a very old and very wise turtle. "Useless! Zese photos zat everyone has seen . . . Printed and stamped and sent halfvay around der vorlt . . . zese are photos with nothing to say. I need photos zat speak in whispers, zat hum, zat sing of life!"

Max had no idea what Eckleberger was talking about, but she was mesmerized by the way he spoke. He leaned forward and dropped his voice, as if he were sharing a delicious secret.

"A sculptor does more than sculpt the nose, the eyes, the ears, and cheekbones." He placed a hand on his chest over his heart. "Vee must sculpt the soul!"

"Spoken like a true artist," Mr. Dumfrey said, dabbing his eyes with his ever-present handkerchief. He coughed delicately. "But as to the, erm, photographs you require, I'm afraid that may present certain difficulties. Perhaps, just this once, you might stick to sculpting the nose and ears and cheekbones?"

Eckleberger's eyes gleamed. "Do not vorry," he said. "I vill see to that. An old dog has his tricks." And he winked at Max.

4

Mr. Dumfrey announced that he had an urgent appointment back at the museum, and after waving to Herr Eckleberger and promising to visit again soon, Thomas, Pippa, Max, and Sam followed him out onto the street, their pockets filled with chocolate-studded sugar cookies wrapped in wax paper.

But it was too hot to move quickly, and Pippa rebelled at the idea of taking the subway, which was as wet and smelly as the inside of a mouth, so the children said good-bye to Mr. Dumfrey at the entrance to the subway and instead made their way leisurely toward Eleventh Avenue and from there turned north. Thomas estimated that they were moving at roughly the same pace as ketchup oozing out of a bottle. But at least there was a slight breeze coming off the Hudson River.

A man in a tall hat and ragged pants was dozing on a bench. A thin woman was dragging a red-faced child behind her. Two fruit merchants were arguing about the position of their pushcarts. And Thomas realized that for the past couple of months, without knowing it, he had been carrying around a weight in his stomach, a squeeze of fear that kept him glancing suspiciously at strangers and searching every crowd for Rattigan's face.

But now he felt a breaking relief: Rattigan was a thousand miles away. They were safe.

"What are *you* smiling about?" Pippa asked.

"Nothing," he said. Instinctively, he threw an arm around her shoulders. Everything was going to be okay. Even knowing that Thomas's real family might be out there somewhere couldn't destroy his happiness. For Thomas, the museum was the only home that mattered.

Pippa swatted him off. "Get off me. You're making my hair sweat."

Definitely back to normal.

As they approached the corner of Eighth Avenue and Thirty-Fourth Street, Thomas spotted a familiar figure: his friend Chubby, a newspaper boy who'd staked every corner from Herald Square to Forty-Second

Street as his own. Chubby was somewhere between fifteen and sixteen years old. Chubby didn't know, exactly, and he often celebrated a birthday several times a year. He had no parents, a fact of which he was very proud, as if he had deliberately ensured they would get rid of him.

"Chubby is as chubby does," he had said, somewhat confusingly, the one time Thomas had ventured to ask him about his name, which did not exactly suit. Chubby resembled nothing so much as a string bean, with a few features not normally found on the vegetable: a great knob of a nose, sharp elbows and knees, bright green eyes, and patchy straw-colored hair that poked out from beneath the filthy cap he always wore. He looked like a stiff wind might knock him backward.

But he had a voice like a foghorn. Even from three blocks away, they could hear him bellowing: "Extra! Extra! Read all about it!"

"Heya, Chub," Thomas said, waving.

Chubby raised a paper to his hat in recognition, but kept on squawking: "Extra! Extra! Read all about it!"

"Does he ever breathe?" Pippa muttered. Pippa disliked Chubby, largely because he was always mispronouncing her name.

As if he'd heard her, Chubby at last turned and

sucked in a deep and wheezy breath. "Heya, Tom. Heya, Sam. Heya, Max. Heya, *Philippa*."

"It's *Pippa*." Pippa squeezed her hands into fists. Thomas knew she hated it when people called her by her full name.

"Like you say." Chubby grinned, showing off the huge gap in his long front teeth, which made his face look endearingly like a rabbit's. He nudged Thomas. "She looks more like a *pip*-squeak though, don't she?"

Pippa looked as if she wanted to punch Chubby in his sunburned nose. Thomas changed the subject quickly before she could decide to do it. He was not altogether certain that Max wasn't rubbing off on her. "What's the latest, Chub?"

"You heard the news?" Chubby asked. He pronounced "heard" as "hoid." Pippa rolled her eyes, but didn't say anything. "This wacko Rattigan's running loose in Chicago. Building an army on the sly. That's what they say." Even as he spoke, he managed to fob a newspaper onto a passing businessman, flipping the dime that was given to him from his palm to his pocket. "The coppers are offering *one hundred dollars* for a reward. Just my luck, huh? One hundred big ones on the table, and not a chance we get even a scratch."

"Oh? And if he was in New York, you think you'd be

the one to bring him in?" Pippa said scornfully.

Chubby's expression shifted. He smiled slyly. "Why not? I hear lotsa things. See lotsa things, too. I got my nose to the street."

"You've got your *ear* to the street, you moron," Pippa said.

Chubby shrugged. "Yeah, sure, ears too." He rocked back on his heels. "All's I'm saying is, Rattigan better not show his mug around here *or else*."

Thomas couldn't agree with Chubby more. Rattigan better stay far away, *or else* Thomas, Pippa, Max, and Sam were in serious danger. Just thinking about Rattigan—his long white fingers, like something dead you find floating in the water; his strange, twisted smile—made his stomach give an uncomfortable lurch, like he'd just eaten too many hot dogs. He decided to change the subject.

"So how's business?" he asked, and then quickly added, as Chubby disposed of another paper, this time to a woman wearing a hat that looked like an upside-down bowl, "The *other* business."

Chubby was the official head of an informal underground gambling ring. He collected bets from neighborhood kids on everything: whether it would rain or not on the Fourth of July, and which color

36

fireworks would be the first to explode over the East River; whether the Yankees were going to win the home game; how many pigeons would perch at any one time on the head of Father Duffy's statue in Times Square; the likelihood that Stewie Horowitz, the nearsighted delivery guy who worked for Manny's deli, would get through the day without clobbering someone on his bicycle; and on and on. Thomas had had a string of good fortune on Chubby's circuit. Chubby had regretfully banned him from placing wagers ever since, but there were no hard feelings.

Chubby's face fell. "Oh, yeah. *That*. Not so good since the flatfoots got wind of it." He looked to Pippa and clarified, "The cops."

"I *know* what you meant," she said haughtily. "The cops are just doing their job, you know, and I think it's very rude of you to—"

Max cut her off. "Don't mind Pip," she said, clapping Pippa so hard on the back that Pippa yelped. "She's got a bad allergy to fun. Makes her pop out in hives all over her body, start itching like crazy."

"Oh, yeah?" Chubby scratched his forehead. "I got a peanut allergy. Makes my throat swell up like a balloon."

"I do not—" Pippa stuttered. Her face was the color of a storm cloud. "*It does not*."

Once again, Thomas jumped in, this time before Pippa could take a swing at Max. "Sorry to hear it, Chubby," he said. "I'm sure you'll be up and running again soon."

"Yeah." Chubby toed the sidewalk with a scuffed-up shoe.

"Want a cookie?" Sam said, obviously hoping to cheer Chubby up. By now, the cookie had mostly disintegrated in his pocket, both from the heat and the fact that Sam had accidentally crushed it. Still, Chubby accepted the sticky mass of wax paper gratefully.

His face brightened. "You been to Mr. E's house?" he said.

Thomas and Sam exchanged a look. "You know Mr. Eckleberger?" Thomas asked.

"Sure I know Mr. E!" Chubby was happily unfolding the wax packet and shaking crumbs onto his tongue. Then he proceeded to lick the wax clean of chocolate. "He takes all the papers—every single one—and pays me extra to deliver 'em direct. Funny bird." Chubby stared regretfully at the now-clean wax paper, as though debating whether he should feed it directly into his mouth. Instead, he crumpled it up and basket-tossed it into a nearby trash can. "Let me see here . . ." After licking clean his fingers, he began fumbling around in various pockets, fingers wiggling through the places where the lining had worn thin. Finally, Chubby fished something out of his pocket: a silver medallion, fitted with a faded silk ribbon. "Check it out," he said. Thomas saw that Eckleberger's name was inscribed in the silver. "Mr. E gave it to me for Christmas. He's a good egg, even if he has got a funny kind of name. He said it would bring me good luck." He frowned. "So far, it ain't working." He slipped the medallion back into his pocket and leaned in, as though about to confess a deep secret. "It ain't just the cops who got it in for me. There's something even worse. There—"

All of a sudden, he stiffened. His eyes became unfocused, and his face went white with terror. His mouth worked up and down, up and down, like a horse trying to chew through a bit.

"What is it?" Thomas cried out. "What's the matter?"

"Are you all right?" Sam started to put hand on Chubby's shoulder, and then obviously thought better of it.

"It's—her," Chubby choked out, his eyes still blazing with terror. "You gotta hide me. You gotta help me! Don't—let—her—take—me."

"Don't let who take you?" Thomas asked.

But no sooner were the words out of his mouth than he felt a shadow fall over them, as though an enormous cloud had skated over the sky. He smelled the sickening perfume, a mix of rotted fruit and mothballs. And he felt the hideous breath tickle the back of his neck.

"Why helloooo, children!" Andrea von Stikk trilled. Thomas, Sam, Max, and Pippa turned slowly to face her, while Chubby cowered behind them, making small whimpering noises.

Andrea von Stikk was wearing her typical getup, despite the sweltering heat: an enormous dress that had been out of fashion for the past twenty years; gloves trimmed with dead animal; and a hat that could have doubled as an umbrella in a sudden storm. Her face was so red it reminded Thomas of a stewed tomato. Her eyes were like two small bruises, simultaneously puffy and sunken. Her mouth was arranged in a customary expression of self-satisfaction. "Fancy meeting you here," she said in her falsetto. "Alone again, I see. Mr. Dumfrey left you to go wandering about the city on your own, did he?"

"We're not kids," Sam said. "We go where we like."

"Mr. Dumfrey had an important business appointment," Thomas said.

"Oh, yes." Andrea narrowed her eyes so much, they

practically disappeared. Her tone turned sour. "Adding to his little . . . collection, isn't he? I heard. Just what this city needs. Another freak."

Max made a strangled noise. Her hand moved to her pocket. Thomas grabbed her wrist and shook his head. He knew Max wouldn't think twice about puncturing Von Stikk like an overpuffed balloon.

"What do you mean, he's adding to his collection?" Pippa asked.

But Von Stikk had spotted Chubby. "Leonard? Leonard! What are you doing skulking around back there?"

"*Leonard?*" Max repeated, looking as if she had just swallowed her tongue.

Chubby straightened up with a groan.

"Surely you don't think Chubby is an appropriate name for a nice young man," Andrea von Stikk snapped, eyeing Max warily. She had obviously not forgotten about the time Max had punctured her hand with a fork.

"Nice young man?" Max's eyes nearly popped.

Andrea von Stikk licked a finger and began vigorously scrubbing at a smear of chocolate on Chubby's—Leonard's—cheek. Chubby looked a bit like a wild dog that had been forced into a tutu and required to perform tricks. Andrea von Stikk prattled happily on, "There now. Much better. You would be so handsome, Leonard, if you only learned to care for yourself a little better. Once you're at school—"

"You're going to school?" Sam interjected. Chubby only grimaced.

"Of course he is," Andrea von Stikk said. "Leonard will be one of the first students at the Von Stikk School for Underprivileged Youths. Isn't it wonderful?"

"Wonderful," Thomas said, sharing a smile with Sam.

Only a few months earlier, Andrea von Stikk had been threatening to remove Sam, Thomas, Pippa, and Max from the museum for another one of her projects: Von Stikk's Home for Extraordinary Children. Luckily, the home had suffered a run of bad publicity after two of Andrea von Stikk's wards simply vanished. Thomas was convinced they'd run away—nearly anything was better than Andrea von Stikk's particular brand of "care," and he was quite sure he'd rather live on the streets than be subjected to her ice pick of a voice every day.

Miss von Stikk had apparently decided that wrangling publicly with Mr. Dumfrey would bring her more trouble than it was worth, and had launched into a new endeavor in order to redeem her name: a chari-table school for runaways, criminals, and, apparently, paperboys.

Help me, Chubby mouthed as Andrea von Stikk placed a meaty arm around his shoulder and began piloting him down the road.

"Come along, come along," she was saying. "We have to get you fitted for your new uniform. And of course you'll need a haircut . . . and what *is* that smell?"

"Poor Chubby," said Sam, shaking his head.

"Better him than us, Sam," Thomas said, clapping Sam on the back and then wincing. It felt like hitting a brick wall. "Better him than us."

5

They heard shouting just before they turned onto Forty-Third Street. Thinking immediately of trouble at the museum, they began moving faster, and tore around the corner as a group.

Several doors down, a man with skin the exact color and texture of ancient parchment was surrounded by a group of kids Max vaguely recognized from the streets. There were five of them. Ruffians, pickpockets, and petty thieves, they traveled in packs, like wild dogs. They were hooting and pegging the old man with eggs—rotten eggs, Max knew, from the stink of sulfur in the shimmering hot air.

Pippa stopped walking. Her mouth fell open, as if

her jaw had become unhinged. "I don't believe it," she said.

Max cupped a palm over her nose. Her skin still smelled a little like chocolate chips. "Believe what?"

"That's Eli Sadowski," Pippa said in a hushed voice, as if she were saying *unicorn* or *winged fairy*. "Or maybe it's his brother, Aaron. I can never tell them apart. I've hardly ever seen them, except in the window. They never leave their apartment during the day. Ever."

"I can see why," Max said, still speaking through her palm. She had heard of the hermit brothers who lived at 346 Forty-Third Street. According to neighborhood legend, the Sadowski brothers were eccentric millionaires who ate nothing but crackers and canned peaches and only emerged at night to scavenge junk from the streets. Though no visitor had been inside their home in fifty years, rumor had it that every inch of their sprawling five-bedroom apartment was crammed from top to bottom with everything from towering heaps of old clothing to ceiling-high stacks of newspapers dating back to the Civil War. Max had occasionally seen their narrow faces peering down at the street from an upstairs window. But she had never seen them up close.

The old man was dressed in a high-collared velvet jacket that must have been stifling—and had surely gone out of style a hundred years earlier. His whole outfit, in fact, looked as if it had been plucked from the grave of a long-dead man. He was wearing ruffled shirtsleeves and a top hat, dusty boots with small brass buttons, and high-waisted pants, all of it covered with a fine, clinging sheen of egg.

Thomas was already sprinting down the street. "Hey!" he shouted, waving his arms, as if the group of teenagers were a pack of pigeons, and he hoped to frighten them into flight. "Leave him alone! *Hey!*"

The kids barely spared him a glance. They continued shoving the terrorized old man as he tried unsuccessfully to fight his way out of their circle.

"Leave. Him. Alone." Thomas had just reached the assembled group. A kid with shaggy dark hair was reaching for another egg. Thomas grabbed his arm and tried to stop him. The boy with shaggy hair shook Thomas off easily, and his friend—a tall boy wearing a battered hat, with buckteeth and a mean, stupid look— gave Thomas a hard shove. Thomas sprawled backward on the pavement.

"Awww, how cute." The boy with the shaggy hair grinned, displaying a mouth missing several teeth. "The little rat wants to play, too." And he cracked the egg in his hand, letting the mess and the stink dribble down over Thomas's shirtfront.

Now it was Pippa and Sam's turn to shout. Max felt a sudden hot surge of anger, like a bright light exploding in her mind. She had always hated bullies. She dropped a hand into her pocket and felt the familiar weight of her knives, a calming force, like a good-luck charm. Just as Pippa reached Thomas and dropped to her knees to help him up, Max threw. For a moment, both blades glittered together like a single weapon; then the wind broke them apart, as Max had expected, as she had *felt*.

One knife whipped the hat right off the bucktoothed boy's head, hitting only a few inches above his hairline. He went stiff and white as if he'd suffered a physical blow. At the same time, his shaggy-haired friend let out a tremendous howl. He had dropped his carton of eggs and was clutching the top of his head—where the second blade had shaved his hair all the way down to the scalp, before embedding itself in the exterior wall of the Sadowskis' apartment building. The three other boys stood gaping, too stupid and surprised to react.

Pippa had just helped Thomas to his feet. As Max approached, she could hear Pippa yammering on in a very Pippa-like way.

"Terrible . . . ought to be ashamed . . . terrorizing

an old man . . . disgusting . . . raised by wolves!" She jabbed a finger into the bucktoothed boy's chest as he sniffled.

"Are you going to let some girl push you around, Robbie?" Another boy in the group spoke up, although Max thought he sounded nervous. He had a face full of acne, and dandruff flaked from his scalp like a swirling, personal snowstorm. He and a redheaded boy had poor Sadowski pinned between them. The old man looked as if he might crumble to dust at any moment. He stood blinking eggs from his eyes and opening and closing his mouth, as if he wanted to scream but couldn't remember how.

"Shut up, Scratchy," the bucktoothed boy, Robbie, muttered. He was still white in the face and keeping a good distance from Max, but he turned his attention back to Pippa. "Get your fat finger out of my face, or I'll—"

"You'll what?" Thomas's hands were clenched, and even his hair stood up wildly, as if it, too, were angry.

"We'll send you screaming back to last Sunday." The redhead, whom Max had originally mistaken for a boy, spoke up. Max saw that she was, in fact, a very square and very ugly girl, with the squashed face and speckled complexion of the frogs that sometimes washed, belly-up, onto the concrete banks of the East River.

Max realized that she *knew* her—Gertrude was her name, though everyone knew her as the Crab, because of her reputation for pinching anything that wasn't nailed down, and even, occasionally, things that were. The Crab would steal the cross off a nun or a pacifier from the mouth of a baby. "We know what you are," the Crab went on, her eyes narrowed to little slits in the flesh of her face. "You're the filthy little monsters from that freakhouse down the street."

"Watch your mouth," Pippa snapped.

Gertrude sneered. "Try and make me, *freak*."

"Don't call her that." Max wished, now, that she hadn't thrown both her knives. The Crab's face was as red and swollen as a bull's-eye. Max's fingers were itching to feel the smooth handle of her knife, the grooves that matched the impression of her fingertips, the blades as sharp as a predator's teeth. She longed to stake the Crab right in the middle of the forehead and watch her face deflate like a balloon.

"Freak?" The Crab grinned. "You don't like that word, do you, *freak*?"

Max dropped and scooped up the first thing she could reach: a battered leather shoe, which had somehow gravitated to the gutter. She was shouting without realizing it. "We're not the freaks! You're the freaks! Nothing better to do than pick on an old man! Why don't you try messing with someone your own *decade*, you pickle-faced bully!"

She threw. The shoe clocked Gertrude directly in the forehead. Gertrude staggered but didn't loosen her grip on Sadowski. A low growl worked its way from Gertrude's throat and began to peak, crest, and turn to a scream.

"Get her!" she screeched. A vivid red bruise was already forming on her head, exactly where the heel of the old shoe had imprinted it. "Get that lousy little worm!"

"Don't talk to her that way," Sam said, taking a step forward. "Or I'll—"

He didn't finish his sentence.

Suddenly, everyone was moving. It was hard to tell exactly what happened: the group was a mass of hands and fists and wide-open mouths, shouting. Pippa was on the ground. Thomas was yelling. Robbie swung at Sam. Sam blinked as Robbie's fist connected. Then Robbie was howling, doubled over, cradling his hand to his chest.

"What's the matter with you?" His face was purple. "You got iron in your stomach or something?"

Scratchy let go of Sadowski and charged. Thomas dropped and stuck out his leg at just the right moment. Scratchy went sprawling, sliding on the pavement. A rock skittered out of his hand, and landed at the toe of Max's boot.

"Don't mind if I do," Max said, bending down to retrieve it.

Then it was Gertrude's turn. She let go of Sadowski's arm and charged. Max wound up and threw. The rock whizzed through the air and hit Gertrude square in the chest. She reeled, turning a full circle and gasping for air like a fish pulled onto a fishing boat.

"Go on, Skeeter," she panted. "Don't just stand there!" The boy whose hair had been cropped close to the head, revealing pink patches of bare scalp, hadn't moved. Now, at Gertrude's command, he made a sudden lunge for Max. With the bare line of scalp in the center of his head, he looked like a particularly ugly variety of skunk.

"You're going to pay for that," he snarled, raising a fist. He was tall—much taller than Max. With her hands and pockets empty, she felt suddenly exposed. "I'll crush you up and pick my teeth with your bones, I'll wring you like a—"

He stiffened suddenly, as if an electric current had gone through him. For a second, he stood there, swaying on his feet. Then his eyes rolled back in his head and he crumpled. Behind him, Sam was standing with his fist raised, looking as if he'd just swallowed a mouthful of dirty sock. Max knew that Sam hated fighting.

"It was just a little tap," he said helplessly as Skeeter moaned at his feet. "Honest."

"You really are a bunch of freaks," Scratchy spat out. But his eyes were wide with fear. He and Robbie hauled Skeeter to his feet, supporting the boy's weight between them. Gertrude was still sucking in breaths. She, too, looked afraid.

"I'd shut your mouth, if I were you," Pippa said, her eyes flashing. She was on her feet again. Her stockings were torn and her knees bleeding. "Unless you want our friend Sam to shut it for you."

"Is it morning already?" Skeeter muttered dazedly. "How long was I asleep?"

Sam was still frowning. "I don't understand it," he murmured. "I barely touched him. . . ."

Scratchy, Gertrude, Robbie and Red took off, bruised and humiliated, dragging the still-dazed Skeeter between them.

"And don't come back!" Max shouted for good measure. "Or I'll stake you on a spit roast and eat you for dinner!"

Eli Sadowski was still rooted in place, trembling, his face an ashen gray color. Pippa approached him cautiously, as though worried he would bite.

"Are you okay?" she asked. "Did they hurt you?"

"Ch—children," he stammered. His voice was as soft as the scratch of dry leaves against a pane of glass. "Mother always said to beware of children."

"It's all right," Thomas said. "We're not going to hurt you."

Eli Sadowski's watery eyes rolled back and forth. "Beware of bees because they sting," he muttered. "Beware of horses because they kick. Beware of dogs because they bite. But most of all—beware. Beware!"

The children exchanged a bewildered look. *Cuckoo*, Max mouthed. Pippa scowled at her, then turned back to Mr. Sadowski. "Can we get you something? A glass of water?"

Sadowski blinked. "Water," he repeated mournfully. "Young lady, water isn't safe nowadays. Hasn't been since the government started testing in 1892."

Pippa swallowed a sigh. "Well, how about some tea? Or some lemonade? If you want to come inside—"

Sadowski snapped into focus. "Certainly not," he said. "I'm far too busy—urgent business—must hurry off for the doctor. My brother, Aaron, is unwell. Must be all the mercury they're putting in the wallpaper . . . or perhaps the poison in the air ducts. There's no time to spare. Good day to you." And with a short bow, he turned and scurried off down the street, his head rotating constantly back and forth, up and down, as if watching for dangers to materialize in the air.

"How about that," Max said. "Not even a *thanks a lot* and *see you Sunday*."

"I feel sorry for him," Pippa said, shaking her head. She was staring up at the smudgy dark window, high above the street, from which they often saw Mr. Sadowski looking. "Imagine being cooped up inside all day long, for years and years and years? He must be very sad."

"He's bonkers, is what he is," Max said. She retrieved the knives she had thrown, feeling better once she had tucked them safely in her pocket.

Back at the museum, Miss Fitch was in a foul mood.

"Where on earth have you been?" she snapped. "What's happened to you? You look as if you've been put through a meat grinder—especially you, Philippa.

Hurry up, hurry up. The afternoon performance starts in less than an hour."

"The performance?" Max repeated. "But we don't have any audience."

"No back talk," Miss Fitch said. She pushed a strand of graying hair from her face. She had changed into her normal clothing—black dress, black shawl, and black stockings—and mostly removed her makeup, although smudges of black mascara still clung to the skin beneath her eyes, giving her the look of a deranged raccoon.

"Besides, Mr. Spotswood is here."

All four children groaned. Mr. Spotswood was ancient—Thomas had once estimated that he was pushing a hundred—and only ever came into the museum because the building now occupied by Dumfrey's museum had formerly housed a florist's shop, where years earlier, Mr. Spotswood had met his wife. Sometimes he spent whole afternoons wandering the exhibits, asking the performers if they had seen Millicent and complaining about the lack of flowers.

"He doesn't count," Max said.

"He falls asleep during the performances," Pippa complained.

"And last time, he clogged the downstairs toilet," Sam pointed out.

"Enough!" Miss Fitch screeched. Thomas, who had been on the verge of saying something, clamped his mouth shut. Miss Fitch sucked in a deep breath. "A visitor is a visitor. The show must go on! Now hurry upstairs and get cleaned up before I take a whip to each of you."

"What's crawled into *her* long johns?" Max grumbled as they started up the spiral staircase at the back of the museum, used exclusively by the performers to access the upper floors.

When they reached the second floor, however, the source of Miss Fitch's bad mood became immediately apparent.

"Howdy, y'all!" Lash was standing in the Hall of Wax, leaning on the handle of his mop. Caroline and Quinn, the albino twins, were sitting, giggling, at his feet, wearing their best dresses, which were identical except for the color of their sashes: red for Caroline, blue for Quinn. "Come on in and join us! I was just telling the little ladies about the time that me and Dumfrey played a show in Longhorn, Texas, and the dust was so bad it blew the ladies' skirts to their ears—"

"We can't," Thomas said regretfully. "Miss Fitch said we have to get ready for the afternoon show."

"Did she now?" Lash straightened up. "All right,

then. You heard the boy. Miss Fitch's orders is Miss Fitch's orders."

"*One* more story, Lash," said Caroline.

"Pretty please," added Quinn.

"Another day, ladies, another day . . ."

"I can't believe it," Pippa muttered as they continued climbing. "A whole show, all for one stupid visitor."

"Quit whining," Thomas said. "At least you don't have to spend half your act folded up like a pretzel in a pillbox."

"At least *you* don't have to read Mr. Spotswood's pockets," Pippa fired back. "Do you know what he had on him last time? A pickle! A single pickle! Just sitting in his suit jacket!"

Max left the others arguing all the way up to the attic—"Neither of you has the right to complain," Sam was saying, "when I'm the one who has to break my back lifting a boulder every day," and Pippa snapped back, "Come off it, Sam, you could lift ten boulders without breaking a sweat." Max decided to duck in and see Mr. Dumfrey. She wanted to ask him about adding her new blindfold trick to her act. His door was closed. She heard the murmur of voices from inside his office. She knocked anyway.

"Ah, Max!" Mr. Dumfrey exclaimed when she

pushed open the door. "Come in, come in. Say hello to Howie—our newest employee!" And he gestured to the dark-haired boy sitting across from him, who turned to her, smiling.

Max opened her mouth to say hi and found she did not remember how. Her mind was a complete blank. All she could think was that Howie was the most beautiful— the most *perfect*—boy she had ever seen. His black hair fell neatly across his forehead. His eyes were a crystal blue, his nose was perfectly straight, his teeth as white as those of a dentist's model.

"Hello," he said with a wave. Even his hands were perfect. Maybe, she thought, he was another knife-thrower, like her. Maybe she was getting replaced. The idea made her heart lurch.

"You're not a freak," she blurted out. "There's nothing wrong with you at all."

"Now, now, Mackenzie." Mr. Dumfrey made a *tsk*-ing sound with his tongue. "You know how I feel about that word. *Freak* is just another word for marvelous. And Howie is quite a marvel. Show her, Howie."

"I don't know, Mr. Dumfrey." Howie blushed prettily. He smiled at Max and her heart made an unfamiliar jumping motion.

"Go on, don't be shy. There's nothing to be ashamed of."

Just then there were footsteps on the stairs behind them. Howie turned around to look at Miss Fitch, who was standing red-faced in the doorway.

Except he didn't turn around in his chair, as Max would have. He didn't turn his body at all. He merely swiveled his head a complete 180 degrees, so that his chin was resting directly between his shoulder blades. Max couldn't repress a gasp.

"You must be the new one," Miss Fitch said in a reproachful tone, as if it were Howie's fault that the museum existed in the first place. She completely ignored Max, and looked instead to Mr. Dumfrey. "Have you seen Lash—I mean, Mr. Langtry?" she asked icily. "There's a smudge on the stage that needs cleaning. It's an absolute disgrace. And I have several buckets of pins I need sorted from my needles."

"I have not seen Lash since this morning," Mr. Dumfrey said, removing his spectacles to polish them. "Have you looked in the Odditorium?"

Miss Fitch's only response was a prolonged sniff. With another withering glance at Howie, she spun around and started back down the stairs.

Max was still watching Howie admiringly as he swiveled his head back to its correct position.

"How—how do you do that?" she asked, before she could stop herself.

"Born that way." Howie leaned toward her and winked. And he swiveled his head in the other direction, so once again his head was turned entirely around to the back, with his chin pointed toward his heels. Max couldn't help but laugh.

Mr. Dumfrey beamed. "Meet Howie," he said, "the Human Owl."

6

There was one person who wasn't happy about Howie's arrival: Sam.

"He doesn't even do anything," Sam muttered, pushing around his oatmeal with a spoon. "He just sits onstage and turns his head a few times. Big deal."

"Shhh," Max said sharply. "He'll hear you." In the week since his arrival, Howie had smiled at her four times, touched her arm twice, and laughed three times at something she had said—though she hadn't been trying to make a joke.

Sam glared at her. "Does he have owl ears, too?"

"Do owls even have ears?" Pippa asked.

"Yes," Thomas replied, without looking up from his book of brain teasers.

"I don't care if he does hear me," Sam said, pushing back his bowl of oatmeal.

Pippa stared at him curiously. "What's the matter, Sam? Howie's not so bad."

"Yeah, Howie's all right," Max echoed, and then ducked her head, blushing.

Sam looked so furious, Max thought a vein might explode in his forehead. "Oh, yeah? Well, *you* don't have to share a room with him. You don't have to listen to him rattle on and on about his gift, and his legacy, and his mom, who could spin her head like a top, and his dad, who could fold his spine in half, and his brother, who has skin like a rubber turkey. I'm sick of it. Sick of it!" And Sam got up from the table so fast, he reversed his chair. He aimed a kick at it. The chair splintered immediately into pieces.

"What's got into him?" Max asked, sliding Sam's uneaten oatmeal across the table to her and digging in.

"Hormones," Betty, the bearded lady, spoke up from her position in the corner. A newspaper was spread across her lap and she was carefully trimming her long brown beard.

"Hot blood begets hot thoughts," said Smalls the

giant, and then paused significantly. When no one responded, he clarified, "Shakespeare." For years, Smalls had hardly spoken unless he was quoting some old poem no one had ever heard of. But ever since he had gotten a poem published in a small literary magazine known as *The Weeping Willow*, he had become practically intolerable.

"Twelve is a very hard year," said the Great Goldini, the museum's resident magician, as he fanned a deck of playing cards out on the table. "Of course, thirteen is even worse. And fourteen—don't get me started on fourteen. Fifteen was no picnic, either. And sixteen—"

"We get your point," Pippa said.

"*Very* hard," Goldini murmured. Then he turned to Thomas. "Pick a card, any card."

"Ace of hearts," Thomas said, without glancing up from his book.

Goldini performed a fancy shuffle of the deck, tossed it up in the air and caught it one-handed, cut it twice, then, with a flourish, turned over the top card. It was the queen of spades. He stared at it for a moment. "That's strange," he said, scratching his head. "Must be a faulty deck."

"The newest buds/are so often shorn/first," Smalls boomed, and once again paused, as though expecting applause. When he was met with another silence, he frowned. "*That* one's an original."

"*Very* clever," Betty said quickly.

"Sounds like something that came out of a book," added Danny the dwarf. Quinn and Caroline both said "Lovely!" at the same time and then jinxed each other, and then double-jinxed each other.

The kitchen door flew open, and Howie appeared. His wavy hair was falling over one eye. He was wearing a neat button-down shirt and pants without a single hole or stain. Howie wasn't an orphan, unlike the other children, as he made sure to remind them daily. (And, of course, there was no way to explain they were orphans only because Rattigan had made sure of it.) He worked the circuit like his parents and brothers. His uncle, who was blessed with the same gift as Howie, had even served as a bodyguard to the president of the United States. The only thing better than having eyes in the back of your head was having a head that could spin around to the back.

"So you see? I was born to be in the business," he'd said to Max two days earlier, smiling his perfect smile.

Max dropped her eyes when Howie's gaze fell on her. For the first time in her life, she felt embarrassed by her shabby jacket and its numerous pockets, and the boys' pants she wore strung to her waist with a rope she'd stolen from a ship's captain, and the cheap shoes Mr. Dumfrey had bought her after her last pair had developed holes. Howie looked like someone who had always had a place in the world, and would always have a place.

Max looked like she'd been plucked off the back of a dump truck and deposited directly in Mr. Dumfrey's kitchen.

"Morning," Howie said cheerfully as he came down the stairs. "What'd I miss? I passed Sam on the way down. He looked like he'd swallowed a snapping turtle."

There was an awkward moment of silence. Thomas pressed his face even closer to his book so that his nose was barely a centimeter away from the print.

"Ah, yes, well." Danny coughed. "Smalls was just reciting us some poetry. . . ."

Fortunately, he was saved from saying any more. Just then, they heard Mr. Dumfrey shout.

"Help!" His voice was muffled through the walls, but it sounded as if he was in the lobby. "Someone! Anyone! Come quickly!"

Max's heart flattened all the way into her shoes. For a second, she was rocketed back in time, to the series of misfortunes that had occurred after Mr. Dumfrey had purchased a hideous shrunken head that resembled nothing so much as a shriveled apple. First, the head was stolen. Then Potts, the janitor, was found poisoned, and Mr. Dumfrey was accused of killing him.

Now something horrible had happened. Again.

She was flying up the kitchen stairs with the others even before she knew she was moving. Danny huffed next to her, and Betty's beard streamed over her shoulder like a silken brown banner.

Together, the residents of the museum thundered into the lobby—

—and saw Mr. Dumfrey, weaving backward and forward, holding a teetering stack of cardboard packages in his arms.

"Someone, help!" Mr. Dumfrey swayed on his feet, desperately trying to prevent the packages from tumbling.

Smalls rushed forward to come to his aid. Max, seeing that Mr. Dumfrey was safe, felt a rush of relief, followed immediately by a quick pulse of annoyance. "You shouldn't scream like that," Max said. "I thought someone had lost a head."

"Quite the reverse, dear Max!" Mr. Dumfrey said, looking quite cheerful now that the packages were safely deposited on the lobby floor. "We've found a head, you see. We've found three of them!"

"Freckles came through?" Thomas asked.

"Indeed he did, my boy. Indeed he did. Max? Lend a hand?"

Max saw immediately what Mr. Dumfrey meant, and came forward with one of her sharpest knives, a small blade that had originally been used for quartering tomatoes.

Max kneeled and neatly slit open each of the three boxes. "Ah!" Mr. Dumfrey gently scooped up the first of the wax heads from the petals of newspaper that enfolded it. He seemed momentarily overcome. For nearly three whole seconds he did not say a single word. His lower lip trembled.

"It's exquisite," he said at last. "It's extraordinary! Behold—Mr. Manfred B. Richstone!"

He spun the head around. Betty gasped. Caroline and Quinn squeaked. Pippa went pale.

It was Mr. Richstone, all right, but nothing like the images that had so far appeared in the papers, in which he had mostly looked confused. This Mr. Richstone was the picture of ferocity. His teeth were bared, his lips drawn back over his gums, like those of an infuriated animal. And he looked *real*. His eyes glittered. His skin was pitted with old acne scars. Max half expected him to start roaring with rage, or snapping away at Mr. Dumfrey's fingers.

"It's . . . it's hideous," Pippa said finally.

Mr. Dumfrey beamed. "Isn't it?" He replaced Mr. Richstone's head and moved onto the next box. "Aha! Here we have Mr. Edmund Snyder—the no-good, fortune-seeking scoundrel who'd been sniffing around Mrs. Richstone. He looks the part of a leech, doesn't he?"

Everyone murmured their agreement. The second head was, if possible, even less attractive than the first. Mr. Synder's head was fitted with oily black hair, a neatly trimmed mustache, pronounced teeth, and small eyes that gave him the look of an overeager beaver. His skin was sallow and his cheekbones sharp as blades.

"Last but not least . . ." Mr. Dumfrey lifted the third head from its box. "Ah, yes," he said softly. "The tragic Rachel Richstone."

Max could now believe that old Freckles had, in fact, crafted statues for the king and queen of Bulgaria and received a medal of honor from the Austrian police. He had made Rachel Richstone as beautiful as he had made her husband and the evil Mr. Snyder ugly. Soft waves of brown hair framed her face. Her skin was as pale as milk. Her blue eyes were wide with terror, and her mouth was open in a scream. For a moment, Max imagined she could hear the faint echo of Rachel Richstone shouting for help.

"Now then," Mr. Dumfrey said, replacing the head and straightening up. "Where has Lash run off to? We'll need to take down the dummies in the Egyptian mummy exhibit right away. With some spiffing up, they'll do quite nicely for bodies. Miss Fitch, follow me, please."

Mr. Dumfrey bustled away, giving rapid-fire orders. As soon as Max, Pippa, and Thomas were left alone in the lobby, Thomas crossed quickly to the box that contained Rachel Richstone's head.

"What are you doing?" Pippa whispered as he kneeled to remove the head. "Dumfrey will slaughter you if you break that thing."

He ignored her. "Look at this," he said, and swiveled the head around so Max was once again confronted by Rachel's pitiful stare.

"Put it back, Thomas." Pippa shivered. "That head gives me the creeps."

"They all do," Max said. "They're so . . ." *Alive*, she almost said.

"Real," Pippa finished.

Thomas shook his head. "You don't see it, do you?" They stared at him blankly. "It's *wrong*. Eckleberger made a mistake. Her teeth are all messed up."

Max squinted. Now she saw a large gap between the head's two front teeth. Thomas was right. In all the newspaper photographs of Rachel Richstone, she had a perfect smile.

"So what?" she said. "It was probably a rush job."

"No." Thomas frowned. "Freckles doesn't make mistakes."

"Let it go, Thomas," Pippa said. "What does it matter?"

Thomas hesitated. "I guess it doesn't," he said at last. Max was glad when he'd returned Rachel's head to its box, and Max could no longer see those big blue eyes, and the silent plea written in them.

7

Even Thomas had to admit that once the heads had been fitted to wax dummies, dressed in clothing expertly tailored by Miss Fitch, and arranged neatly behind glass in furniture reconstructed by Lash to resemble the furniture in the Richstones' bedroom, the result was impressive. Every time Pippa passed through the Hall of Wax and under the shadow of Mr. Richstone's raised arm, she let out a yelp and spun around, half expecting him to bring a fist down on her head. And several times in the early morning, still groggy from sleep, Sam mistook the model of Mr. Snyder, who was dressed in a fur-trimmed cloak similar to one that Goldini used in his act, for the magician and greeted him with a wave and smile as he passed.

But the expected crowds didn't come, even after Dumfrey took out radio and newspaper advertisements trumpeting "An Exact Reproduction of America's Grisliest Crime!" and forced the children to spend an afternoon sweating in the summer heat and distributing pamphlets printed with images of Mrs. Richstone's terrified face.

Only a handful of people were interested: a nun who sprinkled holy water on the floor of the exhibit; an old man with large buckteeth who came two days in a row and was afterward discovered to have pocketed two packs of peanut brittle from the refreshment stand; and Mr. Richstone's legal counsel, who tried unsuccessfully to get Mr. Dumfrey to take down the exhibit on the grounds that it might influence the public against him, an unnecessary concern, since there was no public to influence.

"I can't understand it," Mr. Dumfrey said. The wispy strands of his hair—or what remained of it—usually combed straight across his head, had begun to radiate upward, as they did when he was upset.

It was Thursday, nearly a week after the *Crime of the Century!* exhibit had been added, and another sweltering day with not a single client. Even Miss Fitch could hardly insist under the circumstances that the show go on, and instead, seeming irritated by the children's mere presence, suggested they go out and take some air.

"Go on!" she said, shooing them toward the door. "You're breathing too loudly! I can hardly think!"

"Should we ask Howie to come with us?" Max asked hopefully.

"No," Sam said at once.

Miss Fitch sniffed. "*Howard* is staying here," she said. "I am making adjustments to his costume." And she slammed the door behind them so hard that Pippa jumped.

It was hardly better outside than in, although at least there was a breeze, and Sam was visibly more cheerful since he knew Howie would not be joining them. Thomas had won some pocket change playing Snaps with Danny, a notorious gambler, and suggested they go to the zoo in Central Park. It was always cooler there under the shade of the trees, and Pippa liked the smell of the animals, earthy and sweet, although she sometimes felt sorry for them, too. She knew that this was what some people, like Andrea von Stikk, thought about the performers of Dumfrey's Dime Museum:

that they, too, were like caged animals, forced to perform while visitors gawked.

Pippa's ideas wandered again to the idea of her real parents, and to the home she'd been forced to leave behind. She imagined what her parents might look like, imagined that her mother might have a pointy chin, like Pippa's, and her father might have Pippa's sleek and glossy black hair. Maybe they even lived here, in the city. Maybe Pippa had even passed them in the street—maybe they would even find each other again someday. . . .

"Radio Pippa. Helllooooo. Come in, Pippa."

Pippa blinked. She realized they'd already reached the entrance to the zoo. Thomas and Sam had passed inside the gates already. She had been standing there, staring off into space, like a windup toy that had run out of juice. Max, ever impatient, glowered at her.

"Did you forget how to use your legs or something?" Max said, giving her a nudge. "Come *on*."

Pippa forced her thoughts away from her parents, whoever and wherever they might be, and followed Max into the zoo. They weren't the only New Yorkers to take refuge in the coolness of the winding, shaded walkways. Children darted past, carrying balloons and shouting, while mothers hurried to catch up. Men with shirt-sleeves rolled to the elbow and hats cocked back offered their arm to giggling dates, and ice vendors called out their different flavors. The animals, in their pens and cages, stared out at the procession with such looks of open curiosity that it seemed to Pippa as if the humans were the spectacle, and the animals the observers.

"Let's go see the snakes," Thomas said. He'd picked up a brochure and was squinting over the map. "See? We're close to the Reptile House."

"I want to see the gorillas," Sam said.

Pippa suppressed a smile. It was no wonder Thomas wanted to see the snakes. The way he shimmied and slithered and bent and contorted, he often seemed very much like a snake himself. And although Sam was skinny for his age, all knobby elbows and shoulder blades, he must often feel like a gorilla stuck in a room full of porcelain—Pippa had never met someone more prone to breaking things than Sam was.

"What about you, Max?" she asked. "What do you want to see?"

"Penguins," Max said without hesitation. Pippa, Thomas, and Sam all turned to her in surprise. "What?" she said, a little defensively. "I like how they're all suited up. Plus, it'll be colder over there with all that ice."

They visited the Reptile House first, which was dim

and musty-smelling and only slightly cooler than outside. Thomas pointed out the python and the anaconda, the smaller, green-skinned snakes camouflaged within their habitats, the coral-colored adders. Pippa was glad when they moved on. She didn't hate snakes, exactly, but she didn't like them, either. There was something in the dull flatness of their eyes that bothered her, something that reminded her of Rattigan. . . .

They headed to the gorilla enclosure next. As Pippa walked, she let her mind travel, let it rove through the crowd, bumping up against the minds and thoughts of the other visitors. Trying to read anything in a crowd this size was nearly impossible. There was too much interference. It was like running your fingers over a hundred woolen coats and trying to pick out one by feel. She got nothing but shapes and angles, patchy sensations, as if she were listening to a badly tuned radio.

But it was practice. Months ago, she had managed a single, true vision—an actual image, a memory, lifted from someone else's mind—but since then she'd gotten no closer than brief gobs of feeling, impressions that glommed on to her briefly like wads of chewing gum stuck to a shoe.

The gorilla habitat was in fact a large sunken enclosure, a vast bowl of terrain pitted with rocks and stumpy trees. A dozen gorillas sunned themselves lazily or scampered between the rocks, grunting. Pippa, Thomas, Sam, and Max crowded against the railing, which protected viewers from a steep fall down into the pit.

"I bet that one's the leader." Thomas pointed to one of the largest gorillas, his fur spiky and silver gray, with long arms as thick as tree trunks, lumbering slowly in their direction. His face, strangely human, seemed to be set in a permanent scowl. "See? He's the biggest. Even Sam would have a hard time arm wrestling that one."

"Count me out," Sam said. "That one looks a little like Howie, doesn't it?" He pointed at a smaller gorilla, all black, picking nits out of the fur of his companion.

"Very funny," Max said. "Hey, look at this. It's your old friend Eckleberger." She pointed to a small brass plaque dedicated to a former zookeeper, and engraved with the copper relief of his silhouette. It was one of Freckles's pieces. His signature was clearly stamped at the bottom. "He's like an old wheel—turns up everywhere, don't he?"

"Doesn't he," Pippa corrected her. "And Freckles, for your information, is one of the most well-respected artists in the—"

She didn't finish. She was hit, suddenly, with a staggering wave of anger, a punch of resentment so black and strong she had to tighten her grip on the railing to keep from toppling forward. Dimly, she heard Max saying her name, and was aware that both Thomas and Sam were staring curiously at her. But she couldn't speak. She was in the grip of another person's feeling—of another person's hatred. It was as if instead of brushing up against another person's mind, another person's mind had reached into hers and started squeezing.

It was over as quickly as it had come. She came up out of the depths of the darkness, gasping a little, and whirled around instinctively to search the crowd. What did she expect to see? A man baring his teeth, glaring at her? A woman with her hands balled into fists?

She saw none of these things, and no one she recognized, either. A bum in dingy clothing was edging closer to a boy's ice cream cone, muttering darkly. Fathers sweating in the summer heat mopped their faces with handkerchiefs. There were sticky-fingered children and giggling packs of teenage girls and harried-looking mothers with hats sliding from disheveled hair. But still that dark anger was there, pulsing inside of her, the force of someone's hatred . . .

Someone screamed. Suddenly, the crowd surged forward and Pippa whipped around, forced by the movement right up to the railing, just in time to see a small boy, maybe six or seven, fall straight down into the gorilla enclosure.

"Help!" A woman who must have been the boy's mother was screeching, scrabbling over the railing as if she, too, were thinking of nosediving after him. A man barely managed to restrain her. "Somebody please help! My boy! My baby boy!"

The boy was crying but Pippa couldn't hear him over the noise of the crowd.

"Someone's gotta get him out of there."

"He'll be squeezed like a banana."

"Get a ladder! We need a ladder!"

"Look at that big son of a gun—he's on the move. Watch out, kid! Behind you!"

It was true: even as the boy stood there, frozen in panic, the big silver-backed gorilla was loping toward him. His fur was stiff on his back, bristling with anger. His huge nostrils flared in and out. His teeth were bared and he knuckled the dirt with each powerful stride. He was probably six hundred pounds.

"We need to help," Pippa said breathlessly, but even as she said it she saw another figure drop into the enclosure, landing easily on his feet.

Thomas.

"What's he playing at?" A red-faced man next to

Pippa with an explosion of veins in his forehead was shouting. "He'll get himself killed!"

"He's right," Max said. She was white-faced. "What's Thomas thinking?"

Pippa couldn't speak and only shook her head. Now the gorilla, doubly enraged, let out a bellowing roar that she felt all the way in the soles of her feet.

Thomas managed to coax the little boy onto his back. Pippa saw him test the concrete wall, searching for the smallest crevices and cracks he could use to climb. He must have found one, because slowly, painstakingly, he began to climb, his face tight with concentration.

But it was too late. The gorilla was coming straight for them. Fifteen feet away, then ten, then only five. . .

"I guess that's my cue," Sam said with a sigh. He vaulted over the railing just as the gorilla reached out to swat Thomas off the wall, as if he were no more than a fly. There was another scream, and it took Pippa a moment to realize she was the one screaming.

Sam landed directly on top of the gorilla and went down in a jumble of arms and flying fur. For a good half minute she couldn't tell who was who or which was which and whether Sam had the advantage or the gorilla did. All this time the crowd had tripled in size and everyone—parents and children and even zoo

employees—was shouting. Pippa could hear nothing but the drumbeat of her own panic. She could see nothing but the flash of a knee or an elbow, dark patches of fur, Sam's face occasionally twisted in pain, and the gorilla howling his frustration to the sky.

Meanwhile, Thomas continued to climb, using hand- and footholds no wider than a spaghetti noodle, until at last he reached the railing and was hauled to safety by a half dozen spectators. Thomas thudded to his knees as the little boy's mother fought through the crowd to snatch him up.

"Oh, Eddie," she sobbed into the little boy's hair. "Oh, Eddie. You're all right. It's all right now."

Pippa kneeled to take Thomas by the shoulder. He was breathing hard.

"Sam," he panted out. "Is Sam all right?"

"I don't know." Pippa felt as though her lungs were full of dust. "I can't tell."

But at precisely that moment a cheer went up from the crowd. Pippa helped Thomas to his feet. An exultant Max was jumping up and down, pumping a fist in the air.

"Take that, monkey-brain!" she shouted. "How does that feel, you sorry excuse for a primate?!"

A pale-faced Sam, straggly and exhausted-looking,

had managed to restrain the gorilla's arms behind his back using his leather belt. The silver-backed gorilla now seemed about as dangerous as a ten-day-old kitten. He rocked back and forth on his heels, working his mouth into what looked very much like a frown when at last a ladder was lowered into the enclosure so that Sam could make his escape. The rest of the monkeys hopped and hooted and waved cheerfully at Sam as he began to climb.

Pippa began to giggle. "Looks like the monkeys have a brand-new leader," she said.

"Hey, Sam," Max said as he clambered clumsily over the railing and nearly dropped at their feet. "Have you ever thought of a gorilla for a pet?"

8

They returned to the museum soon afterward. Sam was eager to escape the crush of people asking for his autograph. Thomas wouldn't have minded scrawling off an autograph or two, but knew better than to suggest they stay until the newspapers showed up—not after their adventures earlier that spring with *The Daily Screamer* and its so-called ace reporter.

They found the front doors locked, which was unusual for midday, and had to go around Forty-Fourth Street to enter through the sunken courtyard and the kitchen door. The museum's lower levels were empty. It was so quiet, Thomas could make out the individual squeaks of mice behind the walls. And when they entered the attic, he saw why: every single resident of the museum, including Mr. Dumfrey, was gathered there.

"Ah, children. Excellent timing, excellent. We were just having a bit of a house meeting to discuss finances." It was rare for Mr. Dumfrey to visit the attic, where the performers slept: a vast room filled with old beds, furniture, garment racks, and even a defunct refrigerator, arranged in a mazelike formation to allow each performer a small measure of privacy.

"What finances?" Monsieur Cabillaud grumbled. Monsieur Cabillaud had a very small head, but an excellent mind for math. He was informally in charge of all of the museum's finances.

"Well . . ." Mr. Dumfrey fiddled with his bow tie. "Perhaps if we took another advertisement out in the paper . . . ?"

Monsieur Cabillaud gripped his pin-sized head. "*Non, non,* and more *non!* We have no more money in ze cashbox!"

"There's no need to shout, Mr. Cabillaud," Mr. Dumfrey said. "I heard you perfectly well. We are running low on funds."

Monsieur Cabillaud stood up, stalked over to his

sleeping area, and retrieved the small metal cashbox that held the profits from the museum's ticket sales from under his bed. It was well-known that Monsieur Cabillaud slept with one arm slung around the cashbox. Now, he opened the lock with the metal key he wore around his neck, revealing a box that was empty except for two balls of lint, an ancient stick of bubble gum, and twenty-five cents.

"We are not *low* on funds, Mr. Dumfrey," he said in a trembling voice, drawing himself up to his full five foot three. "We have no more funds. Nothing. Zero!"

Mr. Dumfrey paled. "But . . . but . . . what about the secret fund?"

Thomas exchanged a look with Pippa. They'd never heard of a secret fund.

Monsieur Cabillaud hesitated. Then, with a muttered curse of *"sacre bleu,"* he pivoted and disappeared once again behind his bookshelf. Pippa heard the sound of rummaging and more cursing in French. When Monsieur Cabillaud reemerged, he was carrying a large, unwashed-looking striped sock, in hideous shades of chartreuse and blue.

Smalls let out an outraged cry. "My sock! It's been missing for ages."

"That's your secret fund?" Howie sneered with barely

concealed disdain. Thomas was beginning to understand why Sam disliked Howie so strongly.

"It's camouflage," Mr. Dumfrey explained. "Everyone thinks of stealing a lockbox. No one thinks of stealing a smelly sock."

"*He* stole it." Smalls pointed a large finger in Monsieur Cabillaud's direction. "He stole it from *me*. And it is *not* smelly."

Monsieur Cabillaud inverted the sock over the carpet and shook. A small spider dropped from within the folds of wool, and scurried quickly under the sofa. Mr. Dumfrey gasped and clutched his chest.

"I have told you once," Monsieur Cabillaud said firmly. "And I will tell you again. We are broke."

There was a long moment of silence. Thomas was used to the fact that the museum was often in danger of going out of business. He was used to the fact that Betty mixed water with the milk to stretch it longer, that sometimes there was porridge for dinner and canned sardines for breakfast, that he had to wear his shoes until the soles wore out completely and his toes poked through the leather. But this was worse than usual.

Andrew the Alligator Boy was the first to speak. "I'm sick of it," he said. He thumped his cane on the floor and stood up. "We haven't had a raise in nearly a year.

I've got holes in my shirts and mice in my dresser."

"Just a little more time . . ." Mr. Dumfrey wrung his hands together. "The crowds will come back. They'll *have* to."

"They better," Andrew growled, showing his small, crooked teeth—which did, in fact, give his face the appearance of a reptile's, as did the extreme scaly dryness of his skin. "I heard the Bolden Brothers Circus is looking for freaks. Maybe it's time for a new gig."

This provoked an explosion of sound. Mr. Dumfrey fell backward in his chair, as though he'd been struck by a physical blow. Pippa cried, "Shame on you," and Caroline and Quinn squeaked with dismay. Lash poked Andrew in the backside with his broom and Smalls threatened him with a poetry reading about duty and perseverance. Only Howie looked amused.

"I'm just saying," Andrew said, thumping his old hat farther down on his head. "Something's gotta give." Then he stalked out of the room, hunched over his cane.

"Don't mind him," Betty said. Her thick eyebrows twitched expressively. "You know what Andrew's like. He's always got a bee in his bonnet about something."

"He's right," Dumfrey moaned. He whipped out a handkerchief and buried his face in it. Thomas was terrified he would begin to cry. "I've done a terrible job. . . . I've run this place into the ground. . . . I'm a failure."

"You're wonderful," Thomas spoke up loyally. Even if Mr. Dumfrey did sometimes forget to balance the accounts for months at a time, and even if he sometimes spent too much on banners and newspaper ads and new glass for the exhibit cases, and forgot to stock up on flour and sugar—and even if he occasionally took a gamble on a big exhibit that wasn't worth as much as he had paid for it—Mr. Dumfrey *was* wonderful. Probably the most wonderful man in the world.

Various other performers piped up to agree.

Then Howie said casually, "Did you ever think of selling the place?"

Mr. Dumfrey looked up. His face was white. "S—selling the place?" he whispered.

"Oh, dear," said Betty.

Sam rounded on Howie. "What's the matter with you?" he burst out furiously. "Why would you say something like that?" His fists were clenched.

"Sell the place?" Mr. Dumfrey repeated, gripping the arms of his chair, practically vibrating with distress. He stared, unseeing, into the air.

"This is home," Sam spat out. "Don't you get that?

89 ☞

You can't just show up and start running your mouth about things you don't understand—"

"He just asked a question, Sam, calm down." That was Max.

"Sell the place?" Mr. Dumfrey was by now screeching. His body went totally rigid, as though he'd been electrocuted. Then he slumped backward, in a clean faint.

"See?" Sam was shouting now. His face was purple. Thomas had never seen him look so angry. Howie, on the other hand, looked perfectly calm; he was chewing gum, and didn't even flinch when Sam leaned over him. "See what you did?"

"It's not his fault," Max said.

"I wasn't talking to you," Sam fired back.

"Everybody, just calm down." Thomas stood up and tried to put a hand on Sam's arm.

"Lay off." Sam wrenched away from Thomas. Thomas stumbled backward, and Smalls had to steady him. "Everyone just lay off." Sam, too, stalked out of the room, slamming the door behind him so hard the hinges popped off the walls. The door thundered to the ground, letting up a thick cloud of dust.

"Oh, dear," Betty said again.

"What's his problem?" Max cried, loudly enough

that Sam might have heard. If he did, he didn't answer. Thomas could hear him pounding down the stairs.

Howie laid a hand on Max's arm, smiling his smug plastic smile. "Don't worry about him," he said. "He's just got his wires a little crossed. Anyone would, in his position."

Thomas felt a surge of anger. "In his position? What's *that* supposed to mean?"

Pippa groaned. "Not you, too."

"Don't take his side," Thomas said.

"Everyone, stop screaming!" Caroline said, covering her ears. Two spots of pink had appeared in her cheeks. Against her snow-white skin, it looked as though two gumballs had lodged there.

"Stop being a baby," Quinn said with a toss of her white hair.

"Stop being a nag," Caroline said.

"Both of you, be nice," Betty said.

"Mind your own business," both sisters said at once.

Soon everyone was squabbling. Danny stuck up for Betty, Smalls defended the albino twins, and Goldini was accused of taking no one's side. Caroline burst into tears and Quinn tried to sob even louder. It was so loud Thomas's head began to ache. When Lash attempted to restore order, Smalls inverted a flowerpot onto his head.

It was then—as soil crumbled off Lash's shoulders, and Caroline and Quinn continued wailing, and everyone else was yelling insults and trying to be heard over the din—that there was a loud cough.

Officer Gilhooley and Sergeant Schroeder were standing in the doorway. Side by side, they looked like the number ten: Officer Gilhooley was long and lean as a withered string bean, and Sergeant Schroeder looked like he might move faster if he bounced instead of walked.

Instantly, everyone went silent. Everyone, that is, except Mr. Dumfrey, on whom Betty had just emptied a glass of ice-cold water. He sat up at that exact moment with a startled cry, water dripping from his glasses and spotting the front of his shirt.

"Horatio Dumfrey?" Sergeant Schroeder said—stupidly, since he knew very well who Dumfrey was. He had come to the museum on two separate occasions: once when Dumfrey had reported the theft of the shrunken head and again at the memorial for Potts, the former janitor, who had been poisoned because of his entanglement in the theft.

"Is something wrong?" Mr. Dumfrey said with surprising dignity, given the fact that his hair was plastered to his forehead, and there was water beading at the tip of his nose.

"Is there somewhere we can go to talk? Somewhere *private*?" Schroeder's black eyes were gleaming. It was obvious that Sergeant Schroeder had been the kind of child who delighted in telling other children there was no Santa Claus.

"What's this about?" Mr. Dumfrey heaved himself to his feet.

Schroeder sucked in a breath. It was Officer Gilhooley who blurted it out.

"It's Siegfried Eckleberger, sir," he said. "He's been murdered."

9

"Murdered," Pippa whispered for the seventeenth time.

"I don't believe it." Max's knees were drawn to her chest.

"Murdered," Pippa said again.

Sam couldn't bring himself to speak. He was utterly miserable. Freckles was dead. *Freckles*—who'd been like a grandfather. Who, along with Mr. Dumfrey, was the closest thing to a family that Sam had ever known.

The anger that had been boiling blackly in his stomach for days gave another hearty burp. It was Rattigan who'd made sure that Sam would never have a real family. That was the worst thing he'd done—worse than using Sam and the other children for his sick experiments, worse than changing them, growing them in his laboratory like human houseplants.

Sam knew that his parents were dead. He had once told Max that as a child he'd seen death, and this, his earliest memory, was what he meant. His mother's eyes staring unseeing at the ceiling, his father's mouth frozen in a shout, his parents' hands separated by only a few inches, as if they'd died reaching for each other. The smell of blood. His hands and face sticky with it.

His whole life, he had been afraid that he, Sam, was somehow responsible for their deaths—that he had hurt them accidentally. But now he knew it *couldn't* have been his fault. It seemed possible—even probable—that Rattigan was to blame for this, too.

Still, there might have been an aunt and uncle who remembered him, or even an older sister. Sam had always fantasized that one day he would be shouldering through a crowd at Times Square and hear a shout; he'd look up to see a girl barreling toward him, ready to embrace him, ready to call him *brother*.

But who would claim a boy like him, who'd been twisted and changed and altered? Other performers at the museum might look strange, but normal blood ran through their veins, and normal wires ran through their brains, beating normal signals back to their bodies. Their differences were nature-made, inherent. Born.

Not Sam, though, or Thomas, or Pippa, or Max.

They were well and truly freaks.

And now one of the few people who'd ever treated them kindly was gone.

The news of Eckleberger's murder had affected the residents of the museum like a stiff, cold wind on a pile of old leaves. The performers had scattered to do their mourning in private. Even Max, who had met him only once, was stricken. Although Sam, Pippa, and Thomas had been closest to Freckles, everyone at Dumfrey's Dime Museum had known and loved him.

Everyone, that is, except for Howie. Fortunately, he was steering clear of Sam. Sam was glad. He would never deliberately hurt another person. But for Howie, he might make an exception.

A small panel in the wall behind Pippa popped out and clattered to the ground. An opening no larger than a dinner plate, situated between the life-sized figure of Benjamin Franklin signing the Declaration of Independence and the model of Adam and Eve confronting the serpent, was now revealed. Thomas. The top of Thomas's head came shooting out like a cork from a bottle. A moment later, after several seconds of wiggling, his shoulders emerged.

Soon he was shimmying himself entirely out of the wall, so that he closely resembled the large snake coiled around the tree in the display.

"What's the news?" Pippa asked.

Thomas stood up. He was coated in a fine layer of plaster and dust, as he always was after he'd gone sneaking and sliding through the narrow web of air ducts and pipes behind the walls, which he used as his own private transportation—and eavesdropping—system. He rolled his shoulders, popping them back into place.

"Robbery," he said solemnly. "At least, that's what the cops are saying."

"Robbery . . ." Pippa shook her head. "You saw how many locks were on the door. How'd they get in?"

"And why would anyone want to steal from Freckles?" Sam said. "His studio's a mess. He didn't have anything worth stealing."

"I'm just telling you what I heard." Thomas ran his hands through his hair, releasing a shower of dust. "The cops are bringing Dumfrey over to the studio," he said. "They want to see if he can spot anything missing or weird or out of place." He swiped his eyes with the back of a hand, leaving a dark streak from nose to cheekbone. "He was holed up, you know, working on those stupid heads."

"That means we might have been the last people to see him alive," Pippa said in a hushed voice.

"Except for his killer," Thomas said.

There was a short moment of silence. Sam felt a chill. He stood up. "I want to go, too."

"The cops won't like it," Thomas said.

"Bricks about the cops," Max said. Max had started making up curse words since Miss Fitch had threatened to wash her mouth out with bar soap after she heard Max say a bad word. *Bricks* was one of her new favorites. She, too, stood up. Sam was surprised. She'd been resolutely refusing to look in his direction since his fight with Howie. "We should be allowed to go. Mr. Dumfrey never pays attention, anyway. There could be a bloody handprint on the wall and he'd zoom right by it."

Max was right. So Pippa, Max, Sam, and Thomas descended to the first floor and intercepted Dumfrey as he was following the two cops out the door. Sam was surprised that the police gave them very little resistance when they asked to come along.

"An extra pair of eyes never hurts," Schroeder said, working his jaw back and forth around a piece of gum. "None of you freaks—er, *kids* got special X-ray vision, do you?" Like half of New York City, he'd obviously followed the Case of the Shrunken Head closely. For months, the kids' names had been splashed all over the news. The press had dubbed them freaks and unnaturals and oddities. And that wasn't the worst of it.

"Pippa can read what's in your pockets," Thomas said. Pippa glared at him.

Schroeder squinted. His eyes seemed to recede into the fat pincushion of his flesh. "I don't buy it," he said.

"She can," Thomas said, even though Pippa was giving him a death stare.

"Prove it." Schroeder rocked back on his heels.

Sam felt like screaming. Freckles was dead. *Dead.* And the cops were playing stupid mind games instead of trying to find his killer.

Apparently, Pippa felt the same way. She exhaled impatiently, so hard her bangs fluttered. "A matchbook," she said. "Four nickels and a quarter. A packet of Beech-Nut chewing gum. And a betting slip."

Schroeder patted his pockets quickly, as though Pippa might have reached out with her mind and pickpocketed them. Next to him, Gilhooley stared openmouthed.

"See?" Thomas said. "She's a mentalist. She reads minds."

"Thomas," she muttered. "Shut. Up."

Schroeder was scowling. He didn't like to be proven wrong. "What am I thinking now?" he barked.

"It doesn't work like that," Pippa said.

He snorted. "Too bad. Coulda come in handy. Not like guessing at pocket change." Thomas opened his mouth but Pippa nodded sharply. Sam didn't have the energy to defend her, either. He had just seen Howie's face appear at the second-floor window; Max had looked up, waved, and then blushed when she caught Sam staring. He turned away, feeling heat creep like an itch up his neck.

Freckles was dead. Even when he repeated the words over and over, he couldn't believe them.

"Go on, pile in," Schroeder said, jerking his head toward the squad cars idling in the street. "The captain's waiting. So's Eckleberger, for that matter. But he's likely to wait a long time."

And Schroeder laughed at his own joke.

10

The street outside Eckleberger's studio was packed with onlookers, drawn to the wooden police barricades and swirling lights like ants to a discarded muffin. Pippa saw a man snapping pictures, his battered fedora marking him as a member of the press, and felt her stomach lurch. She still had not gotten over the way it felt to be ridiculed and singled out on the front page of the newspaper. She didn't think she would ever look at a reporter without getting that queasy feeling.

The front door was open, and a police officer was standing guard to keep the crowd away. A plant had been overturned, and dirt had been tracked across the front stoop and into the hallway.

Pippa almost regretted coming. Only two weeks ago she had stood with Mr. Dumfrey and the others here, as the smell of freshly baked *Plätzchen* floated out to them. She felt as though by going inside, by seeing, she would be making it true: Freckles was dead.

But Mr. Dumfrey took off his hat, and followed Schroeder and Gilhooley into the hall, and she followed after them, her heart knocking heavily against her ribs with every step.

And then: they reached the studio and her heart squeezed up into a small, hard knob. The beautiful, sunny space, filled with statues and plaster models and sketches, had been destroyed, ransacked, *ruined*.

"Crill," Max breathed, which was another one of her made-up curse words.

All of Eckleberger's work had been smashed. The ground was littered with plaster and crumbled clay, shattered bits of ceramic, and flakes of paint. The table around which the children had gathered to eat cookies had been knocked over. The drawings were torn from the wall. His pencils had been snapped in half. The drawers of his dresser had been removed and overturned. The fluffy white cat, whose name they had never learned, was crouching under the bed, mewling piteously.

Pippa had a strange sense of unreality, as if she had walked into a dream.

"It's wrong," Thomas spoke quietly, as though echoing her unconscious thoughts.

"I know." Pippa laid a hand on his arm. She was glad, at least, they had already removed the body. She wasn't ready to see it. She wasn't ready to *accept* it.

"No. I mean—" Thomas frowned. "It's too much. Like . . . like a stage show. No normal break-in leaves this much damage. Why is the stove pulled out from the wall? Why are the drawings torn down?" He shook his head. "This wasn't random. It was personal."

"Unless the thief was looking for something specific," Max said. Thomas looked at her, blinking several times, as though she'd just materialized.

"Maybe," he said.

A group of men was conferring on the other side of the room. When Pippa and the others entered, they went silent, staring with either hostility or suspicion or both. Now one of them crossed the room, clomping mindlessly over the shattered remains of Eckleberger's lifework, his fedora pushed back on a large, shiny forehead. Pippa's stomach tightened. Detective Hardaway.

"Dumfrey," he spat out, as if the word were a bad taste in his mouth. His eyes, clear and pale as ice, swept over the children, and his lips curled in disgust. "I see you've brought your . . . *wards* along." He emphasized *wards* as though to make it clear he wished he could use another, more insulting word instead.

Pippa dug her nails into her palms. Hardaway had arrested Dumfrey several months earlier, convinced that Dumfrey was responsible for poisoning Potts, the janitor. And he'd basically accused the children of being mixed up in the whole business. Furthermore, he'd made it clear what he thought of the performers at the museum: that they were freaks of nature and would be better off dead. Pippa could only imagine what he would think if he knew that she, Sam, Thomas, and Max had been made in a laboratory, like Frankenstein's monster.

Just thinking about it made nausea rise up in her throat.

"Ah! Detective Hardaway." Mr. Dumfrey bowed. His smile didn't extend to his eyes. "As perceptive as ever, I see, and a credit to the police academy and the fine state of New York. It's a wonder that the crime in New York City hasn't been entirely obliterated!"

"Yes—well—yes," Hardaway grunted, missing Mr. Dumfrey's sarcasm. He crossed his arms. "So. You were the last to see Eckleberger before he kicked the bucket." It wasn't a question.

"We"—Mr. Dumfrey gestured to the children—"came to pay Siegfried a visit, that is correct."

Hardaway took a step forward so he was only an inch from Dumfrey's face. He leaned in and spoke in a low voice, directing his words straight into Dumfrey's ear, so neither Sergeant Schroeder nor Officer Gilhooley would hear. But Pippa, who was standing next to Dumfrey, could make out every word.

"Listen, Dumfrey. It wasn't my idea to bring you down here. Got that? If I had my say, you'd be leaving this room in a pair of cuffs. Eckleberger's the second friend of yours to get bumped on my watch, and I don't believe in coincidences." He drew back as another man, whom Pippa didn't recognize, joined their group, extending his hand to Mr. Dumfrey.

"Good to meet you, Mr. Dumfrey." This man was older, with bushy white eyebrows, like small clouds tacked to his face. "I'm Captain Burke. NYPD. Heard a lot about you. Been meaning to bring the wife and kids down to the museum. Someday, someday. When people stop bludgeoning one another to death and shooting at strangers in nightclubs."

Pippa liked Captain Burke immediately. He didn't speak to Mr. Dumfrey like other grown-ups did, as if every word was a code for something else that was much worse. And when he looked at the children, he did so with only mild curiosity, instead of a gaping stare or a sneer of disdain. He was wearing a neat suit that looked like something Mr. Dumfrey would own, and he smelled like peppermint.

"I know this must be rough on you," he was saying. "But the idea was to have you take a walk around, see if you can spot anything that looks weird or out of place."

"My dear fellow," Mr. Dumfrey said. "The whole *place* looks out of place!" He gestured helplessly to the dismantled studio. "Are you sure you're dealing with a homicide, and not a hurricane?"

"Whoever broke in did a number on the place," Captain Burke agreed. "Maybe looking for something specific." Max smirked. That had been her idea, too. "Maybe trying to keep us from figuring out what he was after. Or maybe just the violent type. That's why we asked for your help."

Mr. Dumfrey shook his head. He looked unconvinced. "I'll do my best," he said.

"That's all we can do," Captain Burke said, and Pippa decided that if she ever got murdered and needed a cop to search for her killer, she hoped it was Captain Burke. "Now, Mr. Dumfrey, why don't you just come this way. . . . We'll start over here by the kitchen. . . ."

Captain Burke shepherded Mr. Dumfrey across the room and Hardaway stalked after them, glowering from beneath the brim of his hat. The cops in the corner returned to their conversation. Several men crouched and scurried across the space like crabs, snapping pictures of every surface. The children were forgotten.

"Well"—Pippa took a deep breath—"what do we think?" No one answered. She looked around and saw she was alone. Sam was trying to get the cat out from under the bed, and succeeding only in terrorizing it further. Max was sifting through a pile of splintered clay that had once been one of Eckleberger's statues, as though hoping to divine its original shape. And Thomas was standing very still, and staring at something on the ground. Curious, Pippa made her way over to him, stepping carefully around the debris strewn over the floor.

"What is it?" Pippa said.

"Rachel Richstone," he said in a strange voice. He bent and scooped up a half dozen photographs, loosely bound with an elastic band. "I guess Freckles managed to get some photos after all. Check it out."

Pippa fanned the photographs out on Eckleberger's worktable. Even though every newspaper had featured a photograph of Rachel Richstone for the past few weeks, these photos were totally unfamiliar, taken when Rachel was probably no more than nineteen or twenty, though in a few she looked even younger. It was something to do with the wildness of her hair, and the freckles, which in later pictures she must have carefully concealed with makeup.

"See?" Thomas pointed. In two of the photos, Rachel was grinning at the camera, revealing a wide gap in her teeth. "I knew Freckles didn't make a mistake."

"I don't understand." Pippa frowned. In every printed picture she had seen of Rachel Richstone, she was showing off a mouthy grin full of perfect teeth. "Where did the photos come from?"

There was a cough. Pippa and Thomas turned around. Officer Gilhooley was standing behind them, shuffling his feet.

"That was my doing," he said. The large pouches under his eyes gave him the look of a very thin, very pathetic bloodhound. "I knew old Eckleberger. We all did. He did some work for us back in the day, helped us out on some sticky cases. We'd give him a description of a suspect and he'd whip up a bust, realest thing you ever saw. Would never have nabbed Sol Bumstead if it wasn't for him. Best safecracker in the business, at least until Eckleberger helped us get him. I never seen a guy who could make clay come alive like Eckleberger did. The statue was the spitting image of our guy, the spitting image. All based on what some doughnut-shop owner saw from his bathroom window." Officer Gilhooley shook his head. "Old Sticky Fingers Solly wasn't too happy about it. Swore revenge on Eckleberger even as he was heading to the pen. Got sent up to Sing Sing for ten years, all because of good old Eckleberger."

Thomas frowned. "How long ago was that?"

Gilhooley scratched his forehead. "Let's see now. Must have been eight or nine years ago now . . ."

Thomas and Pippa exchanged a look. She knew exactly what he was thinking: if Sticky Fingers Solly had been sprung from jail early, he might very well have come looking for revenge. It was obvious, however, that the idea hadn't occurred to Gilhooley. He was still blinking at them blearily, as if awaiting instruction.

"Okay, so, Eckleberger came to you and asked for some old photographs of Rachel?" Pippa prompted.

Gilhooley nodded. "He wanted something special— the private stash, you know, that hadn't been picked to pieces in the papers. I knew I coulda got in trouble. But he was a friend, kinda. I couldn't say no."

"But where did you get them?" Thomas asked.

Officer Gilhooley looked uncomfortable. "The Richstone place is still a crime scene," he said gruffly. "Even though everybody knows her husband did it. Plenty of people going in and out. I didn't think one more or less would make a difference. I told Eckleberger he could poke around."

"He must have found her secret stash," Thomas said musingly. He bent down and scooped up a picture frame missing its photo. The glass was shattered. "Look at this," he said, passing it over to Pippa.

"It musta got knocked over when the thief was trashing the place," Officer Gilhooley said. Thomas just frowned. Pippa could tell he was puzzling over something—he had the same look on his face as when he was trying to solve one of the riddles from his book—but she couldn't for the life of her imagine what it was.

Pippa shrugged and handed the picture frame back to Thomas. "He's probably right."

Thomas didn't look convinced. "Then why was the photograph removed?" he asked.

"Does it matter?" Pippa said sharply. Eckleberger had been killed, and all Thomas could think about was a stupid broken picture frame.

"Maybe not," Thomas admitted. But as soon as

Gilhooley had turned away, Thomas carefully wiggled a finger between the broken glass and the frame, and extracted a torn piece of brown paper, which looked as though it must have been part of the backing. Someone had jotted down a note on the paper. It read *RVW, June 28*. "RV," Thomas mulled out loud. "RVW. What's RVW?"

"Give it up, Thomas," Pippa said. She was feeling hot and useless and miserable. They were here to help the police catch Eckleberger's murderer. But they weren't helping. Sam was still squatting sullenly in the corner, trying to get the stupid cat to do something other than bare its teeth. Mr. Dumfrey was shaking his head, looking bewildered, while Detective Hardaway smirked.

So far their best lead was on Old Sticky Fingers Solly. But how on earth would they find him?

Pippa had a sudden, sickening realization: Eckleberger's murderer would never be caught.

Across the room, she spotted Max poking around a set of Eckleberger's old tools, probably looking for something she could pocket. Pippa left Thomas still fiddling with the picture frame and stalked toward Max. Max saw her coming and rapidly moved away. Pippa squinted, concentrating, as she did whenever she was reading the contents of someone's pockets or handbag; first, she had to think her way into their *minds*, into the dark folds of their awareness. In Max, she sensed a blockage, a foreign mass that her mind was trying to wrap itself around and conceal. Something hard. Made of metal.

But before she could figure out what it was that Max had taken, the door to the studio banged open and her concentration was broken. She heard the sound of cheery whistling. It was like hearing giggling at a funeral, and everyone turned, surprised.

Chubby sauntered into the studio, a bag of newspapers slung across his chest, his cap pushed back on his forehead. He froze when he saw the police and all the damage. His eyes did a quick spin around the room, so fast that they briefly crossed.

"What—what's happened?" he sputtered.

"What's it look like?" Hardaway practically growled. "There's been a break-in."

"And what in the devil's name are *you* doing here?" Sergeant Schroeder said, puffing out his chest like an over-preening robin.

Chubby's whole posture had transformed. He looked even more frightened than when Andrea von Stikk had approached him in the street. "I—I deliver Mr. E's papers. I brought 'em today, same as usual."

Captain Burke spoke up. "I'm afraid you're too late," he said softly. His eyes never left Chubby's face, and Pippa was reminded of a dog carefully examining a toy, just before chewing it apart. "Mr. Eckleberger's been murdered."

Then something extraordinary happened. Chubby opened his mouth, as if to speak. But instead of saying a word, he turned around and bolted from the room.

11

Instantly, everyone was shouting. The police tore after Chubby, and Sam didn't realize that he, too, was running until he was standing in the street, blinking in the sun. The crowd rippled like water where Chubby parted it. Sam sprinted after him, but by the time he reached the far side of the street, he saw both Chubby and Thomas disappearing around the corner of Fortieth Street. But even Thomas lost him. He reappeared a moment later, shaking his head.

"I lost sight of him for a second and he was gone," he panted.

Hardaway caught up to them a second later, and let out a curse when he saw that Chubby had disappeared.

Sergeant Schroeder waddled out of the thick knot of people a second later, huffing and red-faced.

"I knew it," Hardaway said. "I knew that piece of garbage had something to do with this."

"*Chubby?*" Sam turned to Hardaway, incredulous. He had no idea why Chubby had fled, but he knew for sure that there was no way he'd had anything to do with Freckles's death. "You can't be serious."

But Hardaway wasn't listening. He had turned to Captain Burke, who had also forced his way through the crowd, followed by a winded Mr. Dumfrey. "That little turd's been running an illegal operation on the sly for the past six months. Bet-taking, game-rigging . . . he's a hazard, Chief. I'd bet my boots he's in this up to his neck."

Sam wanted to say that Chubby barely had the brains to keep a penny in his pocket, much less to plan an elaborate crime. But he felt that would be disloyal—and besides, he knew Hardaway wouldn't listen.

"All right," the captain said quietly. "See if you can round him up and bring him in for questioning."

Sam's stomach sank. He hoped that Chubby would be smart enough to lie low for a couple of days. Maybe by then, the police would find the person truly responsible for Eckleberger's death. But watching Sergeant

Schroeder and Gilhooley argue about who got to drive the squad car back to the precinct, Sam seriously doubted it.

They took the subway rather than walk or ride back to the museum in the squad cars, and Sam was glad. He'd had more than enough police for the day. He'd had more than enough police for a *lifetime*.

Mr. Dumfrey was uncharacteristically quiet. Every so often he shook his head and mopped his face with a handkerchief and murmured *"Poor Freckles."* Sam felt strangely exhausted, as if someone had reached into his insides and wrung all the juice from him. Thomas was lost in thought, and even Max had nothing to say, although both times Sam met her eyes she looked quickly away, as if she felt guilty about something. Pippa spent the whole ride gnawing the ends of her sleek black hair, a habit she'd picked up since it had grown longer. Not for the first time, Sam wished he had her talent for mind reading so that he would know what she was thinking.

She didn't speak until they were almost in front of the museum. "Mr. Dumfrey, I was wondering," she said in her sweetest voice, "whether you'd ever heard of a man named Sol Bumstead?"

Mr. Dumfrey raised an eyebrow. "Old Sticky Fingers? Sure I have! Crackerjack bank robber, one of the best in the business. Funny you should mention it—I was just thinking of him the other day. Poor, dear Freckles made the bust the police used to nab him. I used to have it somewhere but for the life of me can't think of where it might have—" Suddenly, he broke off with a small gasp. He turned and glared at Pippa. "No," he said. "No, no, and no."

"What?" Pippa blinked at him, obviously doing her best to look innocent. She did a pretty good job of it, Sam thought. Much better than Max, who always looked as if she'd just swallowed your favorite watch.

"I know what this is about." Mr. Dumfrey placed both hands on his hips, blocking nearly the entire sidewalk. A woman scurried past, shooting them an infuriated look. "I want you to promise me—I want you to swear—that you're not going to go looking for Freckles's killer."

Sam felt a jolt, as if he'd been socked in the stomach by that gorilla he'd wrestled. Was that what Pippa was after?

"No, no, of course not," Pippa said quickly.

"We would never," Thomas added.

"Don't look at me," Max said, crossing her arms,

when Dumfrey glared at her.

"What about you, Sam?" Mr. Dumfrey glared sternly down at Sam, his eyebrows doing their best to meet in the center of his forehead. "Can you promise me you won't go looking for Eckleberger's killer?"

Sam thought of Freckles's liver-spotted hands and quick fingers. He thought of the smell of Freckles's home, like old paper and melting butter and sunlight. Freckles had never forgotten a single one of Sam's birthdays, and once, when Sam was only six and had accidentally broken the model train Mr. Dumfrey had bought him, it was Freckles who painstakingly glued it back together.

Sam slipped a hand behind his back and crossed his fingers. "Promise," he said with the biggest smile he could muster.

Later that night, long after the other residents of the museum had gone to bed, Sam realized he would never be able to sleep. He had dozed temporarily only to find himself back in Freckles's apartment, in even worse disorder than it had been that afternoon, papers and photographs swirling down from the sky through a hole in the ceiling.

"I can't find der cat!" Freckles shrieked. And it was

obvious why: he could hardly look for the cat when he was busy baking cookies.

Sam sprang to search for the fluffy cat, only to find his legs paralyzed. When he turned, he saw a gorilla had locked on to his ankles, and he understood that all along it had been a trap . . . that the gorilla had come to kill them both . . .

He came awake gasping, pressing a hand to his heart. Turning to Thomas's cot, he saw the familiar lumps under the covers that indicated he, at least, was sleeping soundly. Next to Thomas, Howie was so still in his bed he hardly looked alive. Or maybe that was wishful thinking. Easing out of bed, he tiptoed down the performers' staircase—careful not to hold on to the banister, lest he squeeze too hard and crack apart the wood—to the first floor. He went through the Hall of Worldwide Wonders, where the exhibits glinted dully in the moonlight in their dusty glass cases, and the marble floors shone silver, and into the special exhibits room. One of the few benefits of having lost their cook was that they no longer had to be so careful sneaking in and out of the kitchen at night, and as soon as Sam was on the stairs leading into the kitchen, he flicked on the lights.

Instantly, he heard a muffled yelp. Someone, it seemed, had beaten him there.

In the kitchen, Max was standing, holding a butter knife in both hands as if it were a sword.

"Oh," she said, lowering the butter knife. "It's just you."

"Hi to you, too," Sam said, feeling vaguely offended. He had the unhappy feeling that had Howie come down the stairs, she wouldn't try to stick him with a utensil. He moved beyond her to the icebox and reached for the milk, disappointed to find only half an inch left. Not nearly enough for hot chocolate. "Couldn't sleep either, huh?"

Max shrugged. "I *could* sleep," she said. "I just didn't feel like it." But she looked away, biting her lip, and Sam knew she was as upset as any of them about what had happened to Freckles. Unexpectedly, she turned back to him. "Listen, can I ask you a question? Do you think it's still stealing if nobody's gonna know what went missing?"

Sam frowned. "What are you talking about?"

But before she could answer, they heard a muffled sound from deeper in the basement. Max started to speak but he put a finger to his lips. It came again: a thud, a scuffle, a curse.

Someone was with them in the basement.

From the kitchen a narrow door, normally shut, gave

access to a vast and gloomy crawl space crowded with things too old and broken even to have made their way to the attic. Dim, musty and damp, this part of the basement was inhabited by nothing but spiders, mice, and, when he was alive, the equally gloomy Potts, who'd kept a room tucked at the very end of the cluttered space.

Max eased open the door. Sam's hands were shaking so badly, he was likely to have simply yanked it from its hinges. Together they slipped into the crawl space, ducking slightly where the ceiling was sloped, waiting in the darkness while their eyes adjusted. They heard no more sounds, not a single twitch of movement, but Sam knew that there was someone else with them in the darkness—someone else frozen, trying not to move, trying not even to breathe. He could *feel* them, feel their otherness, like something heavy riding on his shoulders. He wondered whether this was how Pippa felt when she tried to read minds.

Suddenly, there was a yelp, a crash, and a whimper.

"What are you—?"

"It's all right, Tom. It's just Sam and Max."

A second later, two flashlights came on, temporarily dazzling Sam's eyes. Then Pippa and Thomas were illumined from the chin up, so that their eyes looked like hollows.

"Sorry," Thomas said. When he grinned, his teeth gleamed.

"Crill," Max cursed. "You scared us."

"Yeah." Sam shivered as he felt something brush his neck. A spider, probably. "We thought you might be a robber."

"Unlikely," Pippa said, sniffing. "Who'd want to steal any of this stuff?" And she cast her light onto an enormous wig, which looked like a huge pile of over-cooked spaghetti mixed with rotting seaweed.

"So what *are* you doing down here?" Sam asked.

"Mr. Dumfrey said that the museum used to keep a bust of Solly Bumstead—Sticky Fingers Solly," Pippa said. "He was a bank robber who got sent to prison and vowed revenge on Freckles. But what if he's out now? What if he got his revenge?"

"Wait, wait." Sam felt the anger that recently seemed so close to the surface give another thrash. "You're trying to track down who killed Freckles—and you didn't tell us?"

"C'mon, Sam," Pippa said. "We would have told you if we found anything. You were sleeping like a baby."

"You were snoring like a baby," Thomas corrected her. "You didn't even roll over when I took one of your pillows. Sorry about that, by the way. I was trying to make it look like I was still in bed. Miss Fitch has been after me ever since she caught me scaling the Great Siberian Woolly Mammoth skeleton after dark."

So that explained the lumpy figure that Sam had mistaken for Thomas. His anger gave a little twitch and then fizzled.

"But if you want to help . . ." Pippa lobbed him an extra flashlight. Sam caught it and felt the handle crack in his palm. Although it was too dark to see her, Sam could feel Pippa rolling her eyes. "Sorry. That was stupid."

"Here, Sam. Share mine," Thomas said.

"No need." Max spoke up suddenly from behind them. She had ventured off a little way into the piles of old junk, so that her voice sounded muffled. Sam remembered then that until only recently she had lived on the streets, making her way in the darkness, living wherever she had to. It seemed impossible to imagine a time when she hadn't been here at the museum. "Can I get a little light, please?"

Pippa swung her flashlight in Max's direction. Max was caught in the glare, holding the large plaster bust of an extremely ugly and very lopsided face. His left eye drooped. His eyebrows bristled. His mouth was thin as a line. At the bottom of a stand a neatly labeled sign read simply SOLOMON "STICKY FINGERS" BUMSTEAD—THIEF AND SAFECRACKER in very large letters.

"Hmmm," Thomas said. "Not much of a looker, is he?"

Pippa gasped. "I know him," she said. Sam swung around to look at her. Unfortunately, she'd lowered her flashlight, so he could only make out her silhouette.

"You know him?" Sam repeated.

"I mean—I've seen him," she stuttered. "At the zoo in Central Park. He was standing right behind me. Max mentioned Freckles and then . . ."

"What?" Thomas prompted, turning his flashlight on her. "What is it?"

In the sudden glare, Pippa's face looked totally unfamiliar.

"I felt hate," she said in a whisper. "Max mentioned Freckles's name, and I felt a wave of hate."

It made sense, Thomas reasoned, that if Solly Bumstead had gotten out of prison early he would have had trouble finding work—or, possibly, his next target, if he was still in the business of looting banks and private houses. In recent years hundreds of down-and-out people had gravitated to Central Park, building makeshift homes out of tents and plywood, so that seen from a distance the long field resembled a patch of misshapen mushrooms sprouting from the ground.

And that, of course, was precisely where Sam, Pippa, Max, and Tom were headed.

They could have waited until morning—they *should* have waited until morning, in Sam's opinion—but Pippa thought that if Solly Bumstead was living in the park, their best chance of finding him was at night. None of them had wanted to risk going upstairs for clothing, but they couldn't exactly go around in pajamas without attracting attention from the police (except for Max, who always slept in her clothing, and she said in a slightly superior voice that it was always for this reason, as though it were common practice to have to sneak out in the middle of the night to track down a possible killer). So they'd all rooted around the basement until they found a trunk filled with moldering clothing and old costumes. Sam was wearing mothball-scented suit pants and a jacket far too small for him. Thomas looked as if he was swimming in a button-down shirt and trousers hitched to his waist with a length of rope, and Pippa had on a shapeless dress she kept tripping over.

Sam did not like the city at night. He didn't like

the empty feel of the streets, the way the landscape so familiar to him felt suddenly cloaked and secretive, like a person in a mask. He didn't like the people who slunk through the shadows, heads down as though they were hiding something, or even the dazzle of Broadway, the flash and glare of the theaters, which in the day seemed so cheerful but after dark seemed to be trying too hard to prove something.

But he especially, especially, did not like Central Park.

The trees, like hobbled people. The grass shushing you every time you took a step. Fires flickering in garbage cans like distant, drowned stars.

And the people, hundreds and hundreds of people, clinging to the earth as if they were in danger of being thrown off into space. It all made him feel as if something huge and heavy were squeezing him.

"This is stupid," he whispered, although there was no reason to be quiet—not when they were already moving into a field of makeshift houses, blankets tacked to rags tacked to cardboard, and the night was alive with babies crying and murmured conversation and the occasional shout. "There must be a thousand people living out here. How are we supposed to find Bumstead?"

Even Pippa looked worried. "We'll have to split up. You've all seen what he looks like now. Believe me, he's as ugly as he was ten years ago."

"Even so, it'll take hours," Sam said.

Pippa huffed a little. "Do you have anything better to do?"

Sam nearly said *sleeping* but closed his mouth when he saw Pippa's face.

"Let's start at the center of the long field," Thomas suggested. "Then I'll go north, Sam will go south, and Pippa and Max can go east and west."

This, however, proved to be unnecessary. No sooner had they begun navigating the clutter of tents and temporary shelters toward the center of the long field than they heard a commotion from nearby. Sleeping babies came awake and started howling. Several men staggered clumsily to their feet before shouting for everyone to *shut up.* An alarm clock went off and was quickly silenced. And a man's enraged voice rose above the din.

"He stole my frying pan! That Sticky Fingers stole my frying pan!"

Thomas, Pippa, Sam, and Max froze.

"Do you think . . . ?" Pippa breathed.

"This way," Max said, already cutting left and

disappearing behind a nest of cardboard boxes hung with laundry. They followed her, weaving between the sorry, soggy little homes, many of them already half collapsing, as the argument only grew louder and more heated.

"I didn't take nothing, you sorry sack of monkey snot," another man said. His voice was a low growl. "Now step off before I make ya."

"I'd like to see you try."

Max, Thomas, Pippa, and Sam burst into a small clearing littered with old metal cans and trash. A single, ragged tent was tied up to a nearby tree, and Sam noticed an overturned bucket holding a filthy bar of soap and a toothbrush. A man Sam immediately recognized as Solly Bumstead was standing next to a smoking campfire, gripping a heavy frying pan. Whatever he'd been cooking smelled roughly like old socks dipped in tuna fish, and Sam had to stop himself from covering his nose.

A second man, this one bucktoothed and bald, was circling Bumstead. "You're telling me," he said, his voice now low and dangerous, "that there frying pan in your hands didn't come straight outta my kit. You're telling me you didn't sneak it off me last night when I invited you to share a drink." The two men were inching closer together, as if they were both swirling toward a central drain.

"I'm telling you," Bumstead said, matching the man's tone, "that if you take one more step, you'll regret the day your mother cooked ya . . ."

For a split second, both men appeared to be frozen. Then, with a shout, the bald one charged. Bumstead gripped the frying pan like a baseball bat and swung. As the bald man ducked, an unidentifiable slop hit Sam directly in the chest.

"You've got to be *kidding* me," he groaned.

Now the two men were on the ground, rolling dangerously close to the fire, wrestling and punching and spitting.

"You stole it!"

"I didn't!"

"Did!"

"Didn't!"

"Maybe we should just let 'em kill each other." Max's eyes were shining. "Save us some trouble."

"Then we won't know the truth about Freckles," Thomas pointed out. He turned to Sam. "What do you say, Sam? Time to break it up?"

Sam sighed. Recently, it seemed, everything was *his* responsibility. "I'll take care of it," he grumbled.

He reached the tussling men in two long strides. The bald man had the advantage. He was on top, pinning Bumstead with his knees. Bumstead's nose was bleeding. The bald man had gotten hold of the frying pan, and now he raised it high, sweat gleaming on his forehead, his eyes wild.

"You want the pan?" he shrieked. "You want the pan? I'll give you the pan!"

Before the bald man could bring the pan down on Bumstead's head, Sam plucked it easily from his hand.

"I'll take that, actually," he said. "Now if you'll just step along, sir. We have some questions to ask our friend Sticky Fingers here."

Bumstead flinched at the sound of his name, as if it pained him. The bald man staggered to his feet.

"Hey. How about you mind your own business, kid?" In the firelight, his buckteeth gave him the look of a deranged jackrabbit. Several other pajama-clad spectators had drawn close to watch the fight, and Sam swallowed a sigh. Once again, he'd become the center of attention.

"You know what? Since you both want the pan so badly . . ." The frying pan was the heavy cast-iron kind. He took the pan in two hands, squeezing and pushing at the same time, until it cracked in two. The noise was sharp as gunfire and several of the onlookers jumped. "There," Sam said. "One portion for each of you. Happy now?"

The bucktoothed man was gaping at Sam, white-faced, as if he'd just seen him step from the grave. When Sam tried to give him his half of the frying pan, he staggered backward.

"W—witchcraft," he rasped. Then he turned and sprinted into the darkness, scattering the spectators in his path.

"Typical. All that work for nothing." Sam shook his head. Solly Bumstead was trying to wiggle backward, away from the firelight, perhaps hoping he could sneak away. Sam tossed the broken frying pan to the ground, missing Bumstead's left ear by inches. "And now on to you, Mr. Bumstead."

And Sam lifted Bumstead easily with one hand, as if he weighed no more than a feather, and set him gently on his feet.

12

"I didn't do it," were the first words out of Bumstead's mouth.

Thomas and Pippa exchanged a look.

"You don't even know what we're here for," Thomas pointed out.

"Doesn't matter," Bumstead said stubbornly. He had a sallow face and a weak chin. His cuffs were filthy and too long, and his thinning hair was coated in pomade that smelled a little like glue. "I know I ain't done it, because I ain't done anything."

"Sounds like you got a guilty conscious to me," Max said, narrowing her eyes.

"Conscience," Pippa corrected her.

Bumstead scowled. "Well, you didn't come to give me no prize, did you? So what? Did some payroll office get knocked over? A jewel robber make away with somebody's diamond necklace? Some fancy old painting go missing from a museum?"

"Worse," Thomas said evenly. "Someone was murdered."

Bumstead startled a little. His expression turned uncertain. "M—murdered," he stammered. "Well, now you're way off the bag. Back in the day I was a top thief, sure. Best in the whole city. But I never went around hurtin' nobody." He worried the ragged hem of his shirt. "I'm a peaceful man, honest. What would I go around killing somebody for?"

"You tell us," Thomas said, watching Bumstead closely. "Siegfried Eckleberger is dead."

"Eckleberger . . ." Bumstead whispered the name like a curse. He closed his eyes. Next to Thomas, Pippa twitched, and he wondered whether she was again feeling a wave of Bumstead's hatred consume her. When he opened his eyes again, he just looked like a tired old man. "I can't say I'm sorry he's dead," Bumstead said. "The man got me shipped off to prison for eight long years. Lost my nerve in lockup. Got scared straight. Now I couldn't steal a tulip from a garden, even if I tried."

"Isn't that a good thing?" Sam ventured to ask.

Bumstead guffawed. "A good thing? A good thing? And how am I supposed to make a living, now I can't do the only thing I was ever good at? No one wants to hire a slug like me, especially not now I got time on my record."

"So you admit you hated Eckleberger?" Max pressed.

"Hated him? Sure. Of course I hated him. There was a time, you know, when I was really worth something." Bumstead's eyes grew unfocused, as if he was peering into the past. "There wasn't a safe I couldn't crack or a door I couldn't open. I once stole the mayor's watch when he was sitting next to me at lunch. You know that Rachel Richstone girl who's been in all the papers? I once took a sapphire necklace off her at her own birthday party. 'Course she wasn't a Richstone yet. She was still a Van der Water back then, and practically oozing money. Her old man did something in metals. Or was it minerals? Either way—" He broke off suddenly when Thomas gave a little shout. "Are you okay?"

Thomas shook his head. "No. I mean yes. I mean go on." He could hardly contain his excitement. His insides were buzzing. Rachel van der Water. RVW—the letters he had noticed on the brown paper backing from the broken picture frame in Eckleberger's studio. At one point, there had been a picture of a young Rachel in that frame. What had happened to it? Had it been taken by the same person who had killed Eckleberger? But why, then, were the other photos left?

And what did it have to do with Eckleberger's murder?

"Ah, forget it." Bumstead scowled again. "All this talking about the past. What good does it do me? That's all done now. Now I'm just some used-up bum, like all the rest." He raised his arms as if to embrace all the people transformed by the darkness into faceless shadows. He dropped his arms again. "But I didn't kill Eckleberger. You can bet your boots on that. Eight years in Sing Sing's plenty for me. I'd never risk doing anything to land me back in that hellhole."

"It's okay," Thomas said. "We believe you."

"We do?" Max turned to him in surprise.

"Sure," Thomas said. "Like he said. He doesn't have the nerves for it."

"No." Bumstead shook his head sadly, as if having failed to commit murder were in itself a crime. "No, I do not."

"Sorry about your frying pan," Sam said sheepishly.

Bumstead flushed a deep red. "Oh, er, that's all right," he said. "I might have—well, I might have exaggerated a little when I said I couldn't steal a tulip from a garden. Not saying I stole it, mind you, since it was just sitting there. . . ." He trailed off.

Pippa sighed heavily. "Don't worry, Mr. Bumstead. Sounds like you'll be back on your feet in no time."

On the way back to the museum, Thomas told Pippa, Sam, and Max about the empty photo frame he'd found at Eckleberger's apartment, and the scrap of brown paper inscribed with what he was sure were Rachel Richstone's former initials.

"It doesn't make sense," Pippa said. "Why would someone steal an old photograph of Rachel Richstone from a frame, but leave a pile of photos next to it, untouched?"

"Sounds like one of those stupid riddles," Max mumbled.

"There must have been something secret in the photograph," Thomas said slowly. Closing his eyes, he could still see the chaos of Eckleberger's studio, the drama of it, as if someone had been staging a break-in for a movie. "Something the thief didn't want anyone to see. With all the other stuff knocked around, he probably thought no one would notice a missing photograph."

"Or she," Max said.

"What?" Thomas looked at her.

"Or she," Max repeated, shrugging. "The thief could have been a woman."

Thomas stopped himself from rolling his eyes. "Okay, he or she probably thought no one would notice."

Everyone was silent for a bit. They'd left Central Park behind. Above them once again the city buildings rose, silent and spectral in a mist sweeping in from the river.

"I still don't buy it," Sam spoke up suddenly. "Who'd want to steal a photo of someone who's already dead?"

"I don't know," Thomas said. "But I'm going to find out."

13

Pippa felt that she'd barely closed her eyes before Miss Fitch was calling for everyone to wake up. Morning sun was streaming hard into the attic, and the other performers were grumbling about having to get up.

It had been four days since they'd tracked down Sticky Fingers in Central Park, and the week was moving at a crawl. The city was in the grips of a heat wave and even with all the windows open, the museum felt like an armpit. By seven o'clock, the hour of the evening performance, everyone was in a rotten mood. Caroline and Quinn were talking about breaking up their act. Caroline, in particular, was no longer content to be one half of the albino sisters, and wanted to go off on her own. Goldini flew into a panic when he discovered his magic wand had been broken in two, and Smalls recited a dull poem about perseverance until everyone wanted to strangle him.

No one noticed that the alligator boy was missing until the finale, which typically ended when Caroline and Quinn cartwheeled into the arms of the alligator boy and Smalls the giant, respectively. At the last second, Goldini ran onstage to keep Quinn from tumbling straight into the audience. Luckily, there was hardly anyone there to witness it. Only three people had arrived to see the nightly performance, and one of them had spent the evening chin-to-chest, snoring loudly.

Quinn was in tears in the kitchen after the performance. "How could he?" she screeched. "When I see him, I'll tear the scales off his face, one by one!"

"Now, now," Lash said, patting her shoulder. "No need to get so riled up."

Quinn promptly threw herself at him and began sobbing into his chest. Caroline was purple with fury, and Miss Fitch glared so hard, Pippa was afraid that her eyeballs would pop out of her head and roll across the floor.

"*Quel désastre*," Monsieur Cabillaud said, throwing his gloves down emphatically on the kitchen table. "Sree people! Sree people to see our show! Zat makes only a dollar fifty—barely enough to keep ze roof over our heads."

"And what about getting paid?" Danny grumbled.

"And what about eating *real* food, for once?" Goldini said, poking at the pile of watery oatmeal that would be their dinner.

"Just a little bit of patience, dear friends," Mr. Dumfrey said. He had joined them for dinner to reassure them, and also to tell them the latest piece of news: that Andrew had decided to take a short "sabbatical" from the museum. At least, that was how he phrased it, but everyone knew that meant one thing only: the alligator boy had quit. "Remember—it's from the rockiest shores that grow the greatest diamonds! Our luck will turn any day now. This is Dumfrey's Dime Museum of Freaks, Oddities, and Wonders—the greatest collection of rarities in the whole known world! And I have one or two ideas up my sleeve—some of my finest work yet."

No one, however, was much reassured. It was clear to Pippa that unless something was done—and soon—Mr. Dumfrey would have a full-on rebellion on his hands.

The only two people who seemed unaware of the

tension in the room were Max and Howie. Max, uncharacteristically, had brushed her hair and tied it with a ribbon, which had so startled Pippa that at first she had mistaken Max for someone else—until Max had threatened to poke her eyes out with a fork if she didn't stop staring. She and Howie were sitting elbow to elbow, and every time Howie said something, Max actually *giggled*. It was obvious to Pippa that Max had gone as stupid for Howie as Miss Fitch had for William "Lash" Langtry.

On the one hand, Pippa could understand why. Howie was the best-looking person she'd ever seen. Certainly Sam, with his pimply forehead and his narrow nose and his look of a dog that had recently been kicked, couldn't compete. And yet Howie was too perfect, too brittle-looking—like one of the porcelain pieces in the museum's collection of priceless, ancient Chinese statuettes. And Pippa hated how he turned his head on his shoulder blades to watch her pass, eyes glittering, as though sizing her up from 360 degrees.

Then, there were the comments—small things, like the way he was careful to emphasize that everyone in his family was *born* with the same talent; and how he leaned in when Pippa came offstage during a particularly bad performance, at which she'd failed to think

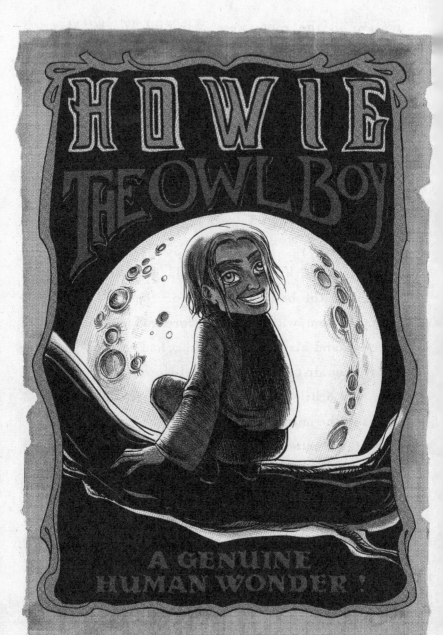

her way even into the pocket of a man's overcoat, and whispered, "Just not coming *naturally*, is it?"

Almost as if he knew what she was—what they all were. But of course, he couldn't know. What Rattigan had done to them in his lab . . . *nobody* knew, except for Dumfrey and Miss Fitch—and, of course, Rattigan himself.

Most of the performers huffed off to the attic right after dinner, and Max and Howie disappeared together, while Sam stared miserably into his untouched oatmeal. Finally, only Mr. Dumfrey, Pippa, Thomas, Sam, and Lash were left in the kitchen.

"I don't know what we'll do," Mr. Dumfrey said, sagging back against his seat, like a balloon drained all at once of air. Pippa realized he'd been trying to put on a brave face for the others. "Unless business picks up, I'm afraid we'll have to close our doors for good."

"Don't worry, Mr. Dumfrey," Pippa said. "You'll think of something."

"You always do," Thomas said.

But Mr. Dumfrey didn't look comforted. "This time, I'm afraid you might be wrong."

There was a moment of depressed silence. Then Lash cleared his throat. All this time, he had been fiddling with one of the kitchen shelves, which was loose, making a big deal of sorting through his tools and testing each one against the screw—and, Pippa was sure, eavesdropping closely on the conversation.

"I been thinkin', Horatio," he said with forced casualness, wiping his hands on a rag, "how about I give the old bullwhip routine a shot? That was always a crowd-pleaser. Brought 'em in like flies to honey."

"Yeah, Mr. Dumfrey. How about it?" Thomas said.

"That's a great idea," Pippa chimed in enthusiastically, She'd been dying to see Lash's old routine since he'd arrived at the museum and started telling them about it. Even Sam smiled for an instant.

But Mr. Dumfrey cut them off. "I—er—appreciate the offer, Lash. Really, I do. But I'm not sure that's such a good idea." He coughed. "We aren't as young as we used to be, you know. Not sure the old acts are up to the gold standard."

"Some of us old dogs got the best tricks," Lash said. "I'm steadier than I was at twenty." Lash held out a hand as if to prove it. Pippa was pained to see that his fingers were trembling very badly. Lash stuffed his hand quickly back into a pocket. "Well, anyway. The offer stands."

"Thank you, Lash." Mr. Dumfrey stood up and laid a hand on his old friend's shoulder. "That's very nice of you."

Lash wouldn't meet Mr. Dumfrey's eyes. He just nodded. As soon as Mr. Dumfrey left the room, Lash hurried out after him, mumbling something about cleaning up the exhibit halls.

Pippa felt sad and anxious. She knew it wasn't fair to blame Howie. But since he'd arrived, everyone was fighting all the time—just when they should have been sticking together. She'd thought that with Rattigan safely gone, everything would return to normal—as normal as they ever were at Dumfrey's, anyway. But things were worse than ever, and she didn't feel as safe as she should. She kept thinking of all those families they'd seen living out in Central Park, and wondering whether she, too, might have found herself there if it weren't for Mr. Dumfrey. If the museum shut down, what would happen to her? Where would they go? She'd been wondering all this time about her real parents, but she didn't have the first idea about how to find them. Even if she could track down her family, she knew deep down that there was no guarantee they'd want her back.

When she'd at last worked up the courage to ask Mr. Dumfrey whether he knew anything about her life before Rattigan got to her, he had practically choked spitting out a no.

"Are you okay?" Thomas laid a hand on her shoulder. She'd been so lost in thought, she hadn't realized that she and Thomas were now alone in the kitchen. Sam had stalked off somewhere. That was another thing that was going wrong—they had only just started to become friends, but for the past few days he'd hardly spoken except to growl.

"Yeah," Pippa said, even though she wasn't sure. "I just feel . . ." She trailed off, uncertain how to describe what she felt.

Luckily, Thomas seemed to know. "Squinchy," he said. "Like when you accidentally step on a snail barefoot."

Pippa turned to him. Thomas's green eyes seemed to pin her momentarily in place.

"Squinchy," she repeated, nodding, and then managed a small smile. "*You* should have been the mind reader."

They sat in silence for a bit. Pippa was surprised that she had grown so comfortable with Thomas in such a short time. For years they had lived side by side and barely spoken except to quarrel. But something had changed after the shrunken head was stolen, after the murders began, after Rattigan. They were joined, all of them—Sam, Max, Pippa, Thomas—whether they wanted it or not. They were connected.

She didn't mean to speak, but suddenly she was saying, "Remember the time Freckles dressed up like Santa Claus, and tried to surprise us by coming down the chimney—"

"And Miss Fitch thought it was a giant rat, and insisted we light a fire," Thomas chimed in. "And he was howling like a maniac until Dumfrey threw the eggnog on—"

"And afterward he sat with us all night, with his trouser bottoms completely burned away," Pippa finished, breathless with laughter, remembering Eckleberger sipping tea in front of the still-smoking fireplace, with his false beard hanging at an angle.

Thomas was laughing, too. "Crazy old Freckles."

"Wonderful old Freckles," she said, and then felt a shooting pain deep in her chest, which drove the rest of the laughter straight out of her body. Freckles would never see another Christmas.

Thomas grew serious also. "I've been thinking," he said, fidgeting a little on the bench, "about the photograph I found. Or rather the one I *didn't* find. I think—"

But just then there was a rustling from the courtyard outside, and a *bang* as something heavy tumbled into the trash bins. Pippa and Thomas both jumped to their feet. Thomas put a finger to his lips, and Pippa nodded. They listened.

The kitchen door led to a small sunken courtyard where the museum placed its trash bins. It was unused except by stray cats and, occasionally, by the performers when they wanted to escape the museum undetected; from the courtyard, a small stone staircase led up to Forty-Fifth Street.

Someone was out there now.

There was another metallic clang, then the sound of muffled cursing. Thomas's eyes widened. Pippa gestured to the shelves behind him. He understood her immediately, and eased two heavy cast-iron pots down from the wall, passing one to her, and gripping the other like a baseball bat.

They took up positions on either side of the door. Pippa's hands were sweating, and the cast iron was so heavy that her arms trembled. If only Sam hadn't gone upstairs. What if a burglar were trying to break in? They would scream; someone would have to hear.

Another fear seized her, like a tight fist closing its hand around her lungs. What if Rattigan had come back . . . ?

No. Rattigan was in Chicago. And he would be caught any day.

There was a scratching sound just outside the door. Pippa's heart was pounding, as if a pair of heavy boots were stomping around inside her chest. The person outside was picking the lock. The door handle rattled. Thomas nodded to her. When the door opened, Pippa would have the first, and clearest, shot. The doorknob rattled again, loose and loud, like an old man trying to cough out phlegm. She felt like she might throw up. Any second now.

There was a click. Then, slowly, so slowly, the knob turned and the door swung open.

Pippa hefted the pan into the air. Fear made the edges of her vision go dark; a face appeared and she swung.

"No, Pippa. No!"

Thomas lunged for her and grabbed her wrist. At the last second, just before she connected with Chubby's terrified face, the pan clattered to the ground.

"What's the matter with you?" Chubby was shouting.

Pippa, still shaking, could only stare. "What's the matter with *me*?" she cried. "What's the matter with *you*?"

"Be quiet, both of you," Thomas whispered.

But it was too late. Sharp footsteps sounded in the hall. Thomas shoved Chubby under the table just as Miss Fitch appeared at the top of the kitchen stairs.

"What's going on? I heard shouting." Her black eyes glittered dangerously. "Why is the door open?"

Chubby was cowering under the table. If Miss Fitch came down the stairs, Pippa knew he would be discovered.

"Nothing," she said quickly. "It was . . . it was . . ."

"A rat," Thomas said. "A big one. It was trying to get in."

Miss Fitch's mouth curled in disgust. "Did you catch it?"

Both Pippa and Thomas shook their heads. Chubby had pulled his knees to his chest, and was making himself as small as possible.

"Disgusting things," she said. "Ought to have their heads snapped off, every one of them. Lock the door. And wash your hands, for Pete's sake. Those vermin carry all kinds of disease." Then she turned and spun around, stalking back into the main hall, and closing the door behind her.

With Miss Fitch gone, Chubby scuttled out from underneath the table and stood up. Their lie hadn't been all that inaccurate. Chubby did look a bit like an overgrown rat. His face was smeared with dirt and crusted bits of things Pippa didn't want to think about. His cap was gone. Lanky dark hair was plastered across his sweaty forehead. His clothes were filthy, and he looked even skinnier than usual.

"What are you *doing* here?" Pippa demanded. "You nearly gave me a heart attack."

"You nearly turned him into a pancake," Thomas pointed out.

It was as though Chubby hadn't heard. "I'm in trouble," he said, pacing the narrow kitchen like a condemned man. "Big, big trouble."

"Slow down," Thomas said. "Start at the beginning."

Chubby took a big gulp of air. Now he *really* looked like a rat—a drowning one. He exhaled slowly.

"Better?" Thomas asked, and Chubby nodded. "Okay, then. Why did you run from the cops the other day?"

He worked the hem of his shirt agitatedly. "I don't know. When I heard Eckleberger was dead I must've lost my top." He looked suddenly green. "I could never stand any of that stuff. Blood and guts and . . . and ghosts." He shivered.

"Don't be an idiot, Chubby," Pippa said, losing patience. "There's no such thing as ghosts."

"Is too," he said. "My friend Alan's got a ghost. Eats the sugar right out of the tin in the middle of the night when no one's looking."

"He's probably eating it himself," Pippa said.

"It was stupid of you to run, Chubby," Thomas said sternly.

Chubby moaned and sank down onto a bench. "I know," he said. "That's why I said I'm in trouble. Big trouble. The cops think *I* killed Eckleberger!"

14

"What?" Thomas and Pippa cried together.

Chubby nodded miserably. "They got it in for me," he said. "Just because I once lifted a bottle of soda or two from a store when no one would miss it. It was wrong!" he added quickly, when Pippa glared at him. "But now they want to pin me with murder. The fat-headed one"—Thomas assumed he meant Sergeant Schroeder—"tracked me down to the Bowery. I got a place to crash down there with a couple of boys. Nice and warm in winter. Cozy, really."

"Focus, Chubby," Thomas said.

"Right, right." Chubby blushed. "So Fat Head tracked me down and tossed my stuff when I wasn't around. He found that medallion I showed you, the one Eckleberger gave me for a present. But he thinks I stole it. Bumped Eckleberger off, just to steal a stupid pin. As soon as he gets his fat hands on me, he's gonna chuck me in a jail cell and leave me to rot."

No wonder Chubby looked so sad and straggly and pathetic, like a boiled noodle left too long at the bottom of the pot. He probably hadn't seen daylight since he'd bolted from Eckleberger's studio. Thomas felt sorry for him.

Pippa obviously didn't. "What do you expect us to do about it?" she said.

Chubby stared at her, wide-eyed, as if it were obvious. "You gotta help me," he said. "You gotta prove I didn't do it."

"How on earth do you expect us to do that?" Pippa said.

Chubby looked stricken. He worked the hem of his shirt harder than ever. "I thought maybe . . . I don't know . . . after the whole mess with the shrunken head. You guys sorted that out, didn't you? The police locked Dumfrey up and you sprung him."

"That was different," Pippa said, flustered. "We were lucky—and besides, we had no choice; the museum was in danger, we were all going to land on the street—"

Much to Thomas's alarm, Chubby thudded down onto his knees, clasping his hands together. "Please," he wailed. "You gotta help me. I'll do anything. Anything! I'll cart your garbage for a month, I'll do your laundry for a year, I'll carry you on my back all the way to Brooklyn—"

"All right, Chubby," Thomas said quickly, if only to get Chubby off his knees. He helped Chubby stand. "We'll help you. On your feet." Chubby obeyed, dragging a hand underneath his nose, leaving a slimy trail from wrist to forefinger.

Pippa stood in stony silence while Thomas and Chubby worked out a plan. Chubby would return to hiding and do his best to stay out of sight while Thomas poked around. Should Thomas need to speak to him, he would hang a pair of red trousers just outside his attic window, and Chubby would knock on the kitchen door at exactly midnight. This precaution was necessary, since they had no other method of communicating; Chubby refused to tell even Pippa and Thomas where he might be heading, and referred shiftily to going "underground."

Finally, Chubby had sufficiently calmed down, and they could tell him goodnight. Thomas watched as Chubby slipped past the garbage bins and was swallowed by the darkness of the street. He closed and locked the door. His eyes were burning. It had been a long night.

Pippa was glaring at him, arms crossed, doing an alarmingly good impression of Miss Fitch.

"You shouldn't have lied to him," she said. "It isn't right."

"I wasn't lying," Thomas said carefully, avoiding her gaze. Even though he knew Pippa's gift was unreliable, when she fixed her dark eyes on him, he sometimes felt as if she was reading the very darkest corners of his mind. "Chubby didn't kill Eckleberger."

Pippa rolled her eyes. "Of course he didn't," she said. "He wouldn't have the brains or the spine for it. But if the police think so, what can we do about it? Nothing." There was a pleading tone to her voice, as if she were trying to convince him. "We've hit a dead end. Anyone in the whole city could have killed Freckles. We've got nothing to go on."

"Look, the same person who took that photograph of Rachel Richstone killed Eckleberger," Thomas said. "I'm sure of it. *So what if he also killed Rachel Richstone? What if the photograph was a clue to Rachel's murder?*"

Pippa looked at Thomas as if he'd gone crazy. "Rachel Richstone was murdered by her husband. He caught her having an affair with Edmund Snyder. Everybody knows he did it."

"Mr. Richstone says he didn't," Thomas said.

"Of course he does," she said. "He isn't likely to confess, is he?"

Thomas shrugged. "I don't see why not. He's getting the chair either way." They were coming up to the second-floor landing. Thomas stopped and put his hands on Pippa's shoulder, lowering his voice so Miss Fitch, sleeping in the costume department not fifteen feet away, wouldn't hear. "What if he didn't do it, Pippa? What if someone else did—the same person who killed Eckleberger, and stole the photograph so he wouldn't be found out? And what if Mr. Richstone's going to get fried for nothing?"

"What if pigs sprouted wings and started parachuting?" Pippa said.

"I'm serious, Pip." Thomas felt a rising frustration, as if his insides were in a tangle and he couldn't figure out how to unwind them. He'd promised to help Chubby. And he wanted to find out who had killed Eckleberger, and see him punished.

But it was more than that. Ever since he'd come face-to-face with Rattigan and learned the truth of his origins, Thomas had felt a constant, needling sense of shame, like a splinter lodged somewhere deep in his chest. He had always known he was different, but now he knew he'd been made that way, engineered in a laboratory—he'd been tweaked and adjusted and turned into a freak. He knew Pippa had recently become obsessed with the idea of a family that had come *before*, but for Thomas the opposite was true. The past was another thing Rattigan had killed. He needed to prove that there was a reason for it; that he could do something good; that he was not like the monster who had created him.

"We need to talk to Richstone—before it's too late."

"You're hurting me," Pippa said, and Thomas realized that he was gripping her tightly. He let her go. She took a step backward. Her eyes were shadowed by the dark curtain of her bangs. In the small patch of moonlight, he could just see her frown.

"I'm sorry, Thomas," she said quietly. "But you're on your own on this one."

Then she turned and fled up the stairs, leaving Thomas alone, in the dark.

Morning brought further trouble: Caroline, insisting that her twin sister was holding her back from fame, had packed a bag and departed for Hollywood. Despite the fact that Caroline and Quinn never did anything but bicker, Quinn was inconsolable, and spent the morning sobbing into her pillow and refusing to speak to anyone.

As the day progressed, everyone's mood only got fouler, as though there were some invisible chemical in the air, turning the residents of the museum against one another. Almost every hour, a new quarrel broke out. Someone was stealing food from the kitchen. A hairbrush had gone missing. A costume was mysteriously stained. Someone had used up the last of the toilet paper. Throughout the day, Lash was forced to abandon his work to break up an argument in the stairwell or the exhibition halls.

There was at least one benefit to all the fighting: Thomas was able to move about freely, without any interference. It was easy for him to nick a piece of paper and a pen from Mr. Dumfrey's desk, since Mr. Dumfrey was busy trying to mollify Miss Fitch, who believed someone had shrunk her undergarments as a joke. It was easy for him to string a pair of red trousers out of the attic window, since Sam was deliberately ignoring him and Howie was too busy complaining about the meager dinner to notice. It was equally easy for him to slip out of bed just before midnight and go down to the kitchens with his letter, now sealed and carefully addressed to *Manfred Richstone*, care of Sing Sing prison. As he had hoped, Chubby showed up right on time, and promised to deliver the letter into the hands of someone who would deliver it into the hands of someone else who would deliver it directly into the hands of Mr. Richstone in his jail cell.

The wait, he knew, would be the hardest part.

15

Pippa had never believed it would be possible, but she almost missed Bill Evans, the reporter who had made their lives so difficult in the early spring with his constant reports about the museum and the children who lived there. But at least—at *least*—he'd brought in some business for the museum. Pippa was getting tired of suiting up in her long velvet dress, which itched and pinched at the same time, only to perform for a single person—most often someone who had come in to escape the heat and take advantage of the Odditorium's many fans. At least the old man who'd been stealing peanut brittle from the refreshment stand hadn't returned. They were running low on candy and couldn't afford to replace it.

And Mr. Dumfrey and Miss Fitch insisted the show would, must, *did* go on—and so, the morning after Chubby's nighttime visit to the museum, Pippa was stitched into her costume and waiting backstage for her cue.

At last, things seemed to be going smoothly. Max had quartered an apple midair and distributed the pieces to the remaining audience members: two old ladies, who sat fanning themselves in the dark, a vastly fat man whose shirtfront was covered with caramel popcorn, and a prim middle-aged woman clutching her purse on her lap as though worried one of the performers might reach off the stage and snatch it. Goldini had performed remarkably well—he had not stuttered, dropped a rabbit, or fumbled a card even once—and was almost finished with his act. It was time for his final trick, the Box of Death, in which Thomas, dressed up like the magician's female assistant, folded himself into a tiny box and was neatly impaled by a dozen swords. It was a guaranteed crowd-pleaser—at least it would have been, had there been any kind of crowd—and even Pippa never got tired of the moment when Thomas sprang, unharmed, from the skewered box. The trick was in the exact positioning of the swords: Thomas had memorized the position he must assume in order to avoid getting even a nick.

Thomas squeezed himself into the box, which was hardly bigger than a child's-sized suitcase. Only his head remained visible, although he was nearly unrecognizable in his costume, which included a blond wig and vivid red lipstick. Each time Goldini produced a sword and, with a flourish, slid it directly through the box—and, to all appearances, directly through Thomas's body—the audience gasped and broke into applause. Goldini's narrow face was flushed with happiness. Only one sword remained; soon, he would be finished with a near-perfect performance.

"So you see," he trumpeted as he raised the final sword so that the blade glittered in the light, "only with magic can the impossible become—"

He didn't finish his sentence. As he shoved the final sword into its position, Pippa had a sudden jolt, a flash of vision: his angle was all wrong. Before she could shout out a warning, she saw the sword plunge between Thomas's ribs. Thomas let out a high-pitched screech and Goldini sprang backward, trembling. In her shock, Pippa wondered at first whether this was part of the act—whether the sword had a trick blade, whether her vision was wrong. Then she saw Goldini's face—white, drawn, terrified—and noticed to her horror several drops of blood spatter to the stage. Thomas's face was contorted in pain. The middle-aged woman in the audience screamed.

"Pull the curtain!" Mr. Dumfrey plunged backstage, panting. "Pull the curtain, for God's sake, and get the boy offstage!"

Lash sprang for the curtain-pull, and a minute too late, the heavy velvet curtains swooshed together, concealing Thomas from the audience's view. But the damage had been done. There were cries and boos from the audience; someone screeched that the price of admission should be refunded. Pippa hurried onstage, where Goldini was frantically trying to free Thomas from the skewered box.

"Don't move"—he gasped, removing blades as fast as he could, while Thomas moaned, his forehead beaded with sweat—"just another minute."

"Thomas!" She dropped to her knees beside the wooden box, wishing that Thomas had at least a hand free so she could squeeze it. "Are you all right?"

"Sure," he said, and winced. "Never been better."

Suddenly, they were surrounded: Danny and Miss Fitch, Betty and Smalls, Sam and Max; all were clustered around the wooden box, shouting out instructions and

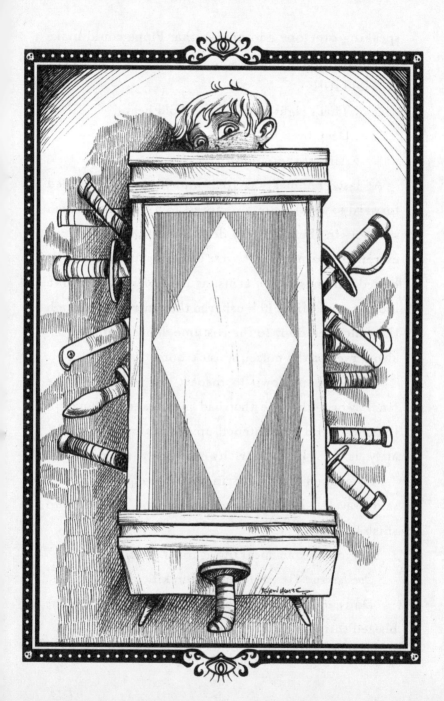

speaking over one another, so that Pippa could make out only snippets of phrases.

"Hold still . . ."

". . . That's right, give it a good old heave!"

". . . Deep breath . . ."

". . . Almost there now!"

At last, Thomas was free, and Miss Fitch rushed forward to administer a compress to his wound—which was not, in the end, very deep, though it still looked extremely painful and was bleeding freely. Smalls hefted Thomas in his arms, as if Thomas were still a toddler, and Miss Fitch ushered them directly through the concealed door to the costume department, which also served as the museum's sickroom.

Goldini bent down to inspect the position of the final sword—the one that had punctured Thomas in the chest—and straightened up again almost immediately, as if a volt of electricity had gone through him.

"Someone's been tinkering with the equipment," he said gravely. "I might have turned poor Thomas into shish kebab."

Everyone began speaking again at once.

"*Quel horreur!* He could have been killed!"

"Don't look at me, Cabillaud, I never touched the blasted thing. Maybe it's *you* who got mixed up."

"Surely you can't think zat I, who once performed great service for ze Belgian government, am to blame!"

"Everybody calm down," Pippa said, before the argument could escalate. She was sick of the squabbling; a sharp headache was crystallizing directly between her eyebrows. "Let's think logically. Who was the last person to touch Goldini's swords?"

"It must have been Lash," Goldini said thoughtfully. "He's responsible for keeping the props in order."

A half dozen faces turned in Lash's direction. He stood a short distance away, trembling, his face the mottled gray of old porridge.

"It's true," he said miserably. "I took the thing apart to give it a good scrubbing. I reckoned I put it back together just fine. But I'll be danged if I didn't make a fine old mess out of things."

"It's all right, Lash," Pippa jumped in quickly, before anyone could begin to lecture him. "It was an honest mistake. Wasn't it?" There was a long pause. Pippa glared at the assembled group until she felt her eyeballs might combust. "*Wasn't it?*" she repeated.

"Of course, of course," Goldini said at last. "No one blames you, Lash. And at least there was no great harm done." The others mumbled their agreement, and Lash looked enormously relieved, and swore up and down to be more careful next time.

But Pippa was left with a sense of unease. Everything, it seemed, was going wrong.

On her way up to the attic to retrieve some books for Thomas to read while Miss Fitch tended to him, she passed Howie on the stairwell. He had removed only a portion of his stage makeup, and his face looked especially pale against the deep hollows Miss Fitch had painted under his eyes to give him a slightly more owlish appearance.

"What's all the fuss about?" he said. "I heard everybody shouting."

"The fuss is about the fact that Thomas almost got chopped in two," she snapped, unreasonably irritated that Howie hadn't been there.

"Chopped in two?" Howie quirked an eyebrow. Even his eyebrows were perfect. Pippa suspected he trimmed, shaped, and perhaps even watered them, like miniature lawns. She had more than once seen a pair of tiny scissors and miniature gold tweezers in his shirt pocket. "What do you mean? What happened?"

"It was during the magic act," Pippa said. "The last trick got botched."

"That's awful," Howie said, but he didn't seem too concerned. He had not, Pippa noticed, asked whether Thomas was okay. Instead, he turned and started up the stairs again. "I guess magic comes more naturally for some people than for others."

"Goldini's a good magician," Pippa protested, even though he wasn't—not really. He tried his best, but he was plagued by nerves, and he often forgot where he had left his props, so that the other performers were always finding playing cards in their dinner rolls and coins wedged between seat cushions, and yet Goldini never had an ace of spades when he needed one. Still, he was a part of their family, much more so than Howie was, and Pippa felt like defending him.

Howie swiveled his head around on his shoulder blades, blinking, as though surprised to see her still behind him. "I wasn't talking about Goldini," he said casually.

Pippa felt a rush of heat to her face as she realized what he meant. "It wasn't Thomas's fault."

Howie shrugged. "Whatever you say."

It was obvious he didn't believe her. She gripped the banister. If she'd had half of Sam's strength, the wood would have splintered in her hand. "You weren't even there," she said. "You have no idea what you're talking about."

"No need to get agitated," he said, which only agitated her further. "I just meant that some people are *born* with a kind of talent. And other people aren't."

Pippa had not missed the slight way he emphasized the word *born*. She was sure of it. Could Howie possibly know about Rattigan, and what he had done? The idea made her feel nauseous and cold all over, the same way she had once felt after learning that Miss Fitch had thrown out a trunk containing several of her journals, believing it was empty: as though her insides had been laid bare only to evaporate suddenly into nothing.

But how could Howie know? Mr. Dumfrey had been careful—obsessive, even—about keeping the children's identities and relationship to Rattigan's experiments a secret. He claimed to know nothing about how Rattigan had picked his subjects, or where they'd come from to begin with.

Then Howie said, "But you know Thomas better than I do. Besides, you're right. I wasn't there," and Pippa's suspicions passed. He was just being a jerk, as usual. She didn't know what Max saw in Howie, other than his big blue eyes and neat white teeth and the swoop of his dark hair over his right eyebrow.

Okay, she *did* know what Max saw in him—but he was still a jerk, pure and simple.

"Hey, Pip," Thomas said, when she squeezed through the costume racks and into the space set apart for the infirmary. "What'd you bring me?"

She grunted a little as she plopped a stack of books down onto the nightstand drawn up to the bed: *Brain Busters, Mind Teasers, Miraculous Mind Benders,* and *The Colossal Book of Puzzlers, Paradoxes, and Impossible Problems,* among others.

"I figured there must be *something* here you haven't read," she said as Thomas began sorting through the pile. "I thought of trying to bring DeathTrap, but I couldn't find the mummy's hand."

"Yeah, Mr. Dumfrey took it back," he said casually. He was sitting up in a small cot, supported by several fluffy pillows. He was shirtless, and Pippa saw cotton gauze packed around his wound. Already, he looked much better. Color had returned to his face and he was breathing easily. "He needed it for the Egyptian exhibit. Besides, you really need the rug to play." DeathTrap was a game of Thomas's invention. Much like chess, it featured a series of moving parts, all of them capable of jumping, biting, skipping, or grabbing in different ways. "Oh, good. You brought *100 of the World's Twistiest Teasers.* I was hoping you would have. I haven't read this one yet."

Pippa was relieved that at the very least, Thomas's accident had seemingly made him forget about the tension of the day before. "Listen to this, Pip. What's white and black and red all over?"

Before Pippa could respond that she had no idea, there was a rattle, a muffled curse, and a squeak of wheels, and the costume racks jumped apart as Mr. Dumfrey came barreling through them.

"The newspaper!" he shouted, clutching a newspaper in one fist and a wrapped football-sized bundle in the other.

Thomas sagged backward. "How did you know?"

"Know what?" Pippa and Mr. Dumfrey said at the same time.

"What's black and white and *read* all over? Get it?" Thomas said.

Mr. Dumfrey blinked at him. "My dear boy, are you sure that sword didn't go straight through your brain? Where's Miss Fitch? Where's Lash?"

Pippa and Thomas exchanged a look. Two mottled spots of color were spreading across Dumfrey's cheeks, and his eyes were shining like highly polished stones. Pippa wondered whether the fact that he had been forced to reimburse the audience members their money—bringing the grand total of the museum's earnings for the week to barely over a dollar—had given Mr. Dumfrey a fever.

"Are you all right, Mr. Dumfrey?" Pippa ventured to ask.

"My girl, I am more than all right! I'm a *genius*. I've just had a brilliant idea! A spectacular idea! All because of a newspaper." He smacked a copy of *The Daily Screamer* onto the foot of Thomas's bed. It was the morning edition, which Pippa and Thomas had already seen. On the front page was a headline trumpeting WIFE-KILLER TO DIE IN HOT SEAT, above a cartoon rendering of Manfred Richstone, strapped to an electric chair.

Thomas went pale. "One week," he muttered, and shoved the paper aside, as if it were a cockroach that had somehow ended up on his coverlet.

"I don't get it," Pippa said to Mr. Dumfrey. "What's your big idea?"

Mr. Dumfrey patted Pippa's shoulder. "It's a once-in-a-lifetime opportunity," he said. "A citywide sensation! Manfred Richstone's execution is our golden goose."

"There's no proof he's even guilty," Thomas said. Pippa knew he must be thinking of the missing photograph from Freckles's studio. She tried to telegraph with her eyes that he should let it go, but he avoided looking at her.

"Proof? Proof is overrated," Mr. Dumfrey said, waving a hand. "It's the *appearance* of guilt people want,

Thomas. And Mr. Richstone has given everyone plenty of that. Illusion and interpretation—that's what magic is all about! The fact is, seven days from now, our friend Manfred Richstone is scheduled for the chair. Which means we have less than a week—less than one week!—to launch our new exhibit." He unwrapped the football-sized bundle he had tucked under one arm, and Pippa shrieked.

It was the wax head—the one Freckles had modeled after Manfred Richstone—looking even more horrible than usual. Its mouth was bubbling with blood and its eyes were rolling to the ceiling, showing only whites.

"It's—it's awful," Pippa said.

"Thank you," Mr. Dumfrey said happily. "I made a few quick adjustments. A splash of paint, a little daub of stage blood. The effect is hideous, don't you think? The Amazingly Lifelike Replica of the Execution of Wife-Murderer Manfred Richstone! It has a ring to it, doesn't it? Of course, we'll need new fliers printed up. Once the news hits the streets, the crowds will be clawing for the doors. It's a surefire win. As sure as sunshine!" Mr. Dumfrey angled the head from left to right, admiring his handiwork.

Just then, a tremendous scream—followed by a crash—ripped through the infirmary. Pippa spun around and saw Miss Fitch, clutching her heart, a shattered glass of milk puddled at her feet.

"Horatio, really." Besides his old friend Lash, Miss Fitch was the only person at the museum who referred to Dumfrey by his first name. "You nearly gave me a heart attack. I thought Thomas's head might have rolled right off."

Dumfrey spared her barely a glance. "Nonsense, Thomas doesn't look a thing like Manfred Richstone. He's a real beaut, isn't he?" And he gave a satisfied sigh before once again tucking the head carefully in its fabric bundle. "Now, Miss Fitch. You know there's no use crying over spilled milk." This, as Miss Fitch had stooped to clean up the ruined glass. "Come. We have business to discuss. We must make immediate preparations for the next exhibit. We need a chair—a big chair, preferably metal—and of course we'll need wires, and some kind of head strap. And fliers! Dozens of fliers! Hundreds of them! Fliers to paper every lamppost in the city . . ."

And Mr. Dumfrey sailed out of the room, leaving Pippa with the uncomfortable feeling of being a wave in the wake of a large boat, unable to shake the feeling that they were all hurtling toward disaster.

16

It had become harder to take food from the kitchen at night—harder but not impossible. Max just had to be more careful.

It was almost dawn, four days after the alligator boy had abruptly quit, and two days after Thomas had nearly had a sword planted in his gut. When, the following morning, Danny had discovered two eggs and a pat of butter missing from the pantry, Monsieur Cabillaud had declared a state of emergency and Lash had volunteered to keep watch all night long over the door that led down from the first floor into the kitchen.

Fortunately, as Max had soon discovered, Lash took periodic sips from a flask hidden in his front pocket—and by five in the morning, was always soundly asleep.

She moved carefully through the dusty attic, marveling that the cluttered room, which had only a few months ago seemed a dizzying maze of junk, now was as familiar to her as her own reflection. Maybe more so, since Max had never cared to look at herself in the mirror, and deliberately avoided it now. Whenever she saw the long scar that reached from her eyebrow to her right ear, she couldn't help but think of Rattigan looming over her, clutching a surgical knife, his grin concealed behind a paper mask.

"What happened there?" Howie had asked her the other day, moving a finger carefully along the tightly sewn scar.

She had jerked away as though she'd been burned. "Car crash," she said automatically, as she always did. Thankfully, he'd let it drop.

She moved past the toilet to the spiral staircase, careful to avoid the third and seventh steps from the top, both of which groaned awfully. She didn't like to steal food from the kitchen but didn't see that she had much choice. For days, she'd been dying to tell someone about her secret, but Thomas was acting weird, Pippa was being her usual snobby, impossible self, and

Sam could suddenly barely look in her direction. And, of course, she couldn't tell Howie. Just the idea made her feel as if she'd been stuck headfirst into a furnace.

Howie, with his clean-pressed shirts and his dazzling smile and his easy manners, was the most normal person she had ever met, despite the fact that he could twist his neck like a corkscrew. Next to him, Max felt as if her body were a suit that didn't fit her very well. She knew that Howie didn't like Pippa, Sam, or Thomas very much—"impostors," he called them, and though Max didn't know what the word meant, she knew it wasn't a compliment.

No. Howie wouldn't understand at all.

But the need to tell someone—anyone—sat like a weight beneath her heart, thumping dully in her chest.

She reached the first floor and slid silently in her socked feet through the galleries, ignoring the prickling of the flesh on her arms and the strange sensation that she was being watched. Most areas of the museum didn't frighten her—not even the Hall of Wax, and the grotesque grinning figures molded from plasticine and wire. But at night, in the darkness, with the vast cool halls filled with shadows, and the exhibits massed behind glass, crouching like misshapen monsters, she couldn't help but feel a small thrill of alarm.

She paused just in front of a vast display case filled with Native American relics, including a pair of worn moccasins that Mr. Dumfrey sometimes removed from the exhibit and wore on special occasions, and a small, sharpened spearhead Max was dying to use in her act. She knew that around the corner, Lash would be parked in a rickety chair pulled from the Odditorium, one hand clutching the leather whip that had made him famous, as if prepared to truss up the thief like a Thanksgiving turkey.

She pressed her ear to the cold glass case and listened. Sure enough, she heard a sound like the distant drag of an ocean wave along a beach—in, out, in, out—and the exhibits rattled very faintly on their shelves. She allowed herself a small smile. Lash was asleep and snoring again.

She slipped out into the open, listening for the neat sputtering of his breath, and stepped carefully over his legs. The door leading into the kitchen step was already open a crack, and she nudged it wider to admit her and then felt for the banisters in the dark. She eased down the stairs and crossed quickly, by touch, to the icebox. She would take a little cheese and some tuna fish, if there was any. Then back up to the little loft above the attic. She would be in bed before anyone knew she'd been awake. . . .

Suddenly, a hand clamped onto her shoulder. She stifled a shriek and whipped around.

"What are you doing here?" It was Thomas, his face ghostly in the moonlight.

"What are *you* doing here?" she whispered back.

"It's you, isn't it?" he said. "You're the one stealing things from the kitchen?"

It was just like Thomas to have caught her. She was momentarily annoyed by the fact that he always saw the solution to a problem before anyone else. Just as quickly, the urge to confess—to explain—overwhelmed her. But she couldn't. Not yet. She didn't know if she could trust him to keep her secret. "Of course not," she said, tearing away from his grasp. "Don't be a nutter. I could say the same thing about you. I came down for a drink of water, that's all." To prove the point, she moved over to the sink, drew a large glass of water from the faucet, and took a gulp. Thomas was still looking at her as if he didn't quite believe her. "So?" she said. "What's your excuse?"

Thomas scratched his left ear, a sure sign that he was about to lie. "My excuse to what?"

"Don't play dumb," she said, crossing her arms. "It doesn't fit you."

Thomas paused. "Waiting," he said finally.

"For what?"

"It's hard to explain."

"Try me."

"Only if you tell me what you're *really* doing down here."

They glared at each other. And then, in the silence, Max heard it: a faint tapping on the door that led out into the courtyard, where the garbage bins were kept, as though a single finger were knocking lightly on the wood. Thomas's face went even paler than before. Max reached instinctively for her pocketknife before remembering that she'd left it upstairs, tucked safely under her pillow.

"Did you hear that?" she whispered. "I think—I think someone's out there."

"I didn't hear anything," Thomas said, too quickly, his eyes ticking nervously toward the door. Max understood at once. So *that's* why Thomas was lurking around in the kitchen—he was waiting for someone, and he didn't want Max to know it.

"Then you don't mind if I take a quick peek around the courtyard," Max said sweetly.

"I'll do it," Thomas said, but it was too late: Max was already unlatching the door.

Thomas was protesting, "Leave off, Max, it's none of your business, you've got no right to stick your nose—"

But he fell silent as the door groaned open.

The courtyard was empty, still, and silent. The garbage cans glistened in the moonlight. A faint wind stirred a candy wrapper on the street. But other than that, there was no movement anywhere—not a single shadow skating across the pavement, nothing disturbed or out of place.

Still, weirdly, as Thomas and Max stood in the open doorway, she couldn't shake the feeling that they were being watched.

"See?" Thomas attempted to sound lighthearted, and failed. "Nobody."

She shut the door quickly, gladly, shutting out the impression of dark eyes watching from unknown corners. "Admit it," she said. "You were expecting someone."

Thomas sucked in a deep breath. "Okay," he said, exhaling. "I admit it."

"Spill," Max said.

Then he told her: about the stack of photographs he'd found at Eckleberger's apartment, taken before Rachel van der Water became Rachel Richstone and fixed her teeth; about the frame and mysterious

missing picture; about his belief that the whole robbery had been staged, and the murder committed, just
for that missing photo. He told her, too, about the letter he had written to Mr. Richstone on death row. He
was expecting a response tonight; by prearranged signal, Chubby's messengers should string a pair of black
sneakers from the traffic lights on the corner once the
letter was in hand.

Earlier in the day, the sneakers had appeared. And
so Thomas was waiting up for a messenger. But no one
had come, and it was almost dawn.

"Now it's your turn," he said as soon as he'd finished
his story.

She took a deep breath. She knew she had no choice
but to confess to being the thief now; she would have
to trust that Thomas would understand once she
explained her reasons.

But before she could speak, there was a loud clatter from the hall. The gentle rhythm of Lash's snoring
stopped abruptly, replaced by a rapid sequence of muttered curses. Max knew at once what had happened: the
flask must have fallen from his hand, startling Lash
awake.

They were trapped. There was no way they could
get through the hall without passing Lash—then they

would both have to give explanations to Mr. Dumfrey.

Thomas looked just as panicked as Max felt. He moved quickly to the stove and shoved aside a small panel in the wall, revealing a network of pipes and looping wires, then looked at Max questioningly. She shook her head. There was no way she could squeeze into a space so small. Only Thomas was limber enough to treat the air ducts and pipes like his own network of private elevators. Max would get stuck like a piece of spinach between two teeth.

She waved him instead toward the courtyard door. They would have to go out past the garbage cans and loop around to the front of the building, then pray they could find a window to jimmy open. At least it was not yet 6 a.m. Even Miss Fitch would not wake for another half an hour.

Max unlocked the door, praying Lash wouldn't hear the click of the bolts, then eased the door open. Thomas darted out first, and she followed, exhaling only when she made it into the damp air. Thomas had already reached the street, as though worried Lash might sniff them out if they stayed too close to the museum.

"Hurry up," he whispered to Max. A distant streetlamp touched his hair white. The sky was a vivid electric blue, as it always was just before the sun wrestled loose of the horizon. Soon the museum would be bustling.

Max swung the door closed carefully. As she did, she noticed an envelope stuck to the door with a fine wad of something that looked like putty. She started to call out for Thomas—his letter had arrived after all—when the letters written across the envelope arranged themselves into words and her voice evaporated.

"Come on, Max. What're you waiting for?"

She reached up with a trembling hand and detached the envelope from the door. She wasn't a great reader—Monsieur Cabillaud had only just taught her—and her eyes scanned over the words once, twice, and again, hoping she'd made a mistake.

But she hadn't. The letter was addressed not to Thomas, but to *The Unnaturals*.

She crossed the courtyard and moved up the concrete steps on feet that felt as bloated as balloons, passing the letter to Thomas wordlessly. He tore the envelope open with his teeth. The noise sounded overloud, as if even the street was holding its breath.

The letter contained a single phrase, so simple even Max had no trouble deciphering it.

SOON, MY CHILDREN.

17

Max felt as if she had been filled head to toe with wet concrete. It wasn't possible. Rattigan was far away—halfway across the country, and, if what the news reports said were true, was likely to be arrested any day. Was this some kind of joke?

But no one knew about Rattigan. No one except Max, Thomas, Sam, Pippa, and Mr. Dumfrey. And Miss Fitch—but even Miss Fitch wasn't that evil.

"Do you think—?" she started to ask, but Thomas hushed her quickly.

"Listen," he whispered.

Almost immediately, she heard it: someone was moving in the shadows. Like a someone who had just delivered a threatening note, and now didn't want to be seen.

Max could hardly swallow. Was Rattigan here, even now, watching from the darkness? Once more, her hand went reflexively to her pocket before she remembered that she was totally unarmed. She thought of calling out for help—surely, someone would wake up and come running.

All these thoughts passed through her head in the space of one second, and before she could resolve to do anything, a shape materialized from the shadows, face concealed by a hat. Max shouted and Thomas sprang.

The stranger turned and bolted up the stairs that led to the street.

"Stop him!" Max shouted, feeling helpless and naked without her knives.

Thomas was still suffering from his injury and had miscalculated his jump; he barely clipped a trash can with his foot and went tumbling to the ground. The trash can clattered down into the courtyard, spilling a mess of bones and pulpy produce onto the stone.

"Thomas!" Max shrieked. But he was up again, unhurt, dashing up the stairs. She sprinted after him, pausing when she saw something glinting in the mess of spilled trash: a metal fork, with two tines missing, but better than nothing. She scooped it up and kept running. Bolting up the stairs, she saw the shadowy figure pass briefly under a streetlamp and careen around the corner of Forty-Fifth Street.

But Thomas, though moving more slowly than usual, was not far behind him. Max watched as he threw himself into the air and vaulted off the side of the corner building, transforming himself into a tumbling ball of momentum, like a human bullet. He disappeared from view. Max pumped her arms faster, tearing around the corner, just in time to see Thomas spread his arms . . .

. . . and belly flop to the ground, a few short inches behind the escaping stranger, with a loud *oof*.

"Don't let him get away," Thomas groaned, rolling onto his side, as Max sprinted by him.

"I won't!" she huffed back. She hoped he wasn't too hurt. She didn't have time to stop and check. She dodged an overturned trash barrel and leaped over a lumpy series of cardboard boxes that had been left in the street for pickup, barely avoiding the tail of an alley cat that was sniffing around in the gutter. The cat let out a startled yowl.

"Sorry!" Max panted out.

Just then, Max had the strangest feeling. It was as

if her mind was a curtain and suddenly, a giant elbow had shoved it aside. All at once, she saw Pippa's face, pinched with disapproval, in front of her. *You'll never catch him that way*, Pippa seemed to be saying. As quickly as the impression came, it disappeared.

The stranger was fast—much faster than Max was. Already, he had turned west onto Forty-Third Street. Max knew that once the intruder had reached the shadowed and abandoned avenues near the river, he could easily slip undetected into an empty warehouse, or hide in a darkened doorway, like a rat passing invisibly through the shadows.

She skidded around the corner and spotted the stranger fifty feet ahead, passing in front of Cupid's Dance Hall. Bernie, the night porter, was nowhere to be seen, and the street was empty—no chance that Max could call out for help. She blinked sweat from her eyes. The dark figure seemed to pass in and out of reality as he threaded between the shadows. It was risky—too dark, and the fork was untested—but she had no choice. She had to throw. Otherwise, the stranger would get away.

He passed into a dark spot between streetlamps. She squinted, trying to distinguish his silhouette from the shadows. There! He moved into the light again. He was directly in front of the museum's steps. Max took aim . . .

Just as a giant black bird came swooping down from the sky . . .

And before the fork even left her hand, the bird and the stranger went tumbling to the ground.

Of course, it wasn't a bird. That, Max realized almost immediately. It was Pippa, wearing her dark bathrobe. She had leaped onto the stranger from the museum's front stoop and pinned him to the sidewalk underneath her.

"Let me go," the stranger was howling as Max approached. "I didn't do nothin'."

"We'll be the judge of that," Max said. She dropped to her knees and shoved the remaining tines of the fork into the soft flesh of the stranger's neck. He instantly went still. With her other hand, she reached up and tore the cap off his head.

She was seized by the sudden, hysterical desire to laugh. She had been half expecting Rattigan himself, or someone with Rattigan's cold blue eyes and pale lips, the color of a dead fish's belly. This boy wasn't much older than she was. He had a flat, stupid face, as if his features had been shaped with a shovel, and he was missing a front tooth.

"Who are you?" she demanded. "What are you doing here?"

"They call me Bits," the boy said, his eyes ticking nervously from Pippa to Max. He began squirming again. "Let me go! Get off me. I'll call for the police. I'll have you locked up for salting a battery!"

"It's assault and battery, you moron," Pippa said, rolling her eyes. "And we're not letting you go until you explain yourself."

Bits licked his lips. "Look, someone paid me a dollar to bring a letter to the freak museum—"

Max dug the tines of her fork a little deeper into Bits's neck. He yelped and hurriedly added, "That's all I know. I was supposed to go down the stairs, knock on the door, and make the drop. I wasn't halfway there and all of a sudden I got two maniacs screaming their heads off and trying to clobber me. I turned tail and ran."

"You're a liar," Max spat out to conceal her confusion. The boy admitted to bringing the note. So why wouldn't he admit to leaving it on the door? "Who paid you to deliver the note?"

Bits's eyes turned suddenly wary. "I ain't supposed to say," he said. "I *promised*."

"I promise *you* I'll turn your throat into spaghetti if you don't answer the question."

"All right, all right!" Bits howled as Max leaned into him. "It was my friend Chubby. He's been laying low. So I been doing some errands for him."

"*Chubby?*" Max repeated. She was increasingly baffled. It didn't make sense. Why would Chubby have paid Bits to leave a threatening letter on the museum door?

"Go on," Bits said. "The letter's in my left pocket. Read it if you don't believe me."

"He's telling the truth," Pippa said quietly. "I can see it."

"But—but—" Max shook her head. "What about the other note?"

Now both Bits and Pippa looked as confused as Max felt.

"*What* other note?" they said at the same time.

Just then, Thomas came limping up behind them, clutching his injured side. "Let him up," he panted, wincing. Max hesitated. "Go on, Max. He didn't do anything."

Max withdrew the fork from Bits's neck. Pippa stood up and extended a hand to help Bits to his feet. He shot her an injured look before accepting.

"That's more like it," he muttered, dusting off his pants—which were quite filthy anyway. "Some thanks I get for doing Chubby a favor."

He fished a wrinkled envelope from his pocket. *PERSONAL* was written across the front in clumsy letters, though the word had been crossed out and replaced with the words: *TOP SECRET. DELIVER TO THOMAS AT 344 W. 43RD STREET.*

Thomas took the letter from Bits. "Did you see anyone when you were on your way to the museum? Anyone at all?"

Bits shrugged. "Took Broadway all the way to Fortieth Street. I saw lots of people. Saw a big fat lady stuck trying to get out of a cab. Saw a man with a dog the size of a rat. Saw two kids pick the pocket of an old guy wearing a cape."

"But no one hanging around the museum?" Thomas pressed.

Bits shook his head. "No one. Not until *you* came rushing at me and screaming like you wanted to swallow my head."

"Yeah, er, sorry about that." Thomas bent down and scooped up Bits's hat from the ground. "We thought you were somebody else. Anyway, tell Chubby we said thanks."

Bits scowled and rammed his hat on his head. "Yeah, sure," he said. "I'll give him a black eye, too." And he turned and stomped away.

Pippa turned to them almost immediately. "Do you want to explain to me what's going on?" she said, crossing her arms.

Thomas hesitated for only a second. "We found this," he said, and passed over the three-word note: *SOON, MY CHILDREN*. Pippa glanced at it quickly, then balled it up in a fist and practically hurled it back to him.

"Where?" she said.

"Outside the kitchen," Thomas answered. "Stuck to the door."

"What were you doing in the kitchen?" A look of suspicion crossed Pippa's face. Max was glad it was dark outside. She could feel herself blushing.

"I was waiting for a note," Thomas said, sighing. "But not that one."

"What about you?" Pippa said accusatorily, turning to Max.

"What about *you*?" Max said. She would sooner spend her life as a nun than let Pippa in on her secret. "What are you doing skulking around and leaping off of stoops?"

Pippa snorted. "Is that a thank-you? If it wasn't for me, Bits would have gotten away."

"I would of pinned him," Max said.

"Not likely. I saw the way you were aiming—you would have been miles off. Even you were scared you wouldn't—" Pippa broke off suddenly, biting her lip.

Max felt a creeping, tingling heat start at her stomach, and radiate up toward her neck. "You," she whispered. She remembered, now, the strange sensation in her mind— as if her thoughts had been forcibly pushed aside. And directly afterward, she had seen Pippa's face. "You . . . you were *in my mind*."

Pippa looked uncomfortable. But she didn't deny it. "I didn't mean to," she mumbled. "It just happened. I woke up and you weren't in your bed. I started to wonder where you were and then . . ." She shrugged. She was doing a terrible job of pretending to be sorry. In fact, she looked almost pleased with herself. "It's never happened before. Not like that. It was easy."

"You . . . you *sneak*." Max squeezed her hands into fists. Bright lights were exploding behind her eyeballs. She felt as if Pippa had split her stomach open and gone picking through her guts. "You sleazy, slippery, no-good *snake*!"

Now Pippa was growing angry. "I told you," she said. "I didn't mean to."

"Yeah, right. Like I'm supposed to believe a *snake* like you."

"Stop calling me that."

"That's what you are."

"Stop!" Before Max could lunge at Pippa, Thomas stepped between them. "Enough, okay? Max, Pippa's sorry. She *is*," he said quickly, before Pippa could protest. "And Max is sorry, too."

"For what?" Max cried.

"For calling Pippa names. And because Pippa was only trying to help." Thomas looked from Max to Pippa and back again. "Okay?"

There was a long moment of silence.

"Fine," Pippa said with a sigh.

"Fine," Max grumbled.

"Good," Thomas said. "We have bigger things to worry about."

"Oh yeah?" Max was still feeling grumpy. "You gonna spill your big secret now, and tell us why Chubby's sending you love notes in the middle of the night?"

"The letter isn't from Chubby," Thomas said. "He was just the go-between." He sucked in a deep breath, and said in a rush: "The letter's from Manfred Richstone."

"What?" Max screeched. High in an apartment above them, several of Miss Groenovelt's cats began to howl. Pippa, Max noticed, didn't react to the news at all. Her eyes were unfocused, soft-looking. Max knew Pippa was reading, feeling her way into Thomas's fingers, into the paper and the ink. No matter how often Max saw Pippa read, she never quite got used to it. It was creepy—there was no other word for it.

Oh yeah? Pippa had replied when Max had once told her so. *Says the girl who sleeps with knives under her pillow.*

Thomas lowered his voice. "You know how I told you I wrote to Manfred Richstone at Sing Sing? Well, Chubby delivered it for me. And he's written back." Thomas shook his head. "I don't think he did it, Max. I'm sure of it."

"Is that why you wrote him? You wanted him to cross his heart and hope to die?" Max said sarcastically.

Thomas ignored her tone. "I wanted him to tell me about the photograph of Rachel Richstone missing from Eckleberger's house," Thomas said. "I think . . . I think it might have been a clue to Rachel's murder. Which means it might be a clue to Freckles's murder."

Max shivered involuntarily. She thought of poor Freckles, his head staved in like a rotten fruit, and his beautiful, light-filled studio, destroyed. "All right," she said, hugging her arms to her chest. "What does he have to say about it?"

Thomas ripped open the envelope with his teeth.

Inside of it were two sheets of paper. The first was stained with what looked like tomato sauce and contained only a short message, badly misspelled.

Look i did what you ask and got the mesage to and fro Like you ask me too so now you Better keep up your end of the ~~bargin bargan~~ bargain your the Only hope I got
—Chubby

The second piece of paper was much cleaner, and covered in a fine web of dense printing. They had to huddle under a streetlamp so that Thomas could read it out loud.

Dear Thomas,

I've received many letters in the short term of my imprisonment—none of them, I'm afraid, very pleasant. Ah, well. I don't blame them. There is no doubt in my mind that my dear Rachel was murdered by a monster, a fiend of only the most evil inclinations.

Unfortunately, most people believe that I am that monster.

Your letter was, as you can imagine, quite an unexpected surprise, and I was relieved to know that someone, somewhere, believes in my innocence—because

I am innocent. I swear it to God and heaven and every angel with the power to hear.

I will do my best to answer your questions, though I admit to some confusion as to their importance. Yes, Rachel had a gap in her front teeth when we first met. I thought it charming; she thought it too "country." (Though she comes from a very good family, she was raised primarily in Virginia, and was particularly eager not to appear unworldly once we moved to New York City.) She insisted on having her teeth fixed after we married—a bit of harmless vanity.

As to your second question, I confess to being slightly baffled. Yes, Rachel did indeed keep a photograph on her nightstand table, in a frame very much like the one you describe: it was wood inlaid with marble, and had a very bad nick on the upper right hand corner. If you're surprised that I should remember it in so much detail, I can explain: the photograph was, in fact, the source of one of our more uncomfortable disagreements. You see, along with Rachel, the people in the photograph were Jennifer Clayton, Rachel's childhood best friend; Jennifer's fiancé, Mark Haskell; and Rachel's first boyfriend, Ian Grantt, who was later killed in the war. And although the photograph dated from well before Rachel and I had even met—she was only sixteen when the photo was taken—and though it was a stupid bit of envy, I disliked that she kept a picture of Ian so close to her bed. I admit that I was the source of the nick on the corner of the frame, which originated after I once threw the photograph during an unattractive fit of jealousy.

Did Rachel and I fight? Yes. It's no secret that I have a beast of a temper, and did not always treat her fairly. Did she infuriate me on purpose, tease me with stories of her past loves, her dalliances, her male admirers? Rachel knew how to anger me, and she knew, just as easily, how to soothe my temper, and turn our storms into easy sunshine. I knew that she was friendly with Edmund Snyder, and I suspected she maintained the friendship just to infuriate me. But I also knew that she loved me and me alone.

What I'm trying to say is: I would never have hurt Rachel any more than I would have split open my own chest to remove my heart.

She was my everything.

Perhaps that's why I did not, at first, have more energy to proclaim my innocence. With Rachel dead, all of life seems like a form of dull imprisonment anyway. Still, so long as the world believes in my guilt it means that out there, somewhere, her real killer goes free, an idea I cannot tolerate. Should my conviction be overturned, I will dedicate my life to hunting down the monster who returned my beautiful angel to heaven long before her due.

It gives me untold comfort to know that there is at least one person in the world who believes in my innocence. Though in all likelihood we will never meet— if my appeals fail, I may breathe my last before this letter reaches your hands—I want to thank you for that.

Sincerely,

Manfred Richstone

There was a long silence after Thomas finished reading. The wind had picked up, and carried with it sounds of distant laughter and car traffic from Broadway. But the street in front of Dumfrey's Dime Museum was still.

"I don't get it," Max said to break the silence. Her voice sounded overloud. She crossed her arms so the others wouldn't notice the gooseflesh on her arms. She didn't like standing out in the open, when they still didn't know how and when the first note had appeared magically on the kitchen door. They were like sitting ducks. "So Manfred *didn't* bump off his wife? Someone else did?"

"Yes," Thomas said. "I'd stake my life on it."

"And you think the same person did Freckles in?" Max said.

Thomas nodded.

Pippa was white-faced under the streetlamp. "Even if Manfred is innocent," she said, "he isn't very much help. He says so himself. He has no idea who might have killed his wife."

"That's where you're wrong." Thomas folded up the letter and once again carefully pocketed it. "He was plenty helpful. There were three other people in that photograph with Rachel. That means there are three other people who might know why it's so important."

"Two," Pippa corrected him. "Rachel's first boyfriend died in the war. Manfred says so."

"Still," Thomas said. "Two leads are better than none."

There was another short pause. Max was desperate to go back inside, but she refused to be the first one to say so. She didn't know why they had to talk about murders and killers on the loose outside, in the weak light of a new dawn. She didn't know why they had to talk about killers on the loose at all.

Pippa's eyes were dark hollows. She took a sharp breath. "All right," she said softly. "So what's our plan?"

18

Back in the attic, Thomas carefully folded up Manfred Richstone's letter and placed it in his secret spot: a velvet-lined jewelry case, supposedly once owned by Napoléon Bonaparte's wife, that he had smuggled up from the exhibit halls and hidden behind the air vent in the wall next to his bed. This contained all his most important possessions, which were admittedly few: the good-luck charm Freckles had brought him from India; a yellowed promotional pamphlet that showed Thomas standing on his head as a grinning, gap-toothed toddler; the first dime Thomas had ever earned; and a slender copy of *Bird Species of America: A Guide,* the first book Thomas had ever read, at the age of three.

The second note—the one with the cryptic, three-word message—he hid between the pages of his heaviest encyclopedia, as if it were an insect that might skitter away if it weren't weighted down.

He dozed for a few hours. His dreams were many and confused. He was chased down a long tunnel by someone he couldn't see. He was arguing with Chubby about how many teeth humans had in their mouths; he was attacked by a dog that gnawed on one of his ribs like a bone.

Then he was with Richstone in a bare room. Richstone was tied to a chair.

"I could never have done it without you," Manfred said. Suddenly he was free. There was a bright light behind his head. His face was a uniform disk of black. "How can I ever repay you?"

Thomas started to ask what Manfred meant—he hadn't done anything—but he found he couldn't move. His hands and feet were lashed to the chair. He had switched places with Manfred. He struggled to get free but he was restrained too tightly. There was an audience of people shouting soundlessly at him from behind a thin pane of glass, and Thomas realized the chair was an electric chair, and everyone had assembled to witness his execution.

"I promise," Manfred was saying, except he wasn't Manfred anymore, but Rattigan. "This won't hurt a bit."

Then Rattigan's hand was on the switch, and Thomas felt a hot rush of pain go through his body. . . .

He woke up stifling a scream.

"Stop fussing." Miss Fitch was standing above his bed. She had removed his old bandage and was ferociously dabbing foul-smelling liquid on his gash. Every time she made contact, Thomas felt as if he were getting stuck with a poker.

"Do you have to do that?" he said through gritted teeth.

"Would you rather get an infection?" she snapped, redoubling her efforts. Thomas stared at the ceiling and tried to focus on something—*anything*—else. Finally, she was done. She re-dressed the wound and straightened up. "There," she said.

"Thank you," Thomas said, sitting up. Already, the burning had turned to a kind of tingling warmth.

Miss Fitch sniffed in reply, which Thomas took to mean: *you are very* un*welcome*.

He dressed quickly and slipped out of the attic, glad to be awake. Betty was using one of the washrooms— she took forever in the bath—and Quinn the other. She screeched at him to leave her alone when he knocked. She was obviously still devastated about her sister. So he washed his face and hands in the Etruscan birdbath on the second floor and sloshed some water on his face, avoiding brushing his teeth altogether.

He was surprised to find Mr. Dumfrey already awake and dressed in his best suit, which included a scarlet bow tie and the embroidered tuxedo slippers that had supposedly been worn by Benjamin Franklin on his deathbed. He was pacing the lobby, muttering to himself. Thomas was starving, and debated taking the shortcut down to the kitchen—which involved an air duct and three quick turns around an old oil pipe—but instead he poked his head into the lobby.

"Is everything okay, Mr. Dumfrey?" Thomas asked.

Mr. Dumfrey started. "Okay?" He beamed. "Everything is better than okay. We're rich, my boy! Come here. Have a look."

Thomas entered the lobby and immediately drew back. The walls were papered with so many multicolored fliers, it looked as if some large animal were molting. Every single one of them featured an image of a grimacing Manfred Richstone strapped to an electric chair: COME SEE THE EXECUTION OF THE NOTORIOUS WIFE-SLAYER! Hundreds of additional fliers were stacked next to the door and perched on the ticket desk.

"Do you know what this is?" Mr. Dumfrey snatched up a flier, waving it over his head as if it were a flag. Thomas said nothing. "It's *gold*, my boy. We're printing money. At nine a.m., we'll start the morning rounds. I want these fliers on every corner from Harlem to the Bowery!"

"Mr. Dumfrey—" Thomas was about to protest when suddenly the front door banged open and Monsieur Cabillaud appeared, a newspaper tucked under one arm, his pinhead shiny with sweat.

"I'm afraid," he squeaked, "zat you will not be needing zose fliers after all."

And he smacked the newspaper down onto the ticket desk so that Mr. Dumfrey and Thomas could read the enormous headline.

MANFRED RICHSTONE SLAIN IN PRISON, JUST DAYS BEFORE ELECTROCUTION!

19

"Cheer up, Mr. Dumfrey," Thomas said half an hour later.

Mr. Dumfrey was doubled over the table, clutching his head in his hands. The other residents of the museum had been awakened by a storm of cursing and by now had trickled down into the kitchen, in various stages of sleep and undress. Only Sam was missing. He had refused to leave his bed, grunting a rude response when Thomas had told him to get downstairs.

"We're ruined," Mr. Dumfrey said in a trembling voice.

"Ruined!" Monsieur Cabillaud wailed.

Howie repressed a small smile. Thomas glared at him.

"Well, here's *two* pieces of good news to cheer you up." Pippa had been reading the article about Manfred's death, which Thomas had skimmed, feeling increasingly sick with every new detail. Manfred Richstone had apparently been stabbed during a prison brawl he'd attempted to stop. Now she turned the page. "'Police have identified the man responsible for the murder of renowned sculptor Siegfried Eckleberger.'"

"What?" Thomas nearly choked on his own tongue.

Pippa raised her eyebrows, then returned her attention to the paper. "At five thirty a.m. this morning, the body of an unidentified homeless man was fished from the East River. In his pockets were Mr. Eckleberger's wallet and gold watch. Police speculate that Mr. Eckleberger was killed when he surprised the man during an attempted break-in."

"Poor Freckles," Mr. Dumfrey murmured in a trembling voice. "My dear friend, killed for a pittance."

Pippa, evidently judging that her attempt to cheer Mr. Dumfrey had backfired, quickly changed tactics. "I've got even better news for you," she said brightly. "Listen to this: 'Rattigan trapped like a rat! The FBI in cooperation with the Chicago police are closing in on Rattigan, according to an unnamed source familiar with the investigation.'" Pippa looked up. "How about that, Mr. Dumfrey? That *has* to make you feel better."

She spoke lightly, but Thomas detected a slight edge to her voice—other than the children and Miss Fitch, the residents of the museum knew nothing about Mr. Dumfrey's relationship to the deranged scientist, and they certainly didn't know that Rattigan had used the children for his terrible experiments.

Or did they? Did *someone* know? Was it possible that the note posted on the door last night was a horrible practical joke? Thomas knew Miss Fitch wasn't to blame. She had no sense of humor, not even a bad one.

Mr. Dumfrey heaved a long sigh. "Thank you, Pippa," he said, absentmindedly patting her hand as he stood up from the table. A little more quietly, he added, "But I'm afraid I won't feel happy until he is in jail." To the others, he said, "I'm afraid that a marching band seems to have taken up residence behind my head. Until further notice, I will be in my study."

"Mr. Dumfrey," Monsieur Cabillaud burst out. "We really must discuss—"

"*Please*, Henri," Mr. Dumfrey said. "Not now."

Monsieur Cabillaud muttered something in French. Thomas could only assume, from the way he was scowling, that it was very rude.

Once Mr. Dumfrey left the room, there was a long moment of gloomy silence. But Thomas couldn't bring himself to care about the museum's troubles. His mind was whirling so fast, he could barely keep his thoughts together.

The police believed that Freckles had been killed by some homeless man during a routine robbery. But why would a random thief have taken Rachel's picture? The thief hadn't even stolen the frame, which he might at least have pawned—and he'd left plenty more valuable items in the studio. It didn't make any sense. But it might mean, at least, that Chubby was off the hook.

Still, Thomas was convinced, more than ever, that the murders of Rachel Richstone and Siegfried Eckleberger were connected. Even if Chubby no longer needed him, didn't he owe it to Manfred Richstone? Now that he was dead, Thomas's might have been the last letter he ever answered.

"Well." Miss Fitch sniffed. "It's ten o'clock already. Curtain's up for the matinee in an hour and we've plenty to do. Thomas, please see to it that Sam hasn't suffocated in his pillows. William—er, Lash—make sure the stage has been properly cleaned. Yesterday I counted *four* black spots."

"Anything you say, Miss Fitch," Lash said with a tip of his hat.

"What's the point?" Quinn wailed. "You heard Mr. Dumfrey. We're ruined. We'll all be put out on the street."

"She's right," Monsieur Cabillaud said. "Zer is no hope for us now."

"Be that as it may," Miss Fitch said, rounding on him, her dark eyebrows quivering with rage, "*the show must go on.* As long as we have a roof over our heads and an audience to perform for—whether it's one person or twelve—we will perform. Is that clear?"

No one argued with Miss Fitch, particularly when her eyebrows were involved. So the performers filed out of the kitchen and up the spiral staircase. Max fell into step next to Thomas.

"Did you hear that?" she whispered. "Rattigan's a thousand miles away, and caught like a fish in a barrel. So he can't be after us."

"I hope not," Thomas said sincerely. With everyone fighting, Dumfrey distracted, Sam sulking, and Max half stupid over Howie, Thomas didn't know what would happen if Rattigan decided to make a reappearance. He did know they would not be as lucky as the last time. "I really, really hope not."

20

Normally, Max found throwing her knife relaxing. But today she was having trouble finding her rhythm.

She hadn't slept well after they'd returned to the attic the night before. Every snore, mutter, and cough had startled her awake, and several times she had reached for the knife she kept under her pillow, watching the shadows pooling in the corners as though they might conceal an intruder.

Then there was the thieving. She was getting tired of keeping her secret, and didn't know how much longer she could go on, especially now that Pippa could creep around in her mind.

Onstage, the morning show was going surprisingly well, despite the fact that the residents of the museum had grumbled and groaned about it after Howie unhelpfully pointed out that they had not been paid in several weeks. Smalls and Danny were performing a two-step, which never failed to amuse the crowd, and the audience tittered appreciatively. Max rolled her shoulders back. It was so dark backstage, she could hardly make out the practice target she'd set up: a soft cloth dummy from Miss Fitch's costume department. But she preferred the darkness. She was gearing up for the blindfold act, anyway.

She wound up, just as Danny waltzed under Small's legs, earning another appreciative chuckle from the audience.

Thunk. Her new knife landed directly in the center of the dummy's chest. She was loosening up. She retrieved her blade and returned to her starting position. She wound up again. But before she could throw, someone grabbed her wrist.

"What are you doing?"

Pippa's voice hissed in Max's ear.

Max tried to shake her off, but Pippa was gripping her too tightly. "Practicing," she whispered back. "What's it look like I'm doing?"

"No." Pippa twisted Max's wrist so she was forced to release the knife. It was the small, teardrop-shaped carving blade that Max had admired at Siegfried Eckleberger's house. Pippa brandished it in front of Max's face, and Max drew back to avoid getting her nose sliced off. "I mean, what are you doing with *this*?"

"Stop waving that around before you hurt yourself." Max snatched the knife back from Pippa and pocketed it.

"I can't believe you!" Pippa cried. Several of the performers who were gathered backstage hushed her. She lowered her voice. "You stole that from a *crime scene*."

"I didn't steal it," Max said. "Freckles said he would leave it to me in his will, didn't he?"

"You—you—you—" Pippa spluttered.

Fortunately, Max didn't hear the insult Pippa settled on, because at that moment, it was her turn to take the stage.

Since Mr. Dumfrey was still feeling too ill to serve as announcer, it was Lash's voice that rolled across the audience from his unseen position backstage.

"Now, for the masterful—*hic*—Mackenzie of the Thousand Blades!" he trumpeted in his best approximation of Mr. Dumfrey's rolling baritone. The effect was somewhat ruined when he hiccuped midsentence.

"And her death-defying assistant, Betty the invincible—*hic*—bearded lady!"

Max took the stage and stood, face out to the audience, while Betty blindfolded her, and Lash continued to prattle on, only fumbling the recitation a little bit. ". . . to perform the once-of-a-kind, one-in-the-world, Spinning Pinnacle of Death . . ."

Once the blindfold was secured tightly, Max could hear the whispers and gasps from the assembled audience. She'd counted seven people—a decent turnout—and felt her spirits lift. She'd give them the show of their lifetime. She'd shock them out of their seats. And maybe the museum wouldn't be forced to close after all.

She felt a familiar tingling in her palms, an itch in her fingers. Her body was aching for her knives, the way a person who loses a hand might still be troubled by the feeling of a hangnail. Her knives were a part of her—she was a part of them.

The stage creaked, and Max stood impatiently, shifting from foot to foot, imagining the scene: Betty, her beard pinned back carefully so that it wouldn't get in the way, secured to a gigantic spinning bull's-eye. Smalls would set Betty to turning and Lash would give Max the signal, and then Max would throw her four knives: two beside Betty's shoulders, one between her

legs, and the last one, the final and most impressive shot, a half inch above Betty's head. It was a difficult trick and even harder blind. But Max had practiced it a dozen times already with no problem.

"Ladies and gentleman, silence—*hic!*—please!"

It was the signal. Max pivoted in Betty's direction. She heard a faint clatter as the bull's-eye began to turn, spinning Betty round and round, head over feet. Other than that, it was silent. No one whispered. No one coughed, or even breathed.

She concentrated. She saw the bull's-eye, and Betty pinned to it like an overgrown insect. She felt the itch in her fingertips grow to an all-over tingle, felt even the air vibrate and hum, *felt* the distance that separated her from the target, every molecule, every current, every breath. As she reached for the first knife she felt a surge of connection, a completeness, as if she were growing fingernails of steel and the blades were just an extension of her hand.

Thunk. Thunk. She released two knives in rapid succession, and someone in the audience gasped. There was a quick swelling of applause: she had thrown the knives at Betty's shoulder blades.

The next knife she threw was longer and heavier. Instinctively, she made minor adjustments to her posture and stance. *Thunk*. The third knife landed and the applause crested again, then rapidly died out as Lash once again demanded silence from his position backstage.

One more knife to go.

The last blade she threw was the small, narrow blade she had taken from Freckles's studio. It was as light as a feather in her hand. She focused . . . she concentrated . . .

The world went totally still. There was nothing but Max, the knife, and the narrow one-inch spot above Betty's head.

Just as Max wound up and released, there was a thunderous clatter from backstage. Someone yelped.

And Max slipped.

Even before she heard the screaming, Max knew that she had made a mistake. She whipped the blindfold off, her stomach heavy with fear. Suddenly, everyone was shouting and rushing the stage. Blood was flowing freely from a cut on Betty's left earlobe. Danny and Smalls were attempting to unpin Betty from the spinning contraption. For one long and horrifying second, the whole stage was open and visible to the murmuring audience; then the curtains slammed shut so that they were concealed from view.

"Nice going," Pippa said as she pushed past Max and ran toward Betty.

"It wasn't my fault," Max said. She was hot all over. *It wasn't her fault.* She spun around and saw Lash hanging back, twisting his hands, his narrow face as pale as a new moon. At his feet was a pile of splintered porcelain. Max recognized it as the remains of a bust of Goldini occasionally used in his act.

The clatter, the yelp, the broken statue—she knew, then, exactly what had happened.

"You," she spat out. "You distracted me. You *made* me throw to the left."

"I'm sorry," Lash said dazedly. "I don't know what happened—I barely touched the darned thing."

There was a growing rumble from the other side of the curtain. Once again, the audience members were calling for a refund.

"First Thomas, and now Betty." Goldini shook his head as Smalls helped a blubbering Betty from the stage.

"It seems like everything's gone wrong lately," Danny said with a significant glance at Lash. Lash's face went from white to a mottled purple color.

"He'll ruin us," Monsieur Cabillaud cried, gesturing to Lash, "even faster zan we can ruin ourselves!"

"I didn't mean it, honest," Lash said, looking around

the assembled group. Danny turned away in disgust. So did Monsieur Cabillaud. Max felt sick to her stomach, and quickly looked down when Lash's eyes landed on her. "I didn't mean it," he repeated, turning pleadingly toward Miss Fitch.

There was a long pause. At last Miss Fitch said, "Of course you didn't." Her voice was strained. "Go on, Lash. We'll speak later."

"You're lucky," Pippa said to Max. "You could have shaved off Betty's nose."

"You're lucky," Max snapped, "I don't carve out your tongue."

Pippa narrowed her eyes. "So long as you don't get *distracted*."

Max stepped toward her, but Thomas intervened. "Come on," he said, resting a hand on Max's arm. "No fighting. We've got more important things to worry about."

"Yeah." Max shook him off. "Like the fact that we're all going to be out on the street. Or maybe we'll be lucky and end up in Central Park with Solly Bumstead and the rest of his crowd."

She pushed roughly past Sam, who was staring at her with his mouth all twisted up, as if someone had just force-fed him a spoonful of salt, and plunged into the darkness of backstage. Quickly navigating the tangle of props and set pieces, she threw open the performers' door and emerged into the costume department and the makeshift infirmary. Beyond the clothing racks, she could hear the trill of Betty's voice and Smalls's murmured reassurances.

"At least," he was saying in his rumbling baritone, "she didn't get even an inch of your beautiful beard. Be thankful, Betty."

Max kept going. She'd apologize to Betty later, although really, it should be Lash who said he was sorry. She was still angry with him, but she was also sorry for getting him in so much trouble. The two feelings wormed around in her stomach and made her nauseous and uncomfortable.

She didn't feel like returning to the attic; she didn't feel like staying in the museum at all. But there was a small cluster of angry customers standing by the ticket booth, demanding their money back, and Max couldn't bear to face them. She turned toward the kitchen but was intercepted by Howie.

"Are you okay?" he said, stepping in front of her so that he was blocking the stairs.

Normally Max was flattered when Howie paid attention to her. But she didn't want his sympathy—or even worse, his pity. Everything Howie did was perfect. Max was sure he'd never tanked onstage.

"I'm fine," she said, once again trying to move past him, and once again failing.

"It's not your fault," he said. His eyes were like dark stones; Max could see herself reflected in them. Her chest tightened. She didn't like it when anyone looked at her the way Howie was now. It was the same way Pippa had looked after she'd broken into Max's brain: as if Max were one of the objects in the museum, to be examined and pointed at.

"I know that," she said. She finally succeeded in ducking past him and started down the stairs.

"I meant, it's not your fault that it's so difficult for you."

The words stopped her. She turned around, clutching the banister, certain she must have misheard.

"What are you talking about?" she said.

Howie shrugged. He was smiling his wide, easy smile. But Max thought she saw something dark flicker behind his eyes. "Come on, Max. Admit it. Some people are just born special. And others aren't."

Max suddenly felt like she was choking. "What—what are you talking about?"

Howie took a step toward her. "Don't be mad," he

said softly. "I'm trying to help you. I'm trying to tell you I—"

"Lay off, Howie. She isn't interested."

Sam materialized in the hallway behind Howie. Max hadn't been so happy to see him in weeks. Howie swiveled his head completely around on his neck so that Max was left staring at the smooth shiny cap of his black hair. "Didn't anyone teach you not to interrupt?"

"Didn't anyone ever teach you not to be such a moron?" Sam responded, color rising to his cheeks.

When Howie turned back to Max, he was scowling. "We'll talk later," he said.

"I could have handled him," Max said quickly, once Howie had retreated. Her heart was beating very fast, like she'd just run a race. She couldn't get Howie's words out of her mind.

Some people are just born special. Others aren't.

What did that mean for her, Max, who wasn't born to be anything? Who was turned, made different, like a pear left to rot in the sun?

Sam made a face. "Like you've been *handling* him so far?"

Max felt a hot flush of embarrassment. "What's that supposed to mean?"

"Come on." Two vivid points of color appeared in Sam's cheeks. "You've been doing nothing but making goo-goo eyes at him since he arrived."

"*Goo-goo eyes?*"

"You know what I mean."

"I know you should mind your own business," Max said. She whirled around and pounded down the stairs.

"Max, *wait!*"

But she didn't wait. She stormed through the kitchen and flew out the back door into the courtyard, where the trash cans were sitting under a shimmering veil of midday heat; up the stairs and onto the street, shoving aside a young couple holding hands and dodging a woman pushing a baby stroller. She heard Sam pursuing her but didn't stop, following the same path she'd followed the night before, when she had sprinted after the shadowy figure she had, in her terror, mistaken for Rattigan.

"Max, wait." Sam jogged around the corner of Eighth Avenue and finally caught up. "Look, I'm sorry. It's just . . ." He had a funny expression on his face, as if his tongue had suddenly tripled in size. "Howie's not exactly my favorite person in the world."

"You didn't even give him a chance," Max said, though she wasn't sure why she was defending Howie to Sam, especially after what he had just said. Maybe because it was the first time Sam had deigned to speak to her in more than a week, and he had still found a way to make her feel like an idiot. "You were awful to him from the start."

"*I* was awful to *him*?" Sam gaped at her.

"You've been awful to him, and to me, and to everyone," she said. They had stopped at the corner of Forty-Third and Eighth Avenue to shout at each other.

"Just because I don't slobber over Howie like some people I know."

"Maybe you're just jealous," Max burst out.

Sam's face had gone very white. He forced a laugh. "Jealous of what?"

Max felt her voice dry up in her throat. Luckily, before she was forced to answer, there was a cough behind her. She turned and saw an unfamiliar man, dressed despite the heat in a three-piece wool suit, dark shirt and tie, and a broad-brimmed fedora hat. Every item of clothing he had looked worn and rumpled, as though he was in the habit of sleeping fully dressed. Even his face looked rumpled—there were smile lines at his eyes and mouth, and Max got the feeling he was trying not to laugh. She realized he must have overheard their whole conversation.

"What do you want?" she spat out, not bothering to try to be polite.

"Hello to you, too," he said, tipping his hat. "I'm looking for the dime museum. You know where it is?"

"Number three forty-four. Look for the big sign," she added pointedly. She turned back toward Sam, but the man coughed again.

"What?" both Max and Sam said together.

"Don't mean to be any trouble," he said. "But I was hoping you might show me the way."

"It's just down the street," Sam said. "You can't miss it."

"Be that as it may," the man said, his eyes twinkling, "I think you'll want to show me all the same. I've got business to talk over with Thomas. I figured it might interest you two as well. Might as well bring Pippa into it, too."

Max felt a sharp current of fear go through her. "How?" She swallowed. "How do you know—?"

"It's my business to know things," he said easily. "Mackenzie, right? And Sam, of course. Pleased to meet you." He extended his hand. When neither of them took it, he reached into his pocket and extracted a small white business card.

It read simply:

NED SPODE
PRIVATE DETECTIVE

21

"Is everyone comfortable?" Spode asked.

Sam shifted a little in the cramped space. He was decidedly *uncomfortable*, but he wasn't going to say so, especially since Max, Pippa, and Thomas quickly nodded.

They were crammed together in the tiny projection booth of an abandoned theater on Forty-Fourth Street, surrounded by dusty projectors and old reels of film. Spode had suggested it, saying it would be safe, dry, and private. It was definitely private. Sam didn't know about dry. Already, he could feel a spot of damp seeping through the seat of his pants.

Thomas had suggested they use the loft instead—the

hidden storage space at the very top of the museum, which earlier in the year they had made their unofficial headquarters—but Max had quickly refused.

"There are mice in there," she said. "Let's go somewhere else."

There had always been mice in the loft, and Max had never seemed concerned before. Still, she held firm. Maybe, Sam thought bitterly, this was Howie's influence, too. Maybe Max would turn into the kind of girl who shrieked when she saw a spider, and insisted on keeping her dress clean.

"All right, then. Let's get down to it." Spode removed his hat and hung it from one arm of a rusted projector. His hair was pale yellow, and tufted like a bird's. His eyes were dark as beads. "I was hired by Manfred Richstone before he died. He wanted me to help clear his name."

"Wait a second. *Richstone?*" Sam shook his head. "The guy who did in his wife?"

"He didn't," Thomas said with a sigh.

Spode twisted up one corner of his mouth into a smile. "That's what I think, too," he said. "Unfortunately, I never got the chance to prove it."

"I don't understand," Sam said, looking around the group. No one looked even the slightest bit surprised at the mention of Richstone's name. Max was picking her teeth with the blade of a knife. Pippa was leaning forward, her arms wrapped around her knees, watching Spode intently. "What's Richstone got to do with us?"

Thomas took a deep breath.

"Go on," Pippa said, nudging Thomas with an elbow. "Tell him."

"Tell me *what*?" Sam stared at Thomas.

The story came out of Thomas in a rush: about Chubby's midnight plea and the letter Thomas had sent to Richstone in Sing Sing prison; about Richstone's response and his sudden death less than a day later; about the connection Thomas was sure existed between the missing picture of Rachel Richstone and Eckleberger's death.

Sam felt heat creeping up from his chest to his head, and fought hard to keep the anger from his voice. "Why didn't you tell me?"

"How could we have?" Pippa said. "You were barely speaking to us."

Sam looked away. He knew it was true. Ever since Howie arrived, he felt like he'd been walking around with his guts turned inside out: everything hurt, everything felt unfair. He had never loved performing—had never liked the feeling of people watching, evaluating, whispering about him in the dark—but now even the idea of being onstage made him sweat, made his stomach cramp. Several times he had even fantasized about running away from the museum, though he knew he never would.

Max, Thomas, and Pippa had been running around, scheming behind his back. It didn't help to know that it was mostly his fault. Part of him wanted to get up and storm out of the room. But the other part of him was too curious—too curious, and also relieved to be back in the group.

"How did you find us?" Thomas asked.

"Richstone showed me your letter." Spode raised his eyebrows. "I gotta admit, it was a nice piece of work. That bit about the missing photograph got me thinking. After Richstone croaked I decided I owed it to him to try to clear him. So I looked you up." Now Spode grinned, showing off teeth faintly yellowed with tobacco. "You kids made a big stir with that shrunken head business."

Sam felt himself blushing.

"Oh yeah," Max said casually. "That wasn't even the half—"

"It was nothing," Pippa said quickly, shooting a warning glance at Max. Sam could tell she wanted to avoid revealing too much about Bill Evans's role, and their ultimate confrontation with Rattigan.

Fortunately, Spode let it go. His expression turned serious. "Let's cut right to the chase. If you got a theory, I'm all ears." This last statement he directed to Thomas.

Thomas hesitated. He looked at Pippa. She nodded slightly. "Well, I don't have any proof. . . ."

"They had no proof against Richstone, and he still ended up with a fist buried halfway in his guts in a prison canteen." Pippa winced and Spode spread his hands. "Sorry, girlie, but that's the way it is. Just start from the beginning and leave the proof to me."

There was another pause. Even the dust motes spinning in the air seemed to hesitate, as if breathlessly waiting for Thomas to speak. A metal projector was digging uncomfortably into Sam's back, but he was afraid to move, fearing it would break the spell.

Thomas took a deep breath. "It started when Mr. Dumfrey—he owns the museum—bought a few wax heads from Eckleberger." Thomas hesitated again, glancing at Spode.

"The sculptor," Spode said. "I looked him up, too, after I read your letter to Richstone. I'd heard about him before, but just the bare bones. He's good at his job, though."

"Was," Sam burst in bitterly. "He's dead now."

Spode turned his hard black eyes on Sam. Sam felt a sudden tightening in his stomach, as if Spode had reached down into the very center of him and started prodding around.

"Yes," he said quietly. "I'm sorry about that, son."

Sam turned away, his cheeks burning, wishing he hadn't spoken. Suddenly, Max reached out and seized his hand. He was so startled he forgot to be embarrassed. He was careful not to squeeze back, so he wouldn't hurt her—and in a split second, she withdrew her hand.

"That's just it," Thomas said. Color was rising to his cheeks. It looked as if all his freckles were blending together. "That's what first got me thinking. What if the whole break-in was staged? What if only one thing was important to Eckleberger's killer?"

"The photograph," Spode mused.

"The photograph," Thomas confirmed. "Otherwise, why go through the trouble to steal it? She wasn't important—Rachel, I mean. Eckleberger had got his hands on plenty of old pictures of her. There was something—or someone—in that picture that Eckleberger's killer didn't want us to see."

Sam chewed thoughtfully on his lower lip. "You

think the same guy who bumped off Eckleberger—"

"It could have been a girl," Max interrupted.

Spode spread his hands. "All right. You think the same guy—or girl—did Rachel in, too." It wasn't a question.

Thomas nodded.

"Could be," Spode said quietly. He was no longer looking at the children. He was staring off into space, his jaw working back and forth, back and forth, like he was chewing on something invisible. "Could be."

"Well, the police don't think so," Sam said. He was still angry that no one had thought to include him in the hunt for Eckleberger's killer, even after Sam had gone on a midnight trek to Central Park to talk to stupid Bumstead, when Sam had perhaps loved Freckles more than anybody—angrier still, that he knew it had been mostly his fault. "Don't you read the papers? The cops think they found their guy. Some bum who drowned with Eckleberger's watch in his pocket."

"Yeah, sure, I heard about that," Spode said, his mouth twisting into a half smile. "I got a friend down at the morgue, even let me pop by for a look." Sam repressed a shiver; even the word *morgue* brought back terrible memories of their adventure earlier in the spring, of the ice-cold room, and the cabinets filled with bodies. Spode shook his head.

"They're barking up the wrong tree. I knew him: old 'Buckets' Tomkins, blind as a bat and harmless as a beetle. No way he could have killed anyone, or stayed sober long enough to do it."

"So how did he get Freckles's wallet?" Pippa asked.

"You tell me," Spode said calmly.

"He might have found it," Thomas said, frowning. "Maybe the killer dumped it, since it wasn't what he was really after."

"Or maybe it was a plant," Sam said, desperate to contribute something to the conversation that would prove he belonged. Everyone turned to him. He felt his cheeks heat up. "Maybe the killer set him up and then gave him a push into the East River." Instantly, he was sorry he'd spoken. The words sounded silly.

To his great relief, Spode nodded. "Could be," he said once again. His eyes were practically black now. "If so, it means we're dealing with someone who's already killed three people: Rachel Richstone, your friend Eckleberger, and good old Buckets. We'll have to be very careful. We might be tracking a very desperate and dangerous man—or woman," he added, at a sign from Max.

This time, Sam couldn't help but shiver.

Spode put his hands on his knees and hefted himself to his feet. Sam noticed he did so only with difficulty. Spode caught him staring. "War injury," he said, reaching down to pat his left knee. "Still gives me trouble once in a while."

"So what's next?" Thomas stood up, too.

Spode took his hat off the projector arm, dusted it off, and placed it on his head. "We need to find out why that picture's so important," he said. "Next I track down Mark Haskell and his old girlfriend, Jennifer. See whether I can shake something out of them."

"What should we do?" Max said.

Spode smiled again, that funny half smile that didn't quite reach his eyes. "You sit tight and stay out of trouble," he said.

"Fat chance of that," Pippa muttered.

"I'll be in touch." Spode opened the door that led, via a narrow, dust-covered staircase, down into the back of the theater. "Remember what I said. Keep your eyes open and your ears up." His voice turned grim. "I wouldn't want anything bad to happen to you."

Sam didn't know why, in that moment, it sounded like a threat.

22

There was no point in returning to the museum
immediately. After the disastrous matinee performance, the evening show would be canceled,
and no one was eager to return to talk of the museum
shutting down.

Instead, they rode the subways aimlessly for a while,
barreling through the hot tunnels and emerging onto
streets sizzling in the sun. Thomas allowed himself
to relax, allowed himself to forget temporarily about
Rattigan in Chicago and poor Manfred Richstone and
the unknown killer here. They ended up at the Fulton
Fish Market, where they stared for a while at the endless wooden stalls and the rainbow-array of seafood,

and tattooed men loading cargo on the docks, and the East River flashing like a coin in the sun.

From there, they made their way toward Chinatown, inching forward with the densely packed crowd, navigating crates stacked with salted cod and seaweed, dried eels and fresh shrimp, the pavement puddled with trampled fishtails and old water. Pippa held her nose and complained the whole way, while Max poked at the live frogs and watched them wriggle away in their barrels.

By then, Thomas was starving. He turned around to suggest to the group that they stop and find someplace to eat, when a meaty kid wearing a dark hat pulled low barreled into him. Thomas stumbled backward, nearly upsetting a large crate of blue crabs, before the boy helped him regain his feet. The shopkeeper, a small, wrinkled Chinese woman, released a string of curses in his direction.

"Sorry," the boy mumbled, before lurching off.

"You all right?" Sam said, carefully squeezing through the crowd.

"Yeah." Thomas rubbed his chest, where the boy's elbow had jabbed him. Fortunately, the spot was several inches away from his puncture wound, which had yet to fully heal. "I'm sure he didn't mean it."

Pippa went suddenly pale. She seized Thomas's arms, startling him so badly he nearly went backward into the crabs again. "Where's your wallet?"

"My . . . ?" But even before his hand went to his pocket and found it empty, Thomas knew. The boy. The "accidental" shove. One hand helping Thomas to his feet, while the other hand dipped into his pocket.

"He took your wallet," Pippa said.

"That snake," Max spat out, even though, Thomas knew, she had picked hundreds of pockets.

"Come on." Sam plunged into the crowd. "There's still time to catch him."

Thomas started to move. But the crowd was too dense, too uniform. Even Thomas, who was used to squeezing and bending through the smallest spaces, found it difficult to move quickly, and Sam, Max, and Pippa were soon left behind, borne back by endless waves of people. Hundreds of faces, thousands of bodies, like an enormous human jigsaw puzzle. The boy might have gone anywhere, in any direction, or turned off the street at any time.

Thomas fought a rising sense of frustration and anger. He didn't so much care about the wallet, a battered leather thing that had, according to Mr. Dumfrey, once belonged to Al Capone and sported a little hole supposedly made by a tommy gun bullet, and he had no more than fifty cents folded into its lining. But his wallet also contained a photograph of Dumfrey holding a baby Thomas on his lap, sitting on the stairs of the museum and squinting into the sun; an Indian arrowhead given Thomas by Hugo the Elephant Man, who had left the museum earlier that spring to marry Phoebe the Fat Lady, and a note written to Thomas from Freckles on his birthday last year. *You're one year older—don't let it bend you out of shape!*

In Thomas's mind, the contents of the wallet proved that he wasn't an orphan—not really. The people at the museum were his family.

Thomas searched the crowd for the floppy brown hat. But from his position, he saw nothing but a dense network of backs and shoulders, a sludgy procession of sweating bodies, oozing down the street like mud through a narrow canyon. He needed a better vantage point. Darting to the side of the street, he hopped up on a pickle barrel—ignoring yet another angry shopkeeper—and, with one neat handspring, catapulted himself from metal arm to awning. From there, it was a single leap to one of the fire escapes stitched neatly up the side of the tenement buildings.

He squatted on one of the landings, catching his

breath, scanning the crowd trudging below him on Canal Street. Old men, fat men; women with powdered cheeks and rouged lips; children squawking and bawling or grinning fat-cheeked smiles. He saw Max, elbowing people out of the way, and Sam following behind her, careful not to touch anyone; and Pippa floundering to keep up, as if she were riding in the wake of an enormous ship. Sweat trickled down his forehead and he swiped it away impatiently.

There! He caught a glimpse of the floppy brown hat just as it, and the boy, turned right on Mott Street.

"Max! Sam! Pippa!" Thomas waved his arms frantically to attract their attention. They looked up, staring at him gape-jawed. He didn't have time to explain how he had ended up on a fire escape high above the street. "That way!" he cried out, pointing to the place the boy had just vanished. "He's heading south on Mott Street!"

Max, Sam, and Pippa plunged gamely on through the crowd. Thomas nearly vaulted over the railing—two quick jumps and a slide down the awning would bring him back to street level—but then thought better of it. He'd never catch up to the thief, not that way. Instead, he turned and threw himself at the nearest window. Locked. Inside, he could see a woman with the puckered face of a wizened apple knitting in a rocking chair, gazing at him impassively, as if it were totally normal to see young boys on her fire escape, attempting to gain admittance to her apartment.

Thomas sprinted up the next set of stairs. Here, he had more luck. The window that gave onto the fire escape was open a few inches, allowing Thomas to shimmy through it. He dropped into the kitchen, landing lightly on his feet directly in front of a young woman wearing an apron, holding a large plate of slightly burned sausages. She gaped at him. A small, animal sound began working its way out of her throat.

"Don't be afraid," he said quickly. "I'm just passing through."

She shut her mouth so hard, so fast, he heard her jaw click.

Thomas dashed through a narrow hallway and found himself in a cluttered living room. In one of the many overstuffed armchairs, an enormously fat man wearing a stained white undershirt was listening to the radio and drinking a soda. The man didn't even look up.

"Martha, can you grab me another soda?" he grunted as Thomas squeezed behind him.

Thomas pinched his throat and made his voice a falsetto. "Right away, sweetie," he trilled, and kept moving.

Down another hallway, where the wallpaper was peeling in strips; through a tiny bedroom and an even smaller bathroom; into a *second* bedroom, fitted with nothing but a washstand and a narrow cot, in which an old lady was (thankfully) asleep. Thomas eased onto the bed, careful not to disturb her, and heaved open the window. Wriggling through it, this time on his stomach, he tumbled headfirst onto yet another fire escape.

Thomas's gamble had paid off: the boy with the floppy hat was just crossing onto Pell Street, dodging a dizzying grid of cars and pull-carts. As Thomas watched, he slipped into a narrow gap between buildings. Thomas pounded down the fire escape, taking the last ten-foot drop easily, rebounding off a fabric cart and dashing across the street. Car horns blared, and tires screeched on the asphalt.

He reached the alley just as Sam, Pippa, and Max finally rounded the corner of Mulberry Street, shouting his name. But he didn't stop. The boy in the floppy hat had almost reached the chain-link fence at the end of the alley, and Thomas knew if he didn't catch up, the boy would soon disappear into the maze of streets and buildings on the other side.

On one side of the alley, trash cans were lined up for collection, clustered like mushrooms after a rain.

Thomas jumped and dashed across them, banging and clattering, using the lids as footstools. His chest ached and his breath was rasping in his throat. The blood was pounding in his ears, transforming the noise of the street—traffic and horns, shouts and catcalls—into a distant rhythm. He was getting closer. Closer.

The boy reached the fence as Thomas vaulted off the final trash can. For one second, he was in the air; then he was swinging from a laundry line stretched tight across the narrow gap between buildings, as a red shirt and a pair of frilly underwear came flapping down around his ears; and then he was dropping, tumbling onto the boy's back. The boy cursed, releasing his hold on the fence. Together they rolled, and Thomas felt his cheek hit the pavement and tasted dirt. The boy elbowed him roughly in the chest, and Thomas saw stars of pain: it was exactly the spot where he'd been stabbed a few days earlier. Thomas rolled onto his back, gasping, and the boy sprang to his feet again, hatless, and swung himself up onto the fence like an overgrown spider.

Thomas struggled to sit up.

"Thomas! Stay down!"

Thomas turned and saw Max positioned at the end of the alley, one arm cocked, knife raised. There was a whoosh of air. The boy yelped and nearly fell, catching himself at the last minute. The point of the knife was buried in the thick rubber sole of his right shoe. Even as Thomas pushed himself to his feet, however, the boy was off again, kicking off his shoe and hauling himself toward the top of the fence, now with one dirty polka-dot sock exposed.

Thomas reached the fence next. Max, Pippa, and Sam weren't far behind. The chain link swayed under their combined weight as they clawed for the top.

They jumped together, landing almost simultaneously on the far side of the fence.

"Stop where you are!" someone shouted.

Thomas looked up. The boy—who was now hatless, revealing a thatch of mud-brown hair, and a face so crowded with dirt and freckles, it was impossible to tell one from the other—was standing in the shadows underneath a makeshift shelter, a half-collapsed shed in a barren courtyard behind an abandoned building. He wasn't alone. From the shadows, several other boys emerged, grim and determined, hands clenched into fists as though preparing for a fight. All of them were dirty, many of them shoeless, and each of them had the desperate look of a trapped animal. They began to circle, pressing closer, like a pack of wolves around their prey.

"Sam?" Thomas whispered.

"Yeah?" Sam was very white. More and more kids were emerging from the shed: six, seven, eight of them, now.

"You know that thing you do with your fists? The one that makes people run away?"

Sam nodded.

Thomas swallowed. "I hope you've been practicing."

There was a long second of ragged tension, like the queasy few moments right before a thunderstorm, when no one moved. Then everything unfroze. Three boys rushed Sam at once. Pippa screamed. Thomas saw a jagged bottle flying in his direction, and barely managed to duck.

Then a familiar voice was shouting: "Hey! Lay off! Leave 'em alone!"

Another boy was shoving his way through the crowd out of the shadows, a battered news cap pulled low over his eyes. His pants were torn at the knees, and his face was streaked with dirt. But there was no mistaking his snub nose, smattering of freckles, and bright green eyes.

"*Chubby?*" Thomas said.

Chubby smiled shyly. "Heya, Tom," he said.

23

"Some creep stole my territory," Chubby said, shoveling a forkful of noodles into his mouth, and chewing—much to Pippa's disgust—with his mouth open. "I lay low for a few days and what happens? I find another guy working the corners from Herald Square to Forty-Second Street. What was I supposed to do? A man's got to eat." As though to illustrate this, he forked a dumpling from Thomas's plate and popped it in his mouth.

They were sitting in an old booth in a tiny Chinatown dive, surrounded by the carcasses of ducks and chickens and other animals Pippa didn't care to identify. She pushed away her egg drop soup, which was barely touched.

"So you decided to go into thieving?" she said sternly.

Chubby blushed. "I never gave the orders for that," he said. "Stick to the food stalls and the fat cats only. That's what I said. Sorry about that business with your wallet, Thomas," he said for the sixth time.

"That's all right," Thomas said. "I got it back, didn't I?"

"It's most certainly not all right!" Pippa burst out, so loudly that several other customers swiveled around to stare. She lowered her voice. "The police are looking for you, Chubby. Are you trying to give them a reason to chuck you in jail?"

"I need money to buy my corner back, don't I?" Chubby wailed. "But how'm I supposed to get money, if I don't have my corner? It's like a pair o' ducks."

"A what?" said Max.

"A pair o' ducks," Chubby repeated. "You know, when two things kind of cancel each other out."

"A paradox," Thomas corrected, without raising his eyes from his food.

"Yeah, that's what I said." Chubby wiped soy sauce from his lips with the back of a hand. Pippa turned away, making a face.

"Well, the cops aren't looking for you anymore,"

Max said. She had gone through a vast plate of chicken and rice in record time. "Some bum killed Eckleberger. That's what they think, anyway," she added when Thomas shot her a look. "You're in the clear."

Chubby paused with his fork halfway to his mouth. "Are you fooling with me?"

Max shook her head.

"For goodness' sake, Chubby." Pippa gave in to her exasperation. "You sell newspapers. Don't you ever read them?"

He glared at her. "I told you. Someone stole—"

"Your corner, yes, I know." Pippa's head was pounding. It was stiflingly hot in the restaurant, and the smell of fry oil was making her nauseous. She wished she had never agreed to help Thomas on his search for Eckleberger's killer. Even with Ned Spode's help, and the possible link between murders, it seemed an impossible task. If the police were satisfied, why couldn't they be?

"So I'm off the hook?" Chubby's lean face lit up excitedly. "I ain't a fungus anymore?"

"I think you mean fugitive," Sam said.

Chubby obviously didn't hear him. He slapped a palm on the table, causing all the flatware to rattle. "I'm a free man!" he bellowed. Once again, everyone turned to stare. "Thanks for lunch, Tom. I owe you one. Soon as I get my corner back, I'll treat you to a king's dinner. See you around, Max. See you, Sam. See you, Pip."

"Pippa," she corrected through gritted teeth. But Chubby had already slipped out of the booth and dashed out of the restaurant, leaving several soggy dumplings on his plate.

"You think he's coming back for those?" Max said, gesturing with her chopsticks.

"Help yourself." Pippa shoved the plate over to Max.

"Well." Sam heaved a sigh. "All's well that ends well, I guess."

"Nothing's well," Pippa said. She didn't know why she was behaving so badly—she had a sense that they had stumbled into a game and only very poorly understood the rules. "And nothing's ended, either. It's just beginning. Manfred was innocent, and he's dead. Eckleberger was killed over a stupid picture. And there's nothing we can do about it."

Thomas laid a hand on Pippa's arm. "We're going to find whoever killed Freckles, Pippa," he said quietly. "With Spode's help, we'll do it."

She wanted to believe him. She turned away, blinking back sudden tears. She realized she wasn't just upset about Freckles, but about Dumfrey and the museum and Howie and all the fighting—by the sense that things were slipping away, like water through her fingers.

"Have a fortune cookie," Max said. "It'll make you feel better."

Pippa shook her head, scowling. Max shrugged and took a cookie for herself, cracking it against the table like an egg. Her fortune fluttered out on a pale paper ribbon. Suddenly, her face turned grim.

"What's it say?" Thomas said, reaching across the table to grab it. His smile faded instantly.

Finally, Pippa's curiosity got the better of her. "What?" she said. "What is it?"

But Thomas didn't even have to show her. Suddenly, the words appeared in her mind, smooth and dark, as if imprinted there.

Disaster is on the way, it read.

Once the other fortunes proved to be gibberish—*The proud man catches no fish*, read one, and another, *You will meet a stranger bearing good tidings*—Thomas, Sam, and Max felt much better. Pippa, too, was reassured, though the nervous feeling wouldn't leave her entirely.

They made their way through the thick crowds toward the Canal Street subway entrance. Thomas paused outside a store selling wind-up dolls and por-celain cat figurines, cheap toys and paper fans. In one barrel were hundreds of miniature turtles, clawing at one another desperately to escape. "Did you ever think about buying a turtle for a pet?" Thomas said, pointing. "Look! Built-in armor."

"Don't even think about it." Max's voice turned shrill.

Sam stared at her. "Why not? It's a good idea."

"I'm allergic, that's why not," she snapped. She grabbed hold of Sam's hand. "Come on, keep it moving."

Sam, Pippa noticed, turned the color of a tomato at Max's touch.

The subway at Canal Street was teeming with people and swelteringly hot. Pippa cupped a hand over her mouth, trying to ignore the overwhelming smells of sweat and breath and old seafood. When the subway arrived at last, there was a massive surge toward the doors. Pippa caught an elbow in the chest, and fell backward, gasping, as Thomas, Max, and Sam were carried forward on the wave of people onto the train.

"Tom!" Pippa shouted. She was caught on the platform behind a fat woman sporting sweat stains in the shape of butterfly wings. Thomas tried to turn around, but the momentum of the crowd was too powerful. The doors slammed shut, sealing Pippa off from her friends.

"Sorry, Pip." Thomas's voice was muffled through the glass. Then the train pulled forward and was gone.

This only increased Pippa's bad mood, especially since she had to wait another twenty minutes for a train, and was pressed so tightly between passengers, she felt like a noodle in a very dense casserole.

Then, at Twenty-Third Street, the train came to a shuddering halt, and a tinny announcer's voice declared the train out of service.

"Worse and worse," Pippa muttered as she oozed with the rest of the slow-moving crowd along the platform, toward the stairs that led up to the street. Her bangs were sticking to her forehead, and her dress clung uncomfortably to her lower back.

She was relieved, when she emerged from the station, to be in open air, though it was not much cooler than it had been on the train, and the streets were knotted with cars shimmering in the sun, horns blaring. Still, she resolved to walk home. She'd had enough of trains for the day.

She hadn't gone two blocks when she spotted Howie on the opposite side of the street. He had his back to her and was moving north, as she was, but she recognized the precise cut of his clothing and the swagger in his walk, as though he was parading in front of an invisible camera. Despite the fact that she didn't particularly care for Howie, she nearly called out to him, thinking they could return to the museum together. But at that moment he stopped, looked furtively right and left as though fearful of being observed, and darted into a narrow, soot-stained building.

Pippa waited impatiently for the light to change, then crossed the street along with a tide of commuters and tourists. She broke free of the crowd with difficulty and made her way up the street to the building she'd seen Howie enter. On the ground floor was a dingy dry cleaner's, but a quick glance revealed that it was empty.

Curious, Pippa pushed inside the building. She was greeted by a sad lobby, hardly bigger than a bathroom, which featured a dying plant and a dust-smeared directory of the building's businesses and residents. Pippa scanned the list quickly, and her stomach seized up.

The top floor of the building was occupied by the Bolden Brothers Circus.

Howie, too, was abandoning ship.

24

"Strike!" Thomas said as both the stuffed two-headed raccoon and the three-legged chicken hit the ground with a thud. He jogged to the end of the Gallery of Historical and Scientific Rarities to retrieve the apple he was using for a bowling ball.

"No fair," Max said. "Your apple's rounder than mine."

"At least you get to play," Sam grumbled. He was sitting cross-legged at the end of the gallery, arms wrapped around his knees, watching the game. His first and only roll had resulted in a pulpy mess.

Thomas squatted and restored the raccoon and chicken to their positions. Just then, Pippa entered the gallery from the main hall, backlit by the late afternoon sun.

"Hey, Pippa," he said, straightening up. "You want to roll a turn?"

She ignored the question. "Have you seen Mr. Dumfrey?"

Instantly, Thomas knew something was wrong. Pippa's voice sounded strange—as if something were choking her.

"What's the matter with you?" Max asked. "You're not still creeped about those fortune cookies, are you?"

"What?" Pippa looked startled, as if she'd forgotten all about their lunch. "No. I mean, not *really* . . ."

"Are you mad because we left you on the platform?" Sam said.

"We couldn't do anything. The doors were closing," Thomas said.

Pippa shook her head, and her bangs shook with her. "I don't care about that," she said. "Look, I really need to talk to Mr. Dumfrey. It's about Howie . . ."

"Hey." Max brightened at the sound of Howie's name, and Thomas noticed that both Pippa and Sam looked a little queasy. "Where *is* Howie? I haven't seen him since we got back."

"That's just it," Pippa said impatiently. "I really

think Mr. Dumfrey ought to know that—"

"Ought to know that what?" Mr. Dumfrey came bustling into the gallery, clutching a long, bone-handled knife in one hand and a bottle of ketchup in the other. He was, Thomas saw, altogether in a different mood than the one they had left him in that morning. The color had returned to his cheeks and his eyes were sparkling vividly.

Pippa blushed. All of a sudden, she seemed nervous. She opened her mouth and then closed it again. "I think . . . I think that maybe . . . some of the performers—"

"Well, go on, girl. Spit it out. I'm very busy. Lots to do, no time to do it, et cetera."

"What's the knife for, Mr. Dumfrey?" Thomas asked curiously, relieved but also slightly bewildered by Mr. Dumfrey's change of mood.

"For stabbing," Mr. Dumfrey said calmly, as if that explained everything. "Naturally, we'll have to make some adjustments. The real weapon would have been handmade and much cruder."

"What are you talking about?" Thomas said patiently.

"I'm talking about the murder of Manfred Richstone," Mr. Dumfrey said impatiently. "The brutal slaying of a man just days before he was to get the chair.

It'll make a beautiful piece, very dramatic. Of course, there's much to be done. Manfred's all right, but that hideous Snyder—Rachel Richstone's boyfriend, you remember, the one who drove Manfred to a fit of jealousy—doesn't fit the role of a jailbird at all. We'll have to rough him up, paint on a tattoo or two. If only Freckles . . . ah, well. The less said about that, the better."

"Are you using the ketchup for blood?" Max said, taking a large bite of her apple. Thomas sighed. The game was over, he supposed.

"What? This?" Mr. Dumfrey shook his head and smiled. "Miss Fitch whipped up some lovely scrambled eggs. I've been so busy I haven't had even a nibble for hours. No, dear. Corn syrup and food coloring makes the best blood. Gives a real dripping effect. Now off I go, off I go. I'm not giving up just yet, you know. This new exhibit could give us just the boost we need."

"Wait!" Thomas called Mr. Dumfrey back before he reached the stairs. "Pippa had something to tell you. Didn't you, Pippa?" Thomas turned to Pippa. Her mouth was all twisted up, as if she were trying to chew through a metal bit.

"Well, what is it, Pippa?" Mr. Dumfrey blinked at her expectantly. There was a split second of silence.

"It's nothing," Pippa said finally, with forced

cheerfulness. "It wasn't important."

"Ah! I'll just scurry along then. Time is money and money waits for no man. Tell Lash to come and see me immediately, if you spot him, will you?"

As soon as Mr. Dumfrey had disappeared up the stairs, Max rounded on Pippa. "What was *that* all about?"

"What do you mean?" Pippa said defensively.

"You storm in saying you got news for Mr. Dumfrey, then tell him it's not important. I don't buy it."

For a second, Thomas thought Pippa might deny it. Then she sighed, and her whole body sighed with her. "I didn't want to ruin his good mood," she said.

"Why?" Sam stood up. He was already so tall that the top of his head nearly grazed the immense hanging exhibit of the world's first airplane, and he quickly ducked. "What's wrong?"

Pippa sucked in a deep breath. "I saw Howie at the office of the Bolden Brothers Circus," she blurted. "I think he might be leaving the show, just like Caroline and the alligator boy."

Now Thomas understood why Pippa looked so miserable. Howie was a draw—there was no doubt about that. The audience—when there *was* an audience—loved him. Thomas knew, deep down, that part of the reason he so intensely disiked Howie was because he was jealous. He envied Howie's confidence, his natural ease. He envied the fact that Howie had a real family—a mother, a father, two brothers, that stupid uncle Howie wouldn't stop boasting about who was the president's bodyguard—all of them, like Howie, odd or special in some way.

If Howie left, it would be a huge blow to the museum. Even if Mr. Dumfrey could convince the crowds to come back, they might soon find that there was no one left to entertain them.

"I knew it," Sam said with a kind of bitter triumph. "I knew he couldn't be trusted."

Max's face had gotten very red. "There might be another explanation," she said.

"Oh, come on, Max." Sam rolled his eyes. "Don't be an idiot."

Max glared at him, then whirled around and stalked out of the room.

"How can she like Howie?" Sam said despairingly, to no one in particular. "Can't she see what a weasel he is?"

Neither Pippa nor Thomas had a good answer for this. Sam scowled.

"Well I, for one, hope he does leave," Sam spat out.

"I hope he leaves all of us alone forever. She can leave, too, for all I care." And he stormed out of the room, stepping so hard that the floor shuddered slightly, like the earth after a quake.

Pippa sighed. "Maybe that fortune cookie was right after all," she said, and Thomas couldn't help but agree.

But they needn't have worried. The afternoon performance went off without a hitch, though admittedly there was only one person there to see it, who afterward confessed he had wandered in by mistake; Howie returned and showed no signs of dissatisfaction, performing his part with the same good-natured casualness as always. There were no midnight visitors, no mysterious notes, no disruptions to the everyday rhythm of the museum.

And in the morning Thomas heard, intermingled with various ringing church bells, a sound that cheered him up immensely: Chubby's voice, loud as an artillery blast, bellowing "Extra! Extra! Read all about it!"

"You hear that, Sam?" Thomas whispered. Sam grumbled a reply. "Sounds like Chubby's back to work."

Sam groaned, rolled over, and drew a pillow over his head.

As always, Thomas was the first one awake—except for Miss Fitch, no doubt, although she hardly counted, since Thomas was convinced she never slept at all. He was up, dressed, and on the street in less than a minute, and he followed the sound of Chubby's voice down Forty-Third Street and onto Ninth Avenue.

The air was sticky with the kind of heat that threatened rain, and Thomas found himself thinking about Ned Spode, and the picture of Rachel Richstone that had started everything. Funnily, he found he could imagine it just through Manfred Richstone's descriptions: the smiling Rachel, somehow even more beautiful because she was imperfect; her first boyfriend, the dashing and mysterious Ian Grantt; Jennifer Clayton and her fiancé, whom Thomas imagined to have the dazed, friendly look of a well-fed cow. For the thousandth time, he asked himself what it could possibly mean. Why was the photo so important?

He hoped Spode would have news for them soon.

He found Chubby strutting along Ninth Avenue between Thirty-Ninth and Fortieth Streets, like a rooster patrolling a particularly sunny patch of yard. In less than a single day, Chubby had been transformed. His hair, which had the day before been stringy with grease, was clean and cropped close to his head. His boots were radiantly shiny, and he was wearing a brandnew pair of suspenders and a clean shirt. There were a dozen newspapers bundled under one arm.

"Tom!" Chubby waved enthusiastically when he spotted Thomas. As Thomas approached, Chubby reached into his pocket and pulled out a thick wad of dollar bills, casually counting out four of them and slipping the money into Thomas's hand. "I told you I'd pay you back for lunch, didn't I? Now we're even. Not a bad racket, is it? I bought my corner back this morning and the papers have been selling like hotcakes."

Thomas frowned as Chubby slipped the money back in his pocket. "You haven't been pickpocketing again, have you?" he said.

Chubby did a relatively convincing job of looking offended. "I'm on the straight and narrow from now on. Scout's honor. I don't need more trouble with the cops." He lowered his voice. "It was the funniest thing. EXTRA, EXTRA, READ ALL ABOUT IT! Yesterday, after lunch, some guy offered me *ten bucks* just to do some errands for him. GET YOUR NEWS, GET YOUR NEWSPAPER, HOT OFF THE PRESSES! Easiest money I ever made." Even as Chubby talked, he never stopped doing business: he dispatched papers, pocketed coins, and made change without even breaking for air.

Thomas couldn't help but smile. Chubby couldn't

stay out of trouble even when he wanted to. "Just be careful, okay?"

"I'm always careful," Chubby said, showing off the wide gap in his teeth when he grinned.

Thomas started to turn around as Chubby was encircled by a new swarm of customers. Chubby called him back.

"Hey, Thomas! You want a paper? Big news today."

"Oh, yeah?" Thomas knew that Chubby said the same thing every day: it was the only way he could convince people to keep buying. "What's that?"

Chubby was counting change, and didn't look up. "That crackpot, Rattigan," he said, and Thomas's whole body went cold, as if the sun had suddenly blinked out. "He was caught."

25

Sam was, for once, having a nice dream. He was
dreaming that he was very small, and a man
with a long white beard—was it Freckles?—was
picking him up and spinning him in a circle. Above
him, birds scattered across a blue sky, thick as a cloud,
and when Sam extended his arms he began to float,
float, float toward them . . . into the mass of soft feath-
ers . . . Then the birds were tickling his nose with their
wings . . . and he felt pressure building behind his eyeballs . . .

"Achoo!" Sam came awake, sneezing, and realized
that Thomas had been tickling his nose with the end of
a supposedly genuine phoenix feather that Sam knew

had been plucked from a perfectly ordinary chicken, and then expertly painted by Miss Fitch.

"Finally," Thomas said. "I couldn't tell if you were sleeping or dead."

Sam sat up, rubbing his eyes, as the birds from his dream scattered once again into unconsciousness. Howie's bed was, as always, impeccably made. Sam scowled and shook off his sheets, leaving them in a piled mess at the foot of his bed. "What time is it?"

"I don't know. Ten? Ten thirty? Sam, you'll never believe it."

"Believe what?" Sam said, yawning, wishing that for once Thomas would let him sleep in past noon.

But Thomas just shook his head. Sam noticed he was practically shaking with excitement. "Where's Pippa? I want to tell everyone at once."

"Tell us what?" Pippa's head appeared over one of the bookshelves that encircled the boys' sleeping area. She had obviously been in the act of getting dressed, since she was wearing a striped sweater and pajama bottoms.

Thomas just shook his head. "Come on," he said. "Let's find Max."

Sam cast one last longing look at his bed and, swallowing a sigh, followed Thomas and Pippa out of the attic. As they stepped into the hall, Max burst out of the stairwell that led up to the small storage area known as the loft. For a second, when she spotted them, she seemed tempted to turn around and retreat. Instead, she stood her ground.

"What were you doing in the loft?" Pippa asked.

"I wasn't doing anything," Max said quickly—too quickly, Sam thought.

"I thought you said you didn't like the loft," Sam said suspiciously. "You said there were mice."

"Exactly." Max's face was as red as a flame. "That's what I was doing—checking for mice."

"And?" Thomas said.

"There are dozens of them—hundreds—piles! It's revolting. Really awful. Stay out of the loft, if you value your fingers and toes." Max's voice was unnaturally shrill, and Sam noticed she wouldn't make eye contact.

"I've got news," Thomas said, before Sam could question Max further. His eyes were glittering, like those of an overexcited owl.

"Did you hear from Spode?" Pippa asked.

Thomas shook his head. "Even better." He looked right and left as though to verify they were alone in the hallway. Then, with a flourish, he whipped a rolled-up newspaper from a back pocket and unfurled it.

MAD SCIENTIST RATTIGAN NABBED IN CHICAGO HIDEAWAY, trumpeted the headline in enormous letters.

Sam stared. He had to read the headline three times before he would believe that it wasn't going to vanish, like trick ink. But there it was, stark black, real and indisputable. As further proof, the front page featured a grainy black-and-white photograph of Rattigan, head down, thin lips pressed firmly together, swarmed by policemen and FBI agents.

Rattigan had been caught.

It was over.

Sam felt if as if a concrete block had been lifted off his chest. In that moment, he felt such a dizzy, heady rush of well-being that even if Howie had strolled into the hall, Sam might have clapped him on the back and called him a friend.

"I don't believe it." Pippa's dark eyes were shining. She ran a finger along the headline as if she, too, believed it might vanish.

"The article says they were closing in on him for weeks," Thomas said. He could hardly keep from crowing. "He'll be chucked in jail for the rest of his life, now. We're free and clear of him."

"He broke out of jail once before," Pippa pointed out, looking momentarily uneasy.

"Not this time," Thomas said.

Sam had a sudden vision of Rattigan's long, pale fingers, his eyes blue and hard as ice crystals, his lips as pink as worms. He imagined him locked in a room built of solid concrete and felt the hysterical desire to laugh. Wasn't that what Rattigan had done to them, in a way? He had imprisoned them not in a room but in their bodies, rebuilt them to be weapons, fiddled with their inner mechanisms like a child with a clock.

"What about the note I found?" Max said, frowning. "*Soon, my children.* Remember?"

Thomas shrugged. "Coincidence. Or some kind of prank. Maybe it wasn't even meant for us."

Sam felt a quick flicker of unease, but he forced his doubts aside. Rattigan was a thousand miles away. By now, he was probably locked up behind steel bars and wearing prison stripes. It was like Thomas said: the note meant nothing.

"Come on." Pippa was smiling one of her rare smiles; it lit up her whole face. "Let's go tell Mr. Dumfrey the good news."

But as they took the spiral staircase and descended toward the main floor, they heard a sound that was by this point becoming familiar: an earsplitting howl, followed by a string of curses.

"What now?" Sam groaned. It seemed a long time that even a day had passed without bringing some new disaster.

As soon as they entered the Hall of Wax, they had their answer: Mr. Dumfrey was standing in front of the shattered shards of what had once been Rachel Richstone's face. Two of the dummies had been toppled. A beady eye Sam recognized as Manfred Richstone's stared up at him from the floor; he saw, further, Richstone's mustache, now detached from the lip and plastered to the heel of Mr. Dumfrey's shoe.

Mr. Dumfrey was white-faced, and shaking like a sail in a strong wind. Behind him, Miss Fitch brought a hand to her chest, quickly making the sign of the cross, as if the dummies had been real people and she had found them dead.

"Who—who could have done this?" Mr. Dumfrey gasped. He lowered himself to his knees and began sifting the shattered remains of Freckles's last work between his fingers. "Monstrous . . . cruel . . . reprehensible . . . all of dear Eckleberger's work, gone. All of our hopes, shattered."

"Come now, Mr. Dumfrey." Miss Fitch placed a hand on Mr. Dumfrey's shoulder, and attempted to draw him to his feet. "You'll hurt yourself."

"Some glue." Mr. Dumfrey's eyes were wild. "That's what I need. Just a bit of glue. We can patch it back together. It'll be as good as new . . . right as rain . . ."

Miss Fitch rounded on the children. "What are you doing, standing around gaping like a bunch of monk-fish?" she snapped. "Make yourself useful. Thomas—go and fetch Mr. Dumfrey some water. Pippa—find Lash and tell him to clean up this mess. Sam—help get Mr. Dumfrey back to his rooms. Max—you go along with Sam, in case he needs your help."

They did as they were told. Sam kneeled down and wrapped an arm around Dumfrey's waist, which felt a little bit like a large sack filled with bread dough. Carefully, gently, Sam helped Dumfrey to his feet.

"Come on, Mr. D," he said quietly. "Let's go upstairs."

Sam guided Mr. Dumfrey toward the stairs. If anyone had seen them, Sam thought, they would have had quite the laugh: Mr. Dumfrey, round as a wrecking ball, listing against the scrawny Sam like a ship during a squall. Luckily to Sam, Mr. Dumfrey felt no heavier than a child, and he soon got Mr. Dumfrey back to his chambers.

"Go on, Mr. Dumfrey. Lie down. Put your feet up for a while."

Mr. Dumfrey said nothing, just made a few

unintelligible noises of distress. But he allowed Sam to ease him down onto the long velvet daybed crammed into one corner of his cluttered office.

The heating vent at Sam's feet wiggled, and then jumped. He stumbled back just as Thomas's head emerged from the floor.

"The stairs were crowded," he explained, panting a bit as he shimmied out of the air duct one-handed, gripping a glass of water. Sam was impressed that not even a drop seemed to have been spilled. "Everyone's heard about what happened by now."

But before they could convince Dumfey to drink, the phone on his desk began to ring.

"Mr. Dumfrey?" Sam called. No response. The phone kept ringing harshly in the silence. "Mr. Dumfrey, you want to get that?"

Mr. Dumfrey groaned and rolled over, so he was facing the wall.

"I guess that's a no," Max muttered.

Sam swallowed a sigh and reached for the phone himself, holding the receiver carefully between only two fingers. The last telephone he had crushed like a paper cup in his palm the only time he had used it.

"Dumfrey's Dime Museum of Freaks, Oddities, and Wonders," he said politely as he had heard Mr. Dumfrey do a hundred times.

There was a pause. Sam could hear crackling on the other end, and the faint rush of distant traffic.

"This is Wolfgang's Deli," said a man's voice eventually. "Someone order ham on rye sandwiches for delivery?"

"No." Sam frowned. "Sorry. I think you have the wrong number."

He was about to hang up when the man burst out, "Wait, Sam. Don't hang up. It is Sam, isn't it? Or is this Thomas?"

"It's Sam," Sam said cautiously, increasingly bewildered. In all his time in the museum, he'd never received a phone call. Everyone he knew was in the museum.

"Who is it?" whispered Max.

"Good stuff. I was hoping one of you would pick up. Just had to be sure. I got some news for you. Can you meet me in the projection booth in ten minutes?"

Sam was flooded, suddenly, with understanding.

"Who *is* it?" Max whispered again, growing irritated.

Sam cupped a hand over the receiver, and checked to see that Dumfrey was still facing the other direction.

It's Ned Spode, Sam mouthed. *The detective.*

26

They once again met Spode in the abandoned projection booth of the old theater, squeezing in between the clutter of old film spools and dusty equipment. Spode looked as though he hadn't slept since the last time they'd seen him. His face was shadowed with stubble; there were pouches, dark as bruises, underneath his eyes; and he was still wearing the same suit, now further creased and stained with evidence of various meals.

"Bad news about Mark Haskell and his wife, Jennifer Clayton," Spode said as soon as they were all settled in. Max liked Spode. She particularly liked that he always got directly to the point.

"Did you track them down?" Thomas asked.

"Sure did." Spode turned his head and spat on the cement floor. Pippa made a face. "But I tracked 'em down too late. They're dead."

Pippa sucked in a quick breath.

"Bricks," muttered Max.

"How?" Thomas looked stunned, as if someone had just driven an elbow into his chest. "When?"

"Just last week. They were on their way to their country place when—bam!—brakes failed on their car. They plowed straight into a telephone pole doing sixty-five. Mark was killed instantly. Jennifer died a few hours later."

There was a long second of silence. Max did the math. All four people in that mysterious photograph were now dead. It couldn't possibly be a coincidence.

"You said the brakes failed," Thomas said slowly. "Could they have been cut?"

Spode's eyes were a stormy color. A muscle flexed in his jaw. "There's no doubt that they were," he said. "I spoke to the mechanic who looked at the wreck."

"First Rachel," Thomas said, frowning. "And now Jennifer Clayton. *And* her husband."

"Don't forget Freckles," Sam said, pushing his long hair out of his eyes.

"And Ian Grantt, Rachel's first boyfriend," Pippa said.

"He died in the war, though," Max pointed out.

"About that." Spode loosened his tie, exposing more of his splotchy red neck. "I did a little digging into Grantt's background, thinking there might be something to it."

"What did you find out?" Thomas asked.

"Not much, strangely enough. No birth records. Nothing before the age of twenty, when he showed up in New York, met Rachel, and then enlisted. He died at the Marne in 1918. Half his battalion was blown to smithereens on the battlefield. They couldn't even put the bodies back together, they were in so many parts."

Max thought of a bunch of human jigsaw puzzle pieces and felt queasy.

"Sounds like a straight story," Sam said.

"Sure does," Spode said. He stood up, dusting off his pants, which had the effect of doing nothing whatsoever, since his hands were filthy. "Still, facts are facts. Someone's gone to a lot of trouble to make sure that everyone in that photograph is six feet under. You know what they say. Dead men can't tell tales."

"But what tales would they have told?" Thomas mused.

"That," Spode said darkly, "is the question."

They exited the old theater in a somber mood, and said good-bye to Spode on the corner.

"I'll be in touch," he said, tipping his hat, and then merged with the crowd flowing down to Times Square. Max noticed he was limping slightly and wondered about all the things he must have seen, the mobsters and gangsters, gunrunners and punks. Maybe, she thought, Spode would take her on one day as a partner. He might need a girl who was good with knives.

Then he was gone. He vanished into the stream of people so quickly it was like a magic trick. For some reason, she thought of Professor Rattigan, the way he'd tailed them earlier in the year without their knowledge, and she shivered. But Rattigan was locked away by now. They were safe.

They walked back to the museum in silence, Max sweating in the jacket she always wore, which had plenty of pockets for her knives. Turning the corner on Forty-Third Street, Pippa stopped and gasped. Max stumbled into her.

"What's your prob—?" she started to ask, but the words dried up in her throat.

Two police cars and an ambulance had pulled up directly in front of the museum.

"Dumfrey," Sam said, his face losing all color.

Instantly, they were sprinting down the block. Max wished she were as fast as Thomas; he was a dozen yards ahead of them within a few seconds. Her heart was hopscotching in her throat. She saw the police loading a stretcher into the back of the ambulance . . . a thin form draped in a spotless white sheet . . .

A *thin* form. She was nearly at the steps of the museum when she realized that the body on the stretcher could not possibly have been Mr. Dumfrey's. At the same time, she noticed several things that, in her panic, she had failed to spot earlier. The ambulance was actually drawn up slightly closer to the neighboring building, number 346. Frank DeSalvo, the owner of the hardware store that leased the first floor, had emerged from his store and was watching the proceedings with interest, chomping on one end of a cigar as if it were a piece of celery. Standing on the front stoop, gripping a cane with one trembling hand, was the frail, paper-white man who Max recognized as Eli Sadowski, whom they had saved a few weeks earlier from a coating of egg wash. He was wearing the exact same outfit in which she had last seen him; she even thought she detected traces of egg on his lapel.

"Out of the way, kid. Give us room." One of the policemen—Max recognized him, too, as one of the meatheads who'd been at Freckles's studio after his death—shoved Max out of the way as he loaded his girth into a squad car, squeezing his stomach in behind the steering wheel. Now that Max was closer, she could see an impossibly thin, liver-spotted hand hanging off the stretcher, and a pair of shining, wing tip shoes identical to the ones Eli Sadowski was wearing.

"My brother," Eli Sadowski said in a moan. "My poor brother. What will they do with him? Hospitals are very bad, very bad. Full of germs and sick people. My mother always said you should never trust a hospital."

Nobody spoke. Thomas, Sam, Pippa, and Max stood in a knot, watching as two beefy emergency workers swung closed the ambulance doors. Eli Sadowski didn't yet seem to realize that his brother wasn't going to the hospital, but somewhere far more permanent. Max thought of the night, months ago, when they'd sneaked into Bellevue Hospital, that hulking beast crouched over the East River. She wondered whether Mr. Sadowski's brother would find his way to the basement morgue.

"Come on, Mr. Sadowski. Let's go inside." Detective Hardaway emerged from number 346, his lips curled into his trademark sneer even as he placed a hand on Eli Sadowski's elbow and tried to pilot him inside. "How about a cup of coffee?"

"Oh, no coffee. No, thank you. They put turpentine

in the coffee nowadays . . . very dangerous . . . very bad for the stomach. . . . It's milk tea and mint water for me. . . ."

The door slammed behind Mr. Sadowski and Hardaway just as the police vehicles and the ambulance pulled away from the curb, sirens quiet and dark. Max called up an image of Detective Hardaway trying to force down some milk tea—whatever that was—and couldn't help but feel a little bit better.

"Poor Mr. Sadowski," Pippa said, sighing.

But Max knew they were all relieved. For today, no disaster had come to the museum.

About this, however, they were wrong; as soon as they heaved open the doors to the museum, Lash came barreling through them, clutching the battered leather duffel bag that contained all his worldly belongings. His eyes were red-rimmed and his lean, weathered face so pale it looked as if he'd been submerged in bleach. It looked as though he'd been crying.

"Lash!" Thomas cried out. "Where are you going?"

"It's over," Lash said in a moan. "It's all my fault, too. I've gone and made a goldanged mess of things. And after Dumfrey was so decent about giving me a chance . . ." His jaw began to quiver.

"What are you talking about?" Max said, horrified

by the sight of the once world-famous William "Lash" Langtry on the verge of tears.

"Those heads!" Lash whipped off his hat, revealing a thatch of blond hair that was starting to thin. He raked his fingers through his hair. "The Richstone exhibit. *I'm* the one who ruined them. I'm the one who shattered them to pieces."

Pippa's mouth fell open. "But . . . why?"

"It was an accident." Lash turned his mournful eyes on Pippa. "I knew the museum was in trouble, see? I thought I could help out. Draw in the crowds with the old bullwhip routine." He patted his leather bag, where Max knew he kept his bullwhip carefully oiled, curled up like a snake. "I used to do a fine trick knocking a grape from a volunteer's head. It got 'em rolling every time. I thought I'd just get in a little practice. . . ."

The realization settled in Max's stomach like a heavy weight. "So you used the Richstone statues as your volunteers."

Lash nodded miserably. "I never used to have any trouble. Never even nicked an earlobe before. But I guess . . . well, I guess ol' Horatio was right. I'm not as steady as I used to be." As though to reaffirm this, he fished a flask from his waistband and took an eager sip. When he finished, the shaking of his hands had only just subsided. "I 'fessed up to Horatio. He had the right to know."

"We can talk to him," Pippa said loyally. "He'll listen to us."

"Sure he will," said Sam. "He'll hire you back in no time."

Lash held up a hand. "Mr. Dumfrey didn't fire me," Lash said. "I offered to quit."

"*What?*" Now all four kids spoke together.

"Don't you see? I've been screwing things up since the start. Because of me, Thomas almost got skewered like a pig. And Max might have carved out Betty's eye! And now this. No. It's better that I go."

There was nothing they could do except stand in dumb silence and watch as Lash shouldered his bag. Max wanted to say something—*it wasn't your fault* or *you'll be okay* or *you'll always have a home here*—but she knew none of those things were true, so she said nothing.

When he was halfway down the stairs, he turned and stopped, his drooping eyes hangdog-sad and his beaten leather bag slung over one shoulder.

"You gotta promise me something," Lash said.

"Anything," Sam said.

For a second, Lash hesitated. And for just that second, Max saw a shift in his expression, a tenseness, a watchfulness, and she felt she was looking back at the same Lash who had once entertained crowds of thousands of people, who had once correctly judged a whip's arc to the space of a millimeter.

"You just promise me to be careful, that's all," he said, and then he lumbered off, and was gone.

27

The alligator boy's departure had been unfortunate, but not unexpected. Moreover, it was something of a relief: he had been unhappy for years, and had made his grievances known at every occasion, loudly and with the greatest possible degree of unpleasantness.

When Caroline left for Hollywood, it had caused a much greater disturbance. She complained, she whined, she hogged the bathrooms and the medieval wall mirror with the winged dragon frame in the Hall of Worldwide Wonders. But she had been one half of Caroline-and-Quinn, and not only had the museum lost one of its more popular acts, but Quinn was left grieving, miserable, and prone to loud fits of sobbing that kept the others up at night, even though at no point before Caroline's sudden departure had Quinn seemed to feel anything for her but constant irritation and jealousy.

But Lash was different. His absence left a vacuum, and seemed less like a sign of bad things to come than the announcement of bad things already arrived. In the two days that had followed since he took his leave, a peculiar silence reigned in the museum. All performances had been suspended—not that anyone was clamoring for them to go on. Even Dumfrey was quiet, grim-faced, and subdued, like a person at a funeral.

Artifacts and objects were disappearing from the museum—taken out by either Dumfrey, Miss Fitch, or a resolute Cabillaud for sale. One morning, there was a small ring of dust in the entryway, marking the place the stuffed bear had once stood proudly, claws outstretched. By afternoon, the moccasins owned by Davy Crockett, which Dumfrey occasionally still wore on special occasions, had been quietly removed from their case. Pippa felt as if she were watching some great, ancient animal slowly succumb to an illness.

As if she were watching the museum die.

As much as possible, she avoided Howie, whom she

could no longer look at without feeling revulsion. It proved harder than she thought. He was suddenly everywhere: lounging in the kitchens chatting with Quinn, telling her how much better she was without her twin sister; volunteering to help Miss Fitch sort through the inventory of tarnished silverware to see whether there was anything worth selling; listening to Smalls recite his newest poems, which grew more and more depressing by the day; or humming along while Danny plucked at his violin. Pippa suspected him of something—he had never been quite so friendly or cheerful—but she didn't know what. At least Max seemed, at last, to be keeping her distance from him, although Pippa caught them once whispering in the stairwell. Max scurried off, cheeks flaming, when Pippa glared at her.

"I only asked him about going to see the Bolden Brothers," Max said later. Before Pippa could protest, she added, "I thought he had the right to speak for himself. Anyway, he was only there on Dumfrey's orders, to see whether they might buy some of our old equipment. He's not as bad as you think," Max finished as pink rushed to her cheeks.

Pippa said nothing. She actually agreed with Max. She thought Howie was likely much, much worse.

A week to the day after Lash had abruptly quit,

Pippa was helping Miss Fitch straighten the attic. Since Lash's departure, the attic had become even more chaotic than usual: piles of paper intermingled with dirty socks, and half the surfaces were obscured by a clutter of personal belongings, cups, combs, half-empty perfume bottles, and long strings of costume jewelry.

"Disgusting," Miss Fitch said, bending over to retrieve what looked like a dirty handkerchief from underneath Smalls's dresser. Miss Fitch's hairstyle was, as usual, a measure of her great unhappiness. Over the past week, as she had grown more and more miserable, her hair had become scraped and parted so severely that Pippa was beginning to think her head might soon split in half. "Animals, all of you. Hasn't anybody heard of dusting? Pippa, run upstairs to the loft. We should have a second mop tucked away somewhere. The floor feels terribly sticky."

Before Pippa could move, Max sprang to her feet with a little cry. "I'll get it," she volunteered quickly, and dashed for the stairs.

"Well." Miss Fitch gave a tight smile—her first in about a week. "I'd say her attitude is improving, wouldn't you?"

"Mmmm." Pippa didn't want to say what she really thought: Max was hiding something.

"Turn the radio up." That was Thomas, who'd been sitting cross-legged on the carpet, trying to figure out new rules for DeathTrap, ever since two of the most critical pieces—the crocodile jaw and the Cyclops eye—had been sold off to keep the museum from having to close its doors. But suddenly his head appeared on the far side of the maze-like formation of bookshelves that divided the room, like a gopher popping up from a hole. "Quick, Pippa. They're talking about Rattigan."

Pippa lunged for the radio and cranked up the volume, just in time to hear the news reporter say:

". . . Multiple reports have now confirmed that the man captured in Chicago and detained for the past seven days at a federal detention center is, in fact, *not* Nicholas Rattigan, but only a very convincing look-alike. . . ."

Pippa felt as if the roof of her mouth were crumbling into dust. Beside her, Miss Fitch gasped and dropped her broom with a clatter.

"Federal investigators confirmed that over the course of the past week, the fraudulent Rattigan was revealed in certain telling details, personal habits, and physical characteristics that over time convinced them that the man was a fake."

"God help us." Miss Fitch was gripping the broom so

tightly her knuckles each showed a single white moon. "That monster."

"At last, after an intense and prolonged interview, the man, whose real name is Richard C. Dobbinshire, confessed that he was paid over the course of several months to study and assume the identity of Professor Rattigan, whom he believed had been wrongly prosecuted in the courts. . . ."

"It can't be true," Thomas said, shaking his head.

"If Rattigan isn't in Chicago," Pippa said slowly, as the dreaded realization knit together in her chest, cold as a creeping mist, "then he could be anywhere."

Thomas's eyes clicked to hers. She knew, in that moment, he was thinking of the note Max had found on the kitchen door: *Soon, my children.*

The floor began to seesaw under her feet. The radio passed on to other news: sports scores, celebrity gossip. How strange, Pippa thought, that the world could keep spinning even after a personal explosion.

"Come on," Thomas said, moving for the door. "Chubby always has the latest news. Let's see what he has to say."

Pippa unfroze. She hurried after Thomas, feeling an urgency she couldn't name.

They pushed past Max, just descended from the

loft, so forcefully that she spun halfway around on the landing.

"Hey!" she shouted. "Hey, where are you going?"

They didn't stop to reply. They pounded down the central stairs and burst into the street, pushing through the small group of reporters that had been clustered for several days in front of the Sadowski brothers' home, hoping to catch a glimpse of the notorious recluse or, even better, be allowed upstairs to his fabled home. It was a dull day, sunless; the sky was the color of tarnished silver, and the wind coming off the river was tinged with an unexpected chill.

Still, the streets were crowded. The Viceroy Theater had already flung open its doors, and tinny music piped onto the street, where women in knee-length skirts and red lipstick stood smoking next to clusters of sailors. The day porter at the St. Edna Hotel was just finishing his shift, dozing on a stool with a paperback on his lap. Sal was shutting down the corner luncheonette candy store, rolling down the grates over the large windows displaying colorful jars of jawbreakers, boxes of bubble gum, and barrels of sugarcoated almonds, and he gave a brief wave as Thomas and Pippa dashed past.

They zigzagged through the neighborhood, listening for the trademark foghorn of Chubby's voice. But on the corner of Thirty-Seventh Street they had an unexpected surprise: not Chubby, but Bits, the gap-toothed messenger who had delivered Richstone's letter to Thomas on Chubby's instructions. He had a bag of papers strapped to his sizable middle, and every so often he croaked out a "Papers! Papers! Get your papers!" but with none of Chubby's trademark enthusiasm.

"What's happened?" Thomas demanded as he and Pippa came to an abrupt halt. "Where's Chubby?"

Bits turned his piggy eyes on Thomas. "Don't know," he said shortly. "Ain't seen him." He started to turn away.

Pippa grabbed his arm. Perhaps remembering how she had previously toppled him, he froze, his eyes suddenly fearful.

A little electric thrill traveled up Pippa's arm. She saw, with a sudden vivid clarity, as if someone had taken a photograph in her mind, a medallion nestled in Bits's pocket: the same medallion Chubby had proudly boasted that Freckles had once given him.

Unconsciously, she tightened her grip on Bits's arm, and he yelped.

"Don't lie to us," she hissed. "What'd you do to him?"

"I—I didn't do nothing," he stuttered, suddenly losing much of his swagger. "I swear."

Before he could protest, she plunged a hand into his pocket and withdrew the medallion. "So how do you explain this?" she spat out. "And if you try to feed us another line," she added when he opened his mouth, "we'll have a friend cut out your tongue."

"Or knock you back to next Tuesday," Thomas said, doing his best to look menacing, although the impression was rather spoiled by a smudge of chocolate around his mouth, left over from lunchtime.

Fortunately, it had the intended effect. Bits lost all pretense of toughness.

"Look, I don't know where Chubby's been," he whined. "I swear. One day he was here, strutting up and down, talking about some top secret mission and driving everybody crazy. The next he wasn't. Poof. He dumped all his stuff, just left it in his squat on Grand Street. Me and the other guys, we figured he wouldn't miss it." He blushed a deep red when Pippa made a squeak of protest. "Well, why would he leave his stuff if he was planning on coming back?"

"Idiot," Pippa said. "He would have *taken* his stuff if he *wasn't* planning on coming back."

Bits scratched his forehead with a stubby finger. The

logic of this statement obviously confused him. "So, what? So, like someone kidnapped him?" Bits shook his head. "What would anyone want with Chubby?"

Pippa had to admit, she had no ready answer to that question. Still, it was suspicious.

Even after they said good-bye to Bits—who offered them a free paper, obviously eager for Pippa and Thomas to leave him alone—Thomas was distracted and moody, kicking at cans in the street and walking, head down, in gloomy silence.

"I'm sure Chubby is all right," Pippa said with forced cheerfulness. "He's done this before, remember, and he's always turned up just fine."

Thomas shook his head.

"Maybe he decided to go underground for a few days," she said, as much to make herself feel better as to cheer Thomas. "Or maybe he's doing a job for someone out of town. Or maybe—maybe Andrea von Stikk finally tracked him down and chucked him into her school."

At last, Thomas cracked a smile. "Poor Chubby," he said, shaking his head. "For his sake, I almost hope he's been kidnapped."

28

At the museum, they were greeted by an unexpected sight: Betty, Quinn, Smalls, Danny, Goldini, and Howie were sitting on the stoop outside the front doors, holding hands. A small crowd had gathered to stare, and the newspaper reporters previously grouped outside Sadowski's building had gravitated toward them, murmuring excitedly and snapping pictures.

Thomas felt as if he'd been jolted out of his own body, as if he were being squeezed and compressed into the lens of a camera. Suddenly, he pictured how it must look to the crowd of outsiders: Betty, with her light brown beard looped over one shoulder; Quinn, snow-pale, with her eyes protected by dark sunglasses, a large sun hat perched on her head; Smalls, towering over all of them, casting an elongated shadow over the stoop; Danny, a mere tenth his size, balanced like a doll on Smalls's left knee; and Goldini, clutching his magician's hat with one hand, sweating freely. And Howie, dark-haired and handsome, a hint of a smile playing on his lips.

Thomas and Pippa pushed through the throng, ignoring the bursts of laughter, the excited mutterings, and the word *freaks, freaks, freaks* following them like a snake, hissing through the grass.

"What are you doing?" Thomas cried.

Betty's hairy cheeks turned pink. "It's a protest," she said.

"To sin by silence when we should protest makes cowards out of men," added Smalls, in a resonant voice.

"Hush now," Pippa said sharply, casting a nervous glance over her shoulder. The crowd had grown even larger; two businessmen were pointing with sausage-like fingers, laughing openly, while their wives tittered behind gloved hands.

"What in the world are you protesting?" Thomas directed the words to Howie, who was as infuriatingly calm as ever. But it was Danny who answered.

"Good work deserves a good wage," he said loudly so as to be heard. Pippa tried to hush him again but he merely glared at her. "I don't care if they do hear me. Let 'em write it up in the papers!"

"I don't believe this," Thomas groaned.

"We haven't been paid in three weeks," Goldini said, turning his hat in his hands.

"So what?" Pippa fired back. "Dumfrey hasn't been paid in *three years*. You know if he had it to give"— she lowered her voice as the reporters leaned closer—"he would give it."

"That doesn't make it right," Goldini mumbled, but he ducked his head. Thomas noticed that Betty shifted uncomfortably, and even Danny looked embarrassed. There was still a chance, perhaps, to fix this—to solve it before the situation got out of control.

"This was your idea, wasn't it?" he said to Howie. He felt as if he had a rubber band around his throat. He couldn't breathe. He was sick with anger. Pippa had been right about Howie—he was trying to destroy the museum.

"It was everyone's idea," Howie said calmly. To Thomas's disgust, Howie spoke clearly, as if he were onstage, and angled his head slightly, flashing a quick smile for the sudden burst of cameras. Thomas felt like clocking him in the face, but knew it would only bring more unwanted attention.

Apparently Pippa had the same idea. Before he could stop her, she'd grabbed the newspaper Thomas had tucked in his back pocket, and, using it as a baton, waded into the small assemblage of performers on the stairs, swatting and swiping. The laughter of the crowd swelled to a roar, but she didn't seem to notice.

"You should be ashamed of yourself," she said. "You, too." In quick succession, she went down the line of performers, raining blows on their heads and shoulders, while they cowered and protested.

"You gave me a paper cut!" Quinn wailed.

"I'll do more than that unless you get inside this instant," Pippa said, leveling the paper at her as though it were a sword.

"No compromise without compensation!" Goldini said in a trembling voice. Thomas had no doubt he'd been fed that line by Howie as well. But the magician squeaked with fear when Pippa knocked the top hat from his hands.

"You heard her. Get inside, all of you, before I stick you through the stomachs like a bunch of moths to a corkboard."

Max had just pushed out of the front doors, glowering menacingly. When no one moved, she drew

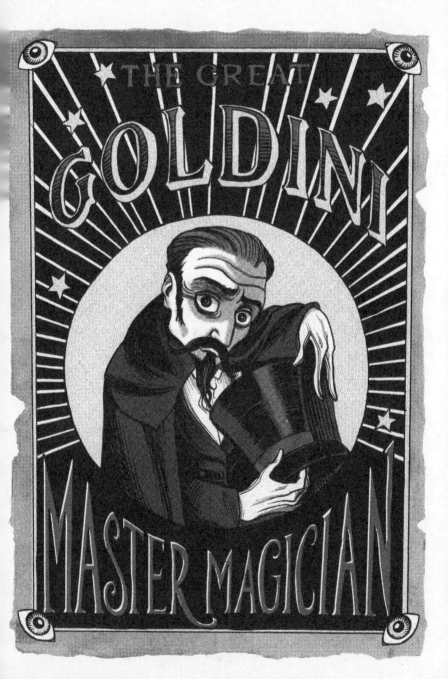

her hand back, as though reaching for a knife in her pocket. There was a sudden frenzied burst of movement. Quinn sprang to her feet and scurried inside, staying as far from Max as possible. Goldini followed her, along with Betty, who ducked her head and murmured, "We didn't mean anything by it."

Only Smalls, Danny, and Howie were left on the stoop. Danny shifted uneasily. Max took a step toward him, and he climbed to his feet, toddling up the stairs and pushing roughly past her.

"We got our rights," he said gruffly, refusing to make eye contact—partly because it would have necessitated that he either crane his neck back, or stand on several stacked chairs.

"I got rights, too," she said. "The right to turn you into mini sausage."

Smalls stood up, and the crowd let out a gasp, and then a titter. Thomas had nearly forgotten they were being observed. Drawing himself up to his full seven foot eight, Smalls took a deep breath, and Thomas braced for another lofty quote. But Max held up a hand, and he shut his mouth so quickly, Thomas heard his jaw click.

"Save it, if you value your tongue," she snarled. With her black hair wild and grown halfway to her waist, she really did look live a savage. Thomas could see, in that moment, why Sam liked her so much.

Smalls obeyed—in silence, thankfully.

Howie was the only performer left on the stairs. There was a moment of electric silence. Thomas wondered what Max would do—whether she would still insist that Howie wasn't so bad, whether she would defend or forgive him.

Next to him, Pippa was very still.

Max's eyes were the hard gray of cold slate. "You, too," she said, and Thomas felt a quick bubble-burst of happiness in his chest. Max, *their* Max, was back.

Howie stood up leisurely, stretching his arms above his head, yawning, as though he had merely tired of the protest and was not being compelled to give up on it. "Come on, Max," he said, giving her a lazy smile. "Don't be mad. You know as well as I do that Dumfrey's packing up shop."

Max didn't blink. "Quickly now," she said, drawing her lips back a little, and displaying teeth that were small and pointed, like a coyote's. "Before I slit that swiveling neck of yours straight down the middle."

Howie's face changed. Gone was the smile, the look of casual unconcern. In its place, in an instant, was an expression of rage. It twisted his lips, distorted his cheeks, made him look feral and ugly.

Howie leaned in. Thomas started forward, afraid he would strike her. But he only whispered something too low for Thomas to hear. He saw Max's face collapse, like a soufflé taken too soon from the oven. But before she could respond, Howie had hurtled through the doors of the museum.

Just as quickly, Max's face hardened again. "That goes for all of you nimrods, too!" she cried to the crowd of onlookers and reporters. "You heard what I said! Get out of here!"

The laughter rapidly died out. Both business-men shepherded their wives away in a hurry, and the remaining crowd broke up just as fast. The reporters, sensing that the moment was over, drifted back toward the Sadowski house.

"That was amazing!" Thomas hurried up the stairs to greet Max, who was still standing, face flaming, practically trembling with anger.

"Yeah," Pippa said. For once, she was smiling at Max and had nothing unpleasant to say. "I wish Sam had seen you."

"I did."

They turned. Sam was crossing the street, carrying a rolled-up newspaper, his face flushed with pleasure. It was the first time in many weeks that Thomas had seen him looking something other than unhappy.

"Nice work, Max," he said when he reached their group, sweeping his long curtain of hair away from his eyes.

Max shrugged and looked away. "Idiots," she muttered. But her lips twitched into a smile.

Then Sam's face clouded. "Bad news," he said. "Rattigan's still on the loose." He indicated the newspaper tucked under his arm. "It's all over the news."

"What?" Max screeched.

"I know, we heard," Thomas said.

"And no one thought to mention it to me?" Max's bad temper had obviously returned.

"We didn't exactly have time," Thomas said. "We just found out ourselves."

"Hmmph." Max shoved past them and jogged down the steps to the street.

"Where are you going?" Sam said.

"And what are you *wearing*?" Pippa added.

Thomas had been so distracted, he hadn't previously noticed that Max was dressed in what appeared to be, at first glance, a shapeless black-dyed flour sack, belted at the waist with a tassel that looked suspiciously like something that might be affixed to a curtain.

Max pivoted to face them, glaring. "Haven't you ever heard you're supposed to wear black to a funeral?"

Thomas, Pippa, and Sam exchanged a look.

"What are you talking about?" Thomas said. "What funeral?"

Max shook the tangled bangs from her face. "Aaron Sadowski's," she said. "They're burying him today." And without a further word, she started for the door of number 346, looking as dignified as possible, given the fact that she was wearing a fabric tent.

"Well," she said, without turning around. "Are you all coming, or not?"

"Do we have to?" Sam muttered. Pippa elbowed him.

"We're coming," Thomas said, swallowing a sigh. It was inconvenient, he thought, that Max had suddenly grown a conscience.

It was strange that in all the years they'd been living next door to the Sadowskis, Thomas had never once climbed the weather-beaten steps to their front door. They passed into a narrow foyer that smelled strongly of old cat pee, and came to a second door, this one locked. Next to it was a cracked buzzer, above which was a handwritten sign: *Go Away, Please*.

"Very friendly," Sam said under his breath.

Max ignored him, jabbing the buzzer repeatedly

with one finger. Nothing happened.

"Maybe he's not home," Pippa said after a minute.

"Of course he's home," Max snapped. "He's always home."

"Well, maybe he doesn't want company," Sam said.

Max made a strangled noise. "His brother just croaked. What's the matter with you?" She turned to Pippa. "Aren't you the one who said I should feel sorry for him?"

"And aren't you the one who said he was cuckoo?" Pippa replied.

Max didn't answer. She punched once again at the buzzer.

This time, they didn't wait at all. No sooner had Max removed her finger from the bell than the door swung open. Thomas had to swallow down an immediate first desire to laugh.

The surviving Sadowski brother was dressed even more strangely than he had been on the two previous occasions. He was wearing a tall top hat and a stiff-necked black coat that looked like something a priest might wear. A withered silk flower, stained yellow from age, was pinned to his chest. His pants were also black, made of a ballooning silk that pooled around his ankles. All in all, he gave the impression of a blind man who'd pulled his clothes from a costume shop. Only the fact that he was obviously in mourning helped Thomas keep a straight face.

Sam didn't conceal his feelings quite so well; he let out a loud snort, which earned him a long, fierce glare from Max.

"Hello," she said, turning back to Mr. Sadowski, and speaking loudly, as though in addition to being absurdly dressed he was also hard of hearing. "We came for the funeral service."

Mr. Sadowski blinked rapidly, his eyes passing back and forth between all four children. "The funeral service—yes, yes. Of course. How very kind. But you see, I can't let you inside. Not without consulting Aaron."

To this, even Max had no immediate reply.

"But isn't Aaron—*oof.*" Pippa elbowed Sam in the stomach before he could say *dead*.

"My dear brother has passed on, yes," Mr. Sadowski said. His lower lip trembled. "It is tragic—very unfortunate. Nonetheless, I don't like to allow guests in without consulting him. Whether or not he is dead, he would find it very rude. Quite intolerable. If you'll just wait here a moment . . . It won't take me very long. He's very opinionated, my brother is." With that, he shut the door in their faces. Thomas heard the *slap-slap-slap* of his footsteps receding.

"He's lost the plot, hasn't he?" Sam said, scratching his head.

"Shhh," Max said. But even she looked uneasy. "He's just upset."

Pippa gaped at her. "Upset? He's going to ask his dead brother whether we can come inside."

"Will you be quiet? He'll hear you."

"I don't care if he does. Max had it right the first time. The man is obviously batty—"

"Quiet, both of you," Thomas said. He had just detected the sound of footsteps again, this time advancing toward them. "He's coming back."

This time, when Sadowski opened the door, his cheeks were pink and his eyes were sparkling.

"My brother says you're very welcome to come in," he announced.

"Great," Pippa said, sounding about as enthusiastic as if she had just won a prize of several-days-old fish.

Fortunately, Sadowski didn't seem to notice. He was already beckoning them to follow him into the gloomy recesses of his apartment. "This way, this way. Sorry that things are a little messy. Aaron is so particular about who he sees. I'm afraid we weren't expecting any company. . . ."

"A little messy" was, Thomas thought, a gross under-statement. The Sadowski apartment made the attic at the museum look as bare as a prison cell. Towers of news-papers surrounded them on either side, stacked from floor to ceiling, some so dry and yellowed they looked as if they might disintegrate when touched. There were piles of broken lamps, tea chests, Thanksgiving platters and old typewriters, interspersed with smaller domes-tic items like balled-up socks and teaspoons. Thomas, Pippa, Max, and Sam shuffled forward in single file. There wasn't any other way to move; the hallway was so narrow, Thomas was forced to keep his elbows at his sides for fear of knocking anything over. Techni-cally, Thomas knew, it wasn't a hallway at all—only a path carved through the mountains of junk.

"What is all this stuff?" Pippa whispered, reaching out to skim a finger over the dusty surface of a carved wooden music box.

Though she had surely spoken too quietly for him to hear, Sadowski spun around.

"Don't touch!" he roared, and Pippa yelped and stepped backward, landing directly on Thomas's right foot. Pain shot all the way to Thomas's knee.

Sadowski whipped out a handkerchief—also black—and mopped his face. He was breathing heavily. "I'm sorry," he said. "It's just that Aaron is very sensitive about our things. That's a very special piece. It belonged to our great-uncle Ezekiel. Neither of us could stomach him—he was a terrible man, a very evil temper—but it's our only reminder of him."

Thomas was tempted to ask why on earth the Sadowski brothers would want to be reminded of someone they couldn't stand, but decided to keep his mouth shut.

"This way, this way. Just through here. Mind the ceiling." The portion of ceiling that Sadowski was referring to was in the process of collapsing, and Sam had to duck to avoid getting plaster and pulpy shreds of wallpaper in his hair. "Here we are. And here's Aaron. Please don't be offended if he's rather quiet today. He's had a terrible week. Really awful."

Thomas, Pippa, Sam, and Max crowded awkwardly in a small circular space at the center of what must once have been a grand sitting room. The chandelier was still visible behind the towers of newspaper and mountains of broken furniture surrounding them, though many of its arms were broken, so it looked like a sorry metal octopus staked to the ceiling.

In front of them was a small coffee table and, at its center, a ceramic urn: here, Thomas knew, were the mortal remains of Aaron Sadowski. Thomas noticed several small efforts to make the cramped space appropriate for a funeral. There was a faded white wreath pinned to the fireplace mantel (the fireplace itself, he saw, was entirely filled with ancient porcelain animal figurines); a black tablecloth was arranged haphazardly over several stacks of newspaper; a faded photograph of the two Sadowski brothers as children was on display next to the urn.

Mr. Sadowski fidgeted with his jacket. "Well, go on," he said, after an awkward pause. "Say hello."

No one moved. Pippa nudged Max forward. Max swatted her hand away. Sam was doing his best to disappear into the stacks of newspaper behind him.

Thomas cleared his throat, stepped forward, and, because he didn't know what else to do, laid a hand awkwardly on the urn. "Hello," he said. His voice sounded overloud in the quiet. The urn was very cold to the touch. "And I'm sorry. You know, about . . . the fact that you're dead."

He was worried that it had, perhaps, been the wrong thing to say. But Mr. Sadowski seemed pleased. His thin lips trembled and tears shone in his eyes. "Lovely," he said. "Aaron is very grateful. Very grateful indeed."

Sam, Max, and Pippa took turns shuffling forward

and repeating the ritual, placing a hand on the urn and muttering, "I'm sorry." Thomas was hoping that, having fulfilled their duty, they could leave. But before he could suggest it, Mr. Sadowski had disappeared and returned with a plate full of dusty-looking cookies.

"Please," he said. "Make yourselves at home. I've just put some milk tea up. Or perhaps you'd prefer some licorice water?"

"Milk tea is fine," Pippa said quickly.

Sadowski obviously didn't have very much practice smiling. He gave a kind of pleasant wince. "Excellent, excellent. It won't be a moment. Sorry there's nowhere to sit. We're in the middle of doing some reorganizing."

"Reorganizing," Sam muttered when Sadowski had once again vanished into the gloom of the apartment. "Right."

"*Look* at this stuff." Pippa thumbed through a stack of newspapers. "All of these date from 1895. That's *last century*. What on earth does he plan to do with all of it?"

"He must have his reasons," Max said.

Pippa rolled her eyes. "Come off it, Max. You nearly flipped when you had to act friendly to a pile of ashes."

"Okay, so maybe he's a little . . . different," Max conceded. "So what? It's not like any of us know a thing about normal."

Mr. Sadowski still hadn't returned. Thomas moved off into the stacks, feeling as if he were an explorer navigating the wreckage of an old civilization: towers, pillars, *monuments* of stuff. He selected a newspaper from the top of a pile at random. From 1916, it felt brittle to the touch, like the dried seaweed they had been served in the restaurant in Chinatown. Somewhere in here, he knew, must be stories about Rattigan dating from his very first arrest. There must be pictures of the cages in which Rattigan had kept his subjects—cages in which Thomas, Max, Pippa, and Sam had once been kept.

He shivered. He didn't like to think about Rattigan still on the loose, and what the mysterious note on the kitchen door could mean. His only comfort was in knowing that if Rattigan wanted to find them, he would have already.

"Hey, Tom. Look at this." Pippa held up a slim book, bound in faded red cloth. The title, *The World's Best Puzzles and Brain Teasers*, was printed in gold lettering. "Want to try your luck?"

"Pass it over." Thomas was grateful for the distraction. His mind felt like a broken jigsaw puzzle, all corners and angles, pieces that wouldn't quite fit together, no matter how much he tried to force them. Here, in the quiet, in the half dark, it was impossible not to think about Rattigan, impossible not to think about Rachel Richstone and her old boyfriend Ian Grantt and poor Freckles and the news Spode had given them about Mark and Jennifer Haskell's deaths.

He flipped to a page at random. It was full of word games.

"What word is an anagram of itself?" he read out loud.

Max groaned. "Really?"

"How about 'mom'?" Sam suggested.

"That's a palindrome," Thomas said. "It's spelled the same backward and forward. An anagram is when you rearrange the letters to spell a different word."

"An anagram of itself . . ." Pippa wrinkled her nose. "How can you rearrange the letters of a word to spell the same word?"

"That's why it's a brain teaser," Thomas said. He was quiet for a minute, letting the problem twist around in his brain, letting it bend and flex. Then there was a click, a settling, as when he found a comfortable position inside the blade box. "Stifle," he announced. "That's an anagram of *i-t-s-e-l-f*."

This time, it was Sam who groaned.

"Hey, look at this." Max was rifling through a stack of old pictures. She displayed a photograph of Eli

Sadowski as a young man, wearing, it seemed, the very same outfit that he still favored most days. The photograph was labeled in a sloping hand: *Elizir Sadowski, 1908*. "Eli's short for Elizir. Funny name, isn't it?"

"Speaking of funny names," Sam said, wincing as he tried to work through one of the ancient cookies Mr. Sadowski had brought out, which looked to have the same texture as a piece of petrified wood. "Have you heard from Spode about Ian Grantt yet?"

Thomas shook his head. Once again, he could feel his brain shifting, like an ocean stirring up waves. What had Sam said that troubled him . . . ?

"It *is* a strange way to spell Grantt," Pippa said. She, too, was sorting through the stacks, lifting yellowed newspapers and shaking her head over headlines from decades earlier. Suddenly, she stiffened. The newspaper in her hands began to tremble.

"What is it, Pippa?" Sam asked curiously.

Wordlessly, she turned and held the paper up for their inspection.

Nicholas Rattigan Arrested in New York, said the headline. *Sick Scientist Performs Human Experiments in Sophisticated Underground Lab.* This must have been the news of his very first arrest—after which Thomas, Pippa, Sam, and Max were scattered and orphaned.

Though Thomas had known for months now about his origins, somehow, seeing the words printed in black and white made them all the more real. The headline began to swim in front of Thomas's eyes. *Sick scientist... Nicholas Rattigan... Underground...*

His mind gave another turn. And suddenly, just like that, he knew. All of those jagged puzzle pieces softened, rearranged, and slid together.

"Give me a pen," he croaked out.

Pippa stared at him. "What's the matter with you?"

"Quick," he said. There was an urgent pressure in his chest: a need to tell, or burst. "A pen."

It took several minutes of rooting to find a pen in the massive piles of old belongings, and another few minutes to find a pen with ink. But at last Thomas, pen in hand, bent over the coffee table and began to scribble in the book of brain teasers.

"Don't let Sadowski catch you," Sam said. "That book might have belonged to his great-aunt's second cousin."

Thomas was in no mood to appreciate the joke. He spelled out IAN GRANTT at the top of the page. "Don't you see?" Thomas said.

"See what?" Max frowned.

"It's an anagram," Thomas said. And he carefully spelled out: N. RATTIGAN.

29

"Here we are. Four steaming milk teas, with a little dash of Epsom salt for the digestion, just like my mother used to make it!" Mr. Sadowski inched back into the room, holding a large pewter tray on which four mugs were rattling precariously. So intent was he on getting the mugs safely from tray to table that it took him a moment to realize that the four children from the museum next door had vanished, as though into thin air. Other than several newspapers that had, much to his disapproval, been disarranged, there was no sign that they had come at all.

"Well," Mr. Sadowski said under his breath. "How very rude." But he was not altogether sorry to be alone with his brother once more.

"Tea, Aaron?" he said, turning to the urn. He was gratified when, as always, his brother said yes.

Meanwhile, Thomas, Pippa, Sam, and Max had already returned to the museum. Luckily, they encountered no hastily assembled protest, no grumbling performers or curious journalists. They saw no one at all. Even luckier, the narrow phone booth nestled underneath the performers' spiral staircase, which was usually occupied, most often by Quinn or Betty, was empty.

Thomas fished Ned Spode's card from his pocket and consulted the number.

Pippa frowned. "I could have read it off for you."

"There's no time," Thomas said. Before he could lift the receiver, however, the phone began to ring. Sam groaned.

"It's probably one of Betty's boyfriends," he said.

"I'll get it," Pippa said, and snatched up the receiver.

"Pippa," Spode said, before she'd even finished saying hello. "This is Pippa, am I right? I have some big news. Gather up the gang. We need to meet as soon as possible."

"We have news, too," she said, tilting the receiver away from her ear, while Sam, Max, and Thomas crowded in to listen. "We don't think Ian Grantt really died. We think he went underground and came back—"

"As Professor Rattigan," Spode said, cutting her off. He spoke with flinty seriousness. "I know. I've got it all figured out. Listen, you're not safe where you are. Let's talk in person. Meet at 712 West Fifty-Eighth. As soon as you can." And he rang off so abruptly, Pippa was left staring at the receiver in her hand, a feeling of buzzing anxiety flowing all the way from her fingers into her chest.

"What did he mean, we're not safe?" Max asked.

"What do you think he means?" Thomas answered grimly. "Rattigan's back. And he's coming for us."

The address Spode had given them turned out to be on a desolate block that dead-ended at the Hudson River. The street was dominated by one hulking building, which looked, due to the narrow, boarded-up windows and the ghostly imprints of old advertising decals, to be an abandoned factory. There was no number. Across the street, a homeless man was dozing in the shadow of a doorway, his hat over his face, using a battered rucksack for a pillow.

"This *must* be it." Pippa squinted up at the side of the building, scanning once again in vain for an identifying mark, or some sign of life in the windows. Nothing. But the previous block had ended with number 710, and there was nothing farther west but water, and seagulls wheeling through the air.

Max shifted from foot to foot, occasionally palming at her pockets, where Pippa could see she'd placed three separate blades in different sizes.

"Should we knock?" Sam asked. Thomas shrugged and Sam stepped forward, raising a fist.

Max intercepted him. "Don't *you* do it," she said. "You'll knock the whole bugging door down." She knocked three times on the door. Pippa could hear the sound echoing hollowly within. After a minute, the door opened, seemingly on its own, revealing a triangle of murky darkness.

Sam stepped forward—to impress Max, Pippa was sure, since his fingers were trembling ever so slightly. She fell into step behind him, and Thomas and Max took up the rear.

"Hello?" Sam called out as they passed inside.

The door slammed shut behind them and Pippa's heart leaped into her throat. She spun around. But no one was there.

"This way!" Spode's voice sounded, very faintly, from somewhere deeper within the building. Pippa felt instantly better. So they were not alone in a creepy building after all.

They moved cautiously, as a group, further into the murky darkness, skirting metal gurneys, dustbins, and coiled cables, and ducking under the chutes that crisscrossed the low-hanging ceiling. The dusty floor was pitted with railway tracks, winding like iron snakes from one end of the factory to another. An old trolley car, only half painted, loomed motionless in the dark. As they skirted around it, Pippa had a sudden fear that it would come blazingly to life, horn blaring, windows flashing with light, and run them down.

There was still no sign of Spode.

"Where are you?" Thomas shouted.

"Just a little further!" Spode called back, although he sounded just as distant as before. Was he *moving*? Surely, he wouldn't be. But Pippa's arms were prickling with gooseflesh. It was cold in the factory, as if they'd passed into a different world, a different season.

Up ahead, Pippa detected a flickering light, as if someone were pacing back and forth with an old-fashioned lantern. Spode. As they drew closer, she could make out the planes of his face, lit up harshly in the gaslight, all ridges and angles. He looked, Pippa thought, like a stranger.

Unconsciously, she began to move faster. Sam had fallen behind. His attempts at bravery had obviously failed him, and he was sticking close to Max.

"There you are," Pippa said, and even she could hear how thin and tremulous her voice sounded. "What are you doing all the way back—?"

She didn't finish her sentence. Several things happened at once. Spode turned to her and there was a sudden, blinding explosion of light, a flare so bright Pippa shut her eyes instinctively. She couldn't see. Her vision was obscured by floating dots of color, and for one terrifying second she believed she'd really gone blind. Everyone was shouting, and someone—it felt like Sam—knocked into her from behind. She went sprawling, hitting the ground hard and biting down on her cheek, tasting blood.

And in that moment of impact, it was as if she was jolted out of her body, like her mind had received a big punt kick. And suddenly she was Pippa but also Max, or Pippa-as-Max, crouching in a corner of Max's mind and feeling her fear and her terror and her desperate, fumbling desire for her knives. . . .

But Pippa-as-Max knew that it was too late. Someone tackled Max from behind, wrestling off her jacket and removing the knives in her pockets. Pippa-as-Max could smell him, the distinctive combination of chemical and sulfur, of something pickled and left too long on a shelf. . . .

And as Max cried out and Pippa was jolted once again into her own body, she knew: they had walked right into a trap.

"Well, well, well." Gradually, a steady light began to penetrate through the blur of Pippa's vision. Another gas lantern flared to life—and standing next to it, his long, pale fingers curled around the handle, was a smiling Rattigan. "So very nice of you to join us."

30

Sam's first reaction was a rush of fury, not at Rattigan but at Spode. "You," he spat out. "You tricked us."

Spode was working a toothpick in his mouth, and appeared unconcerned. "Sorry," he said, shrugging, as if he wasn't the least bit sorry at all. "I'm a paid private eye. Emphasis on paid."

"So Manfred never hired you to clear him at all?" Thomas asked. "That was all a lie?"

"Oh, he paid me all right." Spode grinned. In the low light, his face looked wolfish. Why had Sam never noticed before? "It's just that my old friend Rattigan here paid me more."

"Old friend?" Sam said.

Rattigan and Spode exchanged an amused glance.

"Oh, yes. Edward and I go way back. But there is time enough for explanations later. The truth will *come to light*, so to speak," Rattigan said, and he bent down to retrieve another lantern. Remembering the flash that had nearly burned his eyeballs out, Sam squeezed his eyes shut. Rattigan chuckled. "Never fear, Samson, you'll have no more unpleasant tricks from me. Ingenious device, isn't it? I call it a flare-lantern. This was one of my very first inventions, back when I was just a lowly sergeant in the army. Back when I was Ian Grantt."

"That was a cheap trick," Thomas said, his face flushed with anger. "We figured out that Ian Grantt is an anagram of Rattigan."

"I was certain you would," Rattigan said, nodding encouragingly. "In fact, I was counting on it."

"Was that another one of your tests?" Thomas said, spitting the words as if each one carried a particular bad taste.

"Not at all. At least, not entirely. When I was a young man I decided I wanted a fresh start. With just a few adjustments to my given name, I had a new identity and a new lease on life. I moved to New York."

"And met Rachel Richstone," Thomas said.

"And met Rachel, yes." For just a moment, Rattigan's

face softened. But the result was hideous; now it was like watching a wolf rhapsodize about its first kill. "She was a beautiful girl. Sweet and very faithful. If it hadn't been for the war we might have . . . well, there's no sense thinking about that." Now his face hardened again, and his eyes glittered demonically. "The war changed many men. We all came back with pieces missing, if we came back at all. Isn't that right, Ned?"

Ned spat out the toothpick. "That's right."

"Why don't you show our friends your particular missing piece?" Rattigan said. "Perhaps it will help convince them I am not nearly so monstrous as they believe."

Spode bent down and began to roll up his left trouser leg. Pippa gasped sharply, and Sam experienced a roiling sense of nausea. His leg was a mangled mess of shredded skin and exposed muscle, seamlessly interwoven with metal wiring, rubber tubing, and iron bolts.

Rattigan hardly glanced at it. "We were leading the charge on the German front line, not long before the war officially ended. It was a fool's mission, but we did what we were told. We always did what we were told back then." His voice was full of sudden venom. "Idiot pawns of idiot men playing with power like toddlers with blocks. Hundreds of thousands of men, bloodied and broken—for what? For some lines on a map. For some scraps of dirt."

Sam wanted to look away but he couldn't.

"We were halfway toward cover when the first man had his head blown off. The whole place was a minefield. An artillery blast turned our friend Ned's leg to spaghetti from toe to tibia. It took me the better part of a year to put him back together. But now, you see, he's as good as new."

"Better than new," Spode grunted. Sam was relieved when he yanked down his pant leg, so the horrible confusion of bone and blood and metal and muscle was once again concealed.

"But Spode was lucky compared to some of the others. My best friend, Corporal McMurphy, was blown into so many pieces they could hardly put two teeth together to send home to his wife."

"Stop," Pippa said quietly.

Rattigan turned to her. "You want me to stop?" he said, his voice dropping to a dangerous whisper. "You find this upsetting, these tales of blood and battlefields? But you have to see, my dear Philippa, that I am not the evil one. I don't conceal my true nature. All men are monsters. The only evil is in pretending otherwise."

"You've killed people. That's evil," Sam said. He swallowed when Rattigan's gaze passed to him. His eyes were cold, hardly human. "You murdered Rachel Richstone.

And you killed Eckleberger. He was our friend."

Rattigan didn't blink. "I confess I've had to go to certain lengths to preserve my . . . anonymity. I couldn't risk having the police link me to Rachel's death, you see. Not when I'd gone to such lengths to convince them that I was all the way out in Chicago."

"Why did you kill Rachel?" Max blurted. "What'd she ever do to you?"

"It's what she didn't do, Mackenzie," Rattigan said evenly. "My time as a guest of the federal penitentiary system has left me a little bit short of funds necessary to my work. As you can imagine, I'm quite eager to begin my experiments again . . . especially since I have now seen definitive proof of my success."

Sam's stomach surged into his throat. "We're not proof of anything," he said. "We've got nothing to do with you."

Rattigan waggled a finger. "But you're wrong, Sam. You've everything to do with me. I made you. Your strength, your power, your sense of justice, even your anger—I had a hand in all of it. Oh, I don't doubt you cling to some ideas about Mommy and Daddy," he added with a shrug. "I bet you wonder what life would be like if I had never found you. But don't you see? I'm your true creator. Your mother, father, and future all in one."

The words passed like a fog through Sam's body, invading him with cold. Was it true? Would Rattigan always live inside of him, even after he'd been defeated?

"So you killed Rachel because she wouldn't give you money," Thomas said.

Rattigan studied his nails. "I lost my temper. She was not nearly so stubborn when I knew her."

Thomas frowned. "Where did Eckleberger fit in?"

Rattigan set down the lantern on an overturned crate, clasping his hands together in front of him. "I think you know, Thomas. Don't you?"

"The photograph," Thomas said after a brief pause. "It proved that you'd known Rachel Richstone in the past. It might link you to the murder. And Eckleberger had it. But how did you know that?"

"After our last brief and, I must say, disappointing encounter, you didn't think I'd let you stray too far from my protection, did you?" Rattigan said, revealing his yellowed teeth.

"Your protection?" scoffed Max. "What a load of—"

"It was you," Thomas said, cutting her off. "You came to the museum to see the Richstone exhibit. You stole peanut brittle."

Rattigan shrugged. "It's always been a weakness of mine."

Sam's mind felt like it was fighting to work through a thick mud that had enveloped it. He remembered no one but Richstone's lawyer and a group of leering children and an old man with a thick crop of white hair and buckteeth. . . .

And then he realized: Rattigan. The old man had been Rattigan in disguise. All this time, when they'd believed themselves safe, he'd merely been toying with them, biding his time.

And he was gripped by a sense of hopelessness. Rattigan was too smart. Smarter than all of them, even Thomas.

"A bit of vanity, I suppose," Rattigan said with another flutter of his hand. "I couldn't pass up the opportunity to see some of my work represented."

"You call murder your work?" Pippa said angrily.

"Shouldn't I?" Rattigan said. "It takes planning and dedication to detail. And commitment. Commitment above all." He frowned suddenly. "I was distressed to realize, however, that your friend Eckleberger had misrepresented some critical details of the scene."

"He got Rachel wrong," Thomas said. "He was working from an old picture."

"My thinking exactly!" Rattigan's changes of expression were dizzying; now he was beaming again. "An old picture. But what old picture? The idea troubled me greatly. Rachel and I had once been engaged. She might have hung on to any number of photographs, for sentimental reasons. I was, if I may say so, a very handsome young man."

Max made a choking sound. Rattigan didn't notice, or chose to ignore her. "I became concerned, you see, that your friend Eckleberger might have in his possession evidence that might link me to Rachel. The world believed Ian Grantt had died on the battlefield. That was, to some extent, true. Ian Grantt did die. And Rattigan was reborn."

"So you killed Freckles." Sam was trembling with rage. He thought of Eckleberger, his dark eyes sparkling, passing out warm sugar cookies; Eckleberger dressed up as Santa Claus, distributing presents; Eckleberger, singing old German lullabies in his raspy voice. He wanted to kill Rattigan, to flatten him, to press his vocal cords into paper. Rattigan might be smarter, but Sam was much, much stronger.

Could he do it? Could he kill someone? He wanted to believe that he could, if it was for a good reason. But didn't everyone, even Rattigan, have reasons for doing terrible things?

"I'm not proud of it," Rattigan said shortly. "He seemed like a fine man, and an even better artist. I had no choice. Similarly, I had to kill the Haskells. I realized that they might sooner or later see my picture in the papers—the only downside of my escape from prison is all the publicity it has received—and recognize me as Rachel's old boyfriend in light of her recent murder."

"What about Manfred?" Thomas said. "Did you arrange to have him bumped off, too?"

Rattigan shook his head. "Now you give me too much credit. I would have done, I suppose. Once I learned from Ned that you, Thomas, had gotten in touch with him, I was concerned that idiot might blunder into the truth. As it turned out, I was spared the trouble of acting. Manfred was never very good at making friends, you see."

"So when does it stop?" Pippa said. Her lower lip was trembling. "The running and the hiding and the killing. When does it end?"

Rattigan frowned. "My dear Pippa, you should know I despise any form of violence. Murder is particularly distasteful—it's so common. But again, I had no choice. It was a matter, you see, of survival. And wouldn't you do anything to survive? Wouldn't you, Sam?"

Sam looked away. It was as if Rattigan had just read his deepest thoughts.

"It's the rule of the world," Rattigan said softly. "Dog eats dog. Only the strong survive. That's why I made you strong, Sam." His voice was practically a whisper. In the half-light, his eyes glinted eerily, like those of a cat. "Your father, you know, was supposed to be quite the brute. No one could ever understand how he'd managed to settle down with such a lovely wife."

Sam froze. His breath crystallized in his chest. It was painful to breathe.

"Priscilla, her name was, if I recall correctly," Rattigan squinted up at the ceiling, looking everywhere but at Sam. "Tiny slip of a thing. And your father stumping around with his hands in fists, boasting to everyone he could split a rock with his friend. Joe the Bully, he was called." Rattigan closed his eyes. "But in the end, you see, he was quite weak. Far too weak to stop me."

Sam started for Rattigan. But at the same time, Spode moved a hand almost casually to his pocket, where the bulge of a revolver was visible, and Thomas flung out an arm to stop him.

"Don't," Thomas said quietly. "It's what he wants."

Sam was shaking so hard he could feel his teeth jump together. "You're a liar," he spat out.

Rattigan looked away, as if he found Sam's outburst embarrassing. "I'm explaining to you why I did what I did," he said. "I'm explaining why I made you what you are."

"Stop saying you made us," Sam spat out. "We don't belong to you."

Finally, Rattigan turned back to face him. Now his eyes were like holes, and Sam felt he was falling into them.

"Oh, but I did," Rattigan said simply. "And you do."

31

"I'll be honest with you," Rattigan said, perching on an overturned crate and crossing his legs. All this time, Spode was still standing beside him, motionless, half hidden in shadow. Max had a sudden image of Ned Spode as a soldier under Rattigan's command. Blindly obedient. Determined. Deadly. A cold coil of fear squeezed the lungs in her chest. "I called you here today because I need your help."

"Our help?" Max scoffed. "You think we'll help *you*?"

Rattigan lifted a hand. "Hear me out. You think I'm bad. You think I'm evil. But you've got it all wrong." His eyes were lit up from the lantern, cold and pale as glass, shining with a frightening intensity. "It's the *world* that's evil. I've killed—what?—a half dozen people? That's nothing. Every day, thousands of people around the world are killed by soldiers of one army or another—all supposedly good men, fighting for a supposedly good cause. I want to stop that."

Max remembered what Mr. Dumfrey had told them about his half brother: his deranged fantasy of an army of superhuman soldiers, an unbeatable unit. With power concentrated so heavily in the hands of one group of people, no one else would dare go to war. But it was crazy. Power like that would only lead to more war. Anyone could see that.

"You want us to be part of your army," Thomas said.

"Eventually, yes." Rattigan nodded encouragingly, as if he were a teacher and Thomas a particularly encouraging student. "But first, of course, we'll need funds. In that, too, I'll need your help. Think about it. Do you really want to spend the rest of your life being pointed at? Ridiculed? Mocked? Do you really want to spend your life as freaks, when you could be doing something *important*?"

"Like what?" The anger in Max's chest was uncoiling now, lashing around in her stomach, making her feel careless and dangerous. "Helping you rob little old ladies on the street?"

"Of course not." Rattigan looked shocked. "That would hardly do us any good, would it? No. We'll take money only from the places where it is most abundant."

"So what?" Thomas said. When he was angry, even his freckles darkened. "You want us to help you rob banks?"

"I prefer not to use the word *rob*," Rattigan said. "I like to think of it simply as redistribution. It was the banks and war profiteers that sat back and watched the world go up in flames. Why not settle the score?"

"Sorry to disappoint you," Pippa said. "But you can forget about your big plans. It's like Max said. We'll never help you, not in a million years."

Rattigan hardly blinked. "I'm afraid I'd anticipated a certain amount of . . . resistance," he said with a heavy sigh. "I believe I have ways of persuading you. If you're so disapproving of murder, surely you wouldn't want to be responsible for an innocent person's death?"

A chill went up Max's spine, making even her hair tingle. "What are you talking about?"

"Show them, Ned," Rattigan said with a careless wave of his hand.

Spode had been so motionless, Max had nearly forgotten him. Without a word, he disappeared into the gloomy darkness that surrounded the small circle illumined by lantern light. There was a brief noise of scuffling, as if something heavy was being lifted or dragged.

Then Spode reappeared, pushing a bound-and-gagged Chubby in front of him.

"Chubby!" Thomas cried.

Sam started to take a step forward.

"Don't move, or the boy dies," Rattigan snarled, dropping all pretense of civility. For a moment, Max saw his true face: not the easygoing, smiling scientist who believed that murder was moral and humans were playthings, but the beast, the animal, all madness and hate.

Rattigan stood up, withdrawing a knife from his pocket. Max's stomach turned. It was one of her knives—one of the knives he'd stolen, when he'd tackled her in the dark and wrestled off her jacket. Rattigan tested it against a finger, and a small bright bit of blood immediately welled there.

"Very nice," he said. "I should have known you would take excellent care of your blades, Mackenzie. It shouldn't take more than a single cut to spill this unfortunate boy's guts all over the ground."

Chubby whimpered. Spode shoved him down onto the crate that Rattigan had vacated. Chubby's eyes were rolling like a terrified horse's, and though Max was no mind reader, she could easily see the plea written in his expression. *Help me*, he was saying. *Please help me.*

"Let him go, Rattigan," Thomas said. "Killing him won't do any good."

"I agree," Rattigan said. "That's why I'd like to avoid it. And if you do as I say, the boy will live." Rattigan laid a hand on Chubby's shoulder; Chubby jumped. A whimpering sound worked its way through the gag. "Ned will stay here watching over your friend. You will do what I say, when I say it, and only then, on our return, the boy will be released with not a scratch on him. Well"—Rattigan moved the blade close to Chubby's throat. Chubby was trembling so hard the crate rattled underneath him—"perhaps with one or two scratches."

Max licked her lips, which felt very dry. "And why should we care if you kill him or not?" she said, trying to sound unconcerned. "You made a mistake, Rattigan. He's no friend of ours."

"Oh no?" Rattigan raised an eyebrow. "How unfortunate. But if he's no friend of yours, then surely you won't mind if I make a minor . . . adjustment to his face?"

Rattigan grabbed Chubby's left ear. Chubby screeched in pain. In one fluid motion, before Max could even react, Rattigan lifted the blade and brought it down in a swift chopping motion. . . .

Just then, Rattigan screamed in pain and the knife clattered to the ground. Before Max could register what had happened, what looked like a long leather snake appeared out of nowhere, curling itself around the knife handle and whipping it out of sight.

Then her brain ticked forward and she realized: Lash. He had struck the knife from Rattigan's hand. A split second later Lash was there, whip in hand, his face mottled with fury.

"Lash!" Max cried. But before she could get to him Spode tackled him. He caught Lash square in the stomach and the two men crashed to the floor, bringing down one of the lanterns with them. There was an explosion. Max felt the sudden bite of glass against her cheek. She hardly noticed the pain.

Everything was chaos. Sam lunged for Rattigan, but Rattigan, anticipating his attack, sidestepped him and seized Pippa by the arm. She screamed and tried to shake him off, but he held on firmly, growling at her to be quiet. Max instinctively stepped toward her and felt something cold slide against her ankle. Of course. It was the artist's scalpel, the small blade she'd taken from Eckleberger's studio and had been keeping in her boot. By the time she had it in her hand, Rattigan had snaked an arm around Pippa's neck, holding her close to his chest, like a human shield.

"Not another step, Mackenzie," he said softly. But she could tell he was losing control. His hair was wild, his forehead damp with sweat. It made him look more dangerous than ever. "That goes for you, too, Sam."

Max and Sam froze. Only then did Max realize that Thomas had vanished. She felt a flare-up of hope. Perhaps he had gone to get the police. Then, above them, she saw a brief flicker of shadow, a form darting along the high metal grid of catwalks, and her stomach sank again. What was he *doing*?

"I'm very disappointed in all of you," Rattigan said. "You've given me very little choice." Pippa opened her mouth as if to speak. Nothing but a gurgle came out. Max tested the weight of the scalpel in her hand. She had a clear shot . . . if only Pippa would stop moving . . . if only she had a little more room for *error* . . . Her palm was sweating. She had a sudden flashback to that disastrous performance with Betty, the blood, the sharp gasp from the audience and her roiling guilt . . .

She had to try. It was their only chance.

But before she could so much as lift her arm, Rattigan dragged Pippa backward, kicking over the other lantern, and they were plunged into darkness.

32

Years of shimmying through the complex nest of pipes and ducts within the museum's walls had made Thomas very good at seeing in the dark. As soon as Rattigan seized Pippa, he had sensed an opportunity to attack from above. Melting back into the darkness, he had quickly found an old staircase that led to the factory's upper level: a grid of dusty catwalks, built so that the foremen could easily survey the action down below. When the second lantern shattered, he paused in a crouch, giving his eyes time to adjust to the renewed darkness—listening, too, trying to separate individual strands of sound and weave them into pictures. Shouting and cursing, the muffled sound of blows: Lash and

Spode were still wrestling. Max, commanding Chubby to hold still. Good. At least Chubby would be safe; Thomas prayed Max would tell him to go find help.

Straining now, staying motionless despite the drumming, thrumming urge to do something, to rip Rattigan apart, to scream, he kept listening. What else? A crash from down beneath him, as if someone had overturned old equipment. He stood up again, moving as silently as possible along the catwalk, praying it was still sturdy and would hold. Then he froze.

There was a noise behind him: a shuffling, creaking noise, a vibration that Thomas felt in his feet.

Someone was with him on the catwalk.

Thomas turned around quickly and nearly lost his footing. He windmilled his arms and regained his balance, but his heart wouldn't stop thudding painfully against his ribs. The factory floor must be at least forty feet below him, and cluttered with heavy and sharp equipment. There would be no way to survive a fall.

The shuffling had stopped. But Thomas knew that he was right. He could hear another person breathing heavily in the dark. It occurred to him that Rattigan might have other friends besides Spode. Who knew how many people might be hiding out here in the dark, waiting to attack?

The back of Thomas's neck was sweating. He was losing time. Rattigan had Pippa. He needed to help her.

"Hello?" he risked calling out softly, hoping he didn't sound as afraid as he felt. "Who's there?"

"Oh, it's you." Sam's voice floated back to him. Sam inched forward on the catwalk, eventually becoming visible. "I was worried Rattigan might have more friendly helpers."

"I was thinking the same thing," Thomas said. He was immensely, embarrassingly relieved to have Sam with him. "Did you see which way Rattigan went?"

"That way." Sam pointed to the back of the factory. "At least, I think he went that way. I lost him pretty quickly."

"We have to stop him before he can get to an exit. Once he leaves with Pippa . . ." Thomas trailed off. He didn't even want to think about what Rattigan would do to his best friend. And Pippa *was* his best friend. He realized that all at once with a sudden shock.

They moved forward carefully on the catwalk, pausing every few seconds to listen. Sam was doing his best to tread lightly, but even so the metal shuddered under his feet, and Thomas kept fearing that it would suddenly snap, and send them plummeting toward the factory floor below.

They skirted an enormous bundle of cables, massed like a fist around what looked like a giant engine. The catwalk branched, and Thomas hesitated. Which way?

As he was debating, he heard a loud scream and his heart rocketed into his throat. Pippa.

"This way," Thomas whispered urgently to Sam, taking the catwalk on the right. This one felt even more treacherous than the last, and swayed underneath Thomas's feet as they moved, giving him an awful sense of vertigo. They must be nearing the very back of the factory. Weak light filtered in from several boarded-up windows. Thomas saw a huge set of old trolley rails, dangling from a steel cable hooked to the ceiling, pointing like an accusatory finger toward the floor.

And underneath them: Rattigan, with Pippa still hugged tightly to his chest and a knife to her throat.

"Don't come any closer!" Rattigan's voice was shrill, practically a shriek. He staggered in a circle, hauling Pippa with him, shouting his words up into the dark. "I know you're up there. If you move even a single inch, I'll slit her throat!"

Rattigan was trapped: that much was clear. He had taken a gamble that there would be a secondary exit at the back of the factory, and he had lost. It was a stupid error. But even Rattigan made mistakes. Still, the idea gave Thomas no satisfaction. Rattigan was now desperate and out of control, which made him even more dangerous than usual.

They would have to be very, very careful.

"Where are you?" Rattigan wrenched the knife away from Pippa's throat and slashed at the shadows. "Stay away from me, you hear me? Stay away!"

As Rattigan once again spun around, starting at an imagined noise behind him, Thomas spotted the narrow mouth of a metal chute that ended only a few feet from where Rattigan was now standing. Shaped like a drain spout, the chute hugged the back wall and ceiling, and dead-ended just next to the catwalk. Presumably, Thomas thought, people had once used it to send materials down to the factory floor.

Thomas reached out and squeezed Sam's arm to get his attention. As soon as Sam nodded to show he understood, Thomas took a deep breath and worked himself headfirst into the chute, inching forward on his stomach.

It was hot and very cramped and Thomas's progress felt agonizingly slow. But he didn't want to go faster and risk rattling around or banging his knee, and alerting Rattigan to his progress. Here, there was no light at all. He went forward blindly, hoping he'd encounter no block, until the chute eventually opened up beneath him and he knew he had reached the back wall. Here he spent several minutes turning himself upright. Keeping his back to the wall and his knees to his chest, he was able to work his way down, slowly, slowly, toward the ground. He could hear nothing; the chute acted as a kind of muffler, and all he could hear were the amplified sounds of his own breathing and the *squeak-squeak-squeak* of his shoes. He didn't know what he would do once he reached Rattigan. He knew only that he had to save Pippa.

Once again, the chute turned, this time flattening out as Thomas reached the factory floor. He'd been worried that Rattigan might once again have disappeared before Thomas could reach him, but he was still standing only a few feet away, keeping Pippa restrained with one hand, stabbing at the air with the knife in the other.

"I made you," Rattigan was shrieking as Thomas slid silently out of the chute and stood. His whole body was cold and heavy with fear. Now he saw how mad Rattigan truly was. "I'm your creator. I should be honored like a god!" Rattigan's voice thundered through the space. Above them, Thomas saw the steel railway tracks sway on their cable, as if in response to his words. He inched forward again. He was so close to Rattigan, he might have reached out and touched the back of his neck. His hands were itchy. He was no match for Rattigan in strength. And where was Sam? What was he doing?

"If you won't honor me, we will be enemies for life!" Rattigan bellowed, head tilted back, eyes wild with anger. In that moment, he did look like a vengeful god. "I demand *sacrifice*. Sacrifice, do you hear me?"

It happened so quickly, Thomas barely had time to react. All at once Rattigan spun Pippa around, gripping her by the throat, and raised the knife.

"No!" Thomas screamed.

Rattigan pivoted, surprised. The railway tracks above them gave another lurch and suddenly Thomas knew where Sam was and what he was doing. At the same time, Pippa stamped, hard, on Rattigan's foot. Rattigan lost his grip on her neck. Thomas sprang forward, grabbing Pippa's elbow and yanking her out of the way.

Just then the steel cable above them succumbed, with a groan, to the pressure of Sam's hands, and three tons of steel came crashing down directly on top of Rattigan.

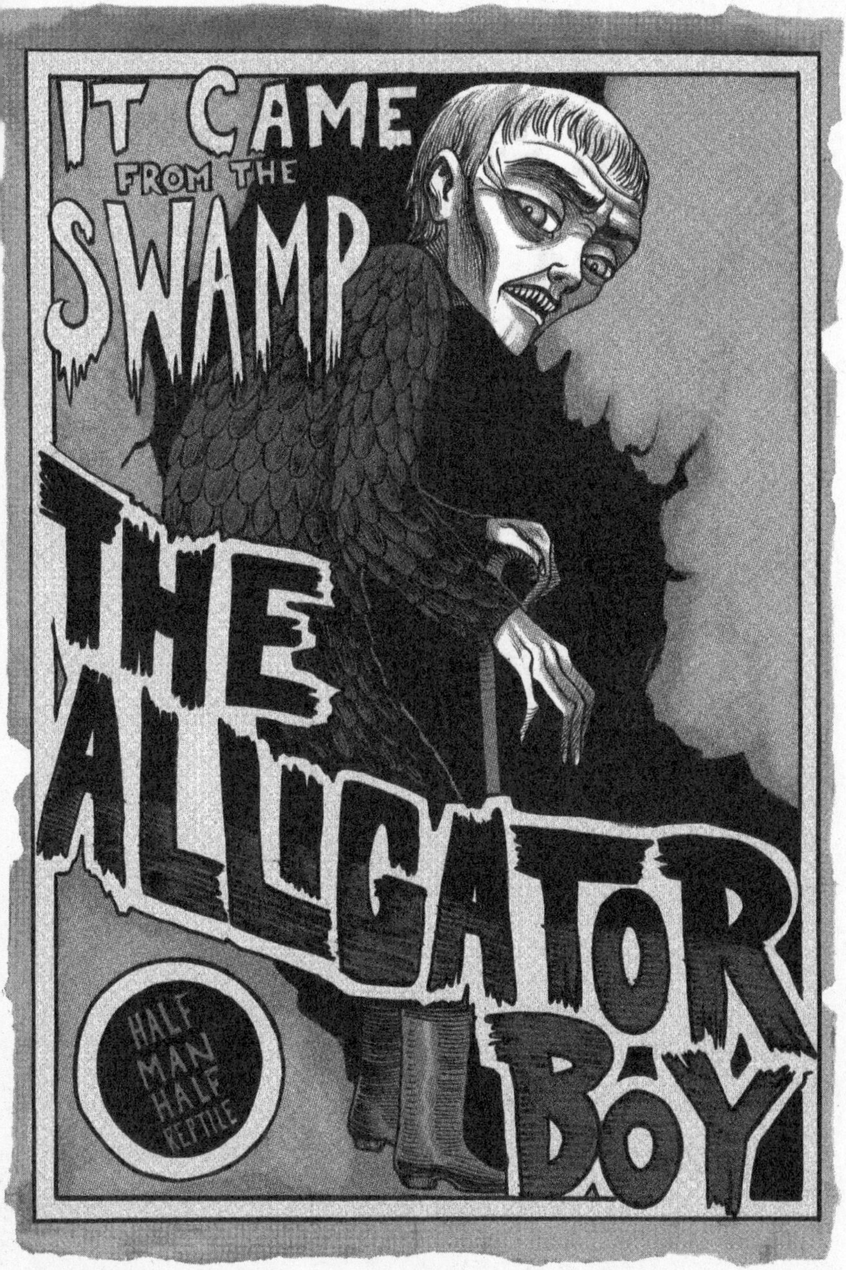
IT CAME
FROM THE
SWAMP
THE ALLIGATOR BOY
HALF
MAN
HALF
REPTILE

It was a somber group that made its way, several hours later, back to the museum. Mr. Dumfrey took the lead. For once, he had nothing to say. Pippa wasn't in the mood to speak, either—no one was. She was relieved that they had gotten away safely, and doubly relieved that Lash, though badly injured, would surely survive as well.

Spode had not been so lucky. They had found him dead next to the bleeding Lash, the bullwhip wrapped three times around his throat, embedded so deeply in his flesh that the coroner expected to have to remove it with a razor blade. But Pippa couldn't bring herself to feel even vaguely sorry for him.

She had never been so tired in her whole life. Even her hair felt tired, and hung limply against her neck. They had told their story, over and over again, both to the cops who had arrived at the factory with Chubby, and to Mr. Dumfrey, who had been summoned there by a call from the police and had arrived with shaving cream still slathered over half of his face.

It was obvious that no one, least of all Schroeder and Detective Hardaway, believed their story about Rattigan, especially when the pile of old trolley rails was cleared and no body was found beneath it. True, there was a steel-reinforced trapdoor set in the floor, but the heavy hinged lid was closed and latched. No man, the police insisted, could have flung it open, jumped inside, and swung the door closed again in the seconds before the rails came crashing down on him.

Sam, Pippa, Thomas, and Max knew better. Somehow, Rattigan had once again made his escape.

Detective Hardaway made no secret of his theory: that Max, Pippa, Thomas, and Sam had, like Chubby, been hired by Spode to make special "deliveries." It turned out Spode had been blackmailing half the rich people in the city, and using Chubby to drop off incriminating photographs and retrieve payouts and hush money. The kids had gotten in over their heads, they'd tried to back out, and Spode had turned violent. Lash—who admitted that after leaving the museum he'd been keeping an eye on the children from afar—had rushed in to save them at the last moment. They'd cooked up the Rattigan story to avoid getting in trouble.

Case closed. And nothing anyone could say would persuade him otherwise—which meant that Rattigan was once again a free man.

Pippa was relieved when they turned onto Forty-Third Street and she saw the familiar contours of the museum's weathered face. But even this pleasure was dampened by the knowledge that the museum was facing almost certain closure. The performers were unhappy. Dumfrey hadn't found a way to bring the crowds back. How much longer could they possibly last? Even now, as they approached, she felt as if she were not really seeing it, but already only remembering it: the wide stoop and vivid red doors with their smudgy brass handles, the old casement windows that were forever sticking, the flag waving proudly from one of the attic windows . . .

She blinked, realizing several things simultaneously: first, that the museum *had* no flag, and second, that what she had at first mistaken for one was in fact a brightly colored shirt that was fluttering through the air. As she watched, another shirt, followed quickly by a set of dress socks, and then a pair of dark trousers, catapulted out of one of the attic windows and swished softly to the ground.

"What in the . . . ?" Mr. Dumfrey stopped, clucking his tongue. "What *now*?"

A shoe came spinning out the window, and thudded directly at Pippa's feet, so she was forced to skip sideways to avoid being clobbered. Max kneeled and scooped it up.

"This is Howie's shoe," she said slowly. "And those are his shirts."

Faintly, from above, they heard Miss Fitch screech: "And *stay* out!" The second shoe followed the first, and this time it was Max who had to avoid it.

"Come on," Thomas said. "Hurry. Before she starts in on his underwear, too."

They raced up the stairs—at least Pippa, Thomas, Sam, and Max did. Mr. Dumfrey followed behind them, panting, pausing on the landings to catch his breath.

"You . . . go . . . ahead," he huffed. "I'll . . . catch up . . . soon."

In the attic, they found the performers assembled in a semicircle, motionless and stunned, watching as Miss Fitch tore through Howie's possessions, tossing them one by one out the window. Pippa had never seen Miss Fitch look so angry. Her hair, usually arranged so exactly, was wild around her shoulders—a situation so absolutely unheard-of, so unimaginable, that Pippa all at once mirrored the other performers' shocked expressions.

Miss Fitch never stopped screaming, not even for an instant.

"You filthy, two-faced louse!" Out went Howie's leather wallet and another pair of pants. The object of her abuse, Howie, was glaring at her, his face dark as a storm cloud, his fists clenched, but making no move to try to stop her. Perhaps he knew there was no point; she was moving with such speed it was almost dizzying to watch. "You slimy snake! Taking advantage—smiling and nodding and all the time plotting against us! You're sickening, truly sickening, you should be absolutely ashamed—"

"Miss Fitch." Mr. Dumfrey had finally reached the attic. Taking his hands off his knees, he straightened up, drawing in a deep gasp of air. "What's going on? What's the meaning of this?"

Miss Fitch turned to him, still trembling with anger, and clutching one of Howie's sweaters, which had obviously been next on her list for the window. "The *meaning* is that this—this—this rat has been scheming all along to shut down the museum." Howie opened his mouth, but before he could speak, she broke in, "Don't say a word. Don't even try to deny it. I have the proof right here." And she whipped out a piece of paper and passed it to Mr. Dumfrey.

Mr. Dumfrey scanned the letter quickly, his face growing paler and paler, his mouth thinning to a narrow line. Pippa closed her eyes and thought her way into his fingers, into the small space between his eyes. It was getting easier to find her way in. Suddenly, she was reading along with Mr. Dumfrey:

From: the desk of Roger Hebbsworth, Secretary, NYC Department of Criminal Justice
To: Mr. Howard Bubo, Superior President
Re: Your letters dating July 18, 22, 28, Aug 1, 6, and 15

Dear Mr. Bubo,

Thank you for your various letters concerning the children currently residing at 344 West 43rd Street. I apologize for the delay, especially in light of the increased urgency of your tone, but I was forced to bring the matter to my superior's attention.

Our conclusion is that though we have heard of Rattigan and his unfortunate experiments, we do not feel our department is qualified to investigate whether the four persons you refer to in your letter might indeed have suffered at his hands, nor to name them, as you requested, "dangerous and unlawful, and a threat to society and humanity at large." We suggest that you perhaps take the matter up with the New York City Department of Health. As for shutting down the museum, you must communicate your written request to the Better Business Bureau of New York.

Thank you for your time, and I wish you luck with your organization, Stop Unnatural Phony Entertainers from Ruining and/or Impairing Our Reputation.

Sincerely,

Roger Hebbsworth

"SUPERIOR?" was all Pippa could stutter, when she finished reading, and slid out of Dumfrey's mind and squarely back into her own. "You started a club called SUPERIOR?"

Thomas, meanwhile, had snatched the letter from Dumfrey. He, Max, and Sam crowded close together to read it.

"It's not a *club*," Howie sneered. "It's an organization

to make sure that monsters like *you* don't get to roam around and mingle with the rest of us."

With a wordless cry of rage, Miss Fitch hurled his sweater out the window. "Out!" she screeched. "Out! Get out!"

"You heard what Miss Fitch said, Howie," Mr. Dumfrey said with quietly suppressed rage. "Take your things and get out."

"Let me help," Quinn said. She sashayed over to Howie, plucked up his hairbrush and hand mirror, and then tossed both over her shoulder, out the window. "Ooops," she said, batting her eyelashes.

"Oh, Quinn. How could you? That isn't the way it's done at all." Betty hurried to Howie's aid and grabbed the delicate, ivory-tooth comb he always used. But instead of passing it to him, she ground it to splinters beneath her heel. "*That's* how it's done."

Howie's eyes were narrowed to slits, and his lips drawn back in a sneer. "Very funny," he said. "But I'm the one who's going to be laughing. This place is doomed and you know it. Even if I hadn't helped things along, you'd still be going under."

Pippa felt a chill race up her spine. "Helped things along?" she said. "What are you talking about?" But as soon as the question was out of her mouth, she knew.

"It was you," Thomas said. "You were the one who messed with Goldini's blade box. It wasn't Lash's fault at all." His face flushed. "I could have been killed."

Howie shrugged unconcernedly. "Sorry," he said, smiling, showing his big, white teeth. "Hazards of the business."

"You distracted me when I was throwing knives," Max said. "You were the one rummaging around backstage, weren't you?"

Howie turned to look at her. His eyes, Pippa saw, held nothing but cold disdain. She thought of all the weeks he'd spent giggling and whispering with Max, finding excuses to touch her elbow or back. It had all been an act, a mask he'd slipped on so he could play the part, stay nestled within the museum like an insect in a piece of fruit, intent on destroying it from the core. And she felt that this was what Rattigan was like, too. They weren't men at all, but only pretending to be. They were the monsters.

"I figured you were the weak link. You had plenty to say about the museum and Mr. Dumfrey, and Caroline and Quinn and the alligator boy, about who was unhappy, and why."

Max's face was storm colored. "You used me," she whispered.

Howie sneered. "Of course I did," he said. "Surely you didn't really think I'd be interested in a half-breed mongrel like—"

He didn't finish his sentence. With a wordless cry of rage, Sam launched himself at Howie. He hit him square in the chest with his shoulder, and they crashed to the ground, skidding straight through a bookshelf, which split cleanly in half, as if Sam were a knife and the bookshelf a lump of butter. It took Smalls, Goldini, Danny, and Dumfrey to haul Sam away from Howie. Howie's face was completely white. He was opening and closing his mouth, making no sound, like a fish dragged up onto shore.

"That's enough, son," Mr. Dumfrey said, placing a hand on Sam's shoulder.

"Yeah," Max said. "He's not worth it."

"Show's over, kid." Danny toed Howie in the ribs with his boot. Howie groaned. "Time to pack it in, or else you're the very next thing that goes out that window."

Once Howie was gone, Miss Fitch settled down and returned to her usual rigorously commanding self. Under her barked instructions, the attic was rapidly set back to order. Everyone pitched in to help, and Quinn,

Danny, Goldini, Smalls, and Betty worked particularly industriously, perhaps in an attempt to make up for the fact that they'd fallen under the spell of Howie's influence.

"SUPERIOR," Danny muttered as he picked splinters from the carpet. "SUPERIOR. Who does that little swivel-headed pip-squeak think he is?"

"The boy's got all the brains of a blunt-headed beetle," said a voice behind them. Lash, his arm in a cast, was standing in the doorway, grinning.

"Lash!" Pippa barreled toward him but he stopped her with an outstretched arm.

"Easy," he said, wincing. "I took quite a bruising."

"You came back!" Sam said, smiling for the first time all afternoon.

"Of course he did." Mr. Dumfrey was sitting in a corner armchair, surveying the work without actually lifting a finger. "I asked him to report here immediately after leaving the hospital. It's his home, after all."

Pippa felt a bubble of happiness growing inside of her. She was almost afraid to breathe or it might pop.

"Well." Miss Fitch hastily adjusted her hair. Obviously, Miss Fitch's crush had not waned in Lash's absence. "I suppose in your condition, we can't ask you to fetch a broom—"

"A broom!" Mr. Dumfrey scoffed. "Lash is one of our star performers, Miss Fitch. Surely you don't mean to waste his skill on housework. No. We're just going to have to advertise for a new janitor."

Miss Fitch stared at Mr. Dumfrey wordlessly.

Lash let out a laugh that sounded half like a wheeze. "That's all right, Miss Fitch. You can put me to work. So long as it's one-handed work."

"Nonsense!" Mr. Dumfrey cried. "You need to rest up. Just as soon as you're back, I'm putting you on the stage. Spode's death will be all over the news. Imagine what people will pay to see the man, and the whip, that killed him!" He frowned suddenly. "Miss Fitch, will you make a note to speak to the coroner about getting the whip back?"

"I don't mind sweeping, Miss Fitch," said a woman shyly. Pippa gasped as Caroline stepped out from the hallway behind Lash, clutching her little blue suitcase and looking contrite.

"Caroline!" Quinn took a step forward, then promptly collapsed in a clean faint.

"Oh, fiddle," Caroline said, her meek expression immediately replaced by one of supreme annoyance. "Of course she has to ruin *my* big moment. Did you ever meet a more selfish creature in your life?"

Quinn, reviving slightly due to the application of smelling salts to her nose, choked out, "I didn't mean to, you heartless monster. Not everything is about *you*."

"Well, it isn't about *you*, either."

"I wish you hadn't come back. . . ."

"If you don't like it, you can pack up and leave. . . ."

Pippa's bubble of happiness had expanded, swelling to include the bickering twins, and Lash with his arm in a sling, and Mr. Dumfrey already making schemes for the future, and Betty and Goldini and Smalls and even Miss Fitch. Everything was back to normal.

All of a sudden, Max let out a sudden shriek and sprang to her feet. "Kitty!" she exclaimed. "I forgot all about Kitty. He must be starving by now." Then, immediately, she clapped a hand over her mouth, as if she could physically force the words back in her mouth.

Sam stared at her warily. Howie had left a large scratch across his cheek. Pippa thought it made him look very rugged. "What are you talking about? Who's Kitty?"

Max shifted from foot to foot. "It was supposed to be a secret," she said, lowering her voice, and checking over her shoulder to make sure Miss Fitch wasn't listening. "I was planning to give him to you for your birthday. But then . . . I don't know. You were being weird and we were fighting, and then . . . it just never seemed like the right time."

"The right time for what?" Pippa said impatiently.

Max sucked in a deep breath. "Maybe it's just easier if I show you."

Thomas, Sam, and Pippa followed Max up the narrow set of stairs to the loft. Max hesitated with her hand on the doorknob. "Are you ready?" she said.

"Enough with the mystery," Pippa said, growing annoyed. "Just open the door."

Max did. First, Pippa saw nothing but a blue blanket and an empty saucer Miss Fitch had been complaining was missing for some time. But then, almost immediately, she saw a flash of pale fur.

"It's okay," Max cooed in a voice that was distinctly un-Max-like. "Don't be afraid."

Slowly, quietly, a cat emerged from the shadows, its pale whiskers trembling. Pippa recognized it immediately as the cat Freckles had rescued, the one Sam had been so desperate to befriend. Apparently it remembered his earlier efforts, because it headed straight for Sam, twining itself around his ankles and purring loudly.

"What do you think?" Max asked, hugging herself.

Sam was holding himself totally still, as if the

slightest movement might send the cat running. "I . . . I . . . This . . . You . . ."

"He loves it," Pippa clarified.

"So that's why you were stealing milk and cheese from the kitchen," Thomas said. "You were sneaking them to the cat."

"I almost told you a dozen times," Max said. "I don't know why I didn't."

"It's the best birthday gift I've ever had," Sam said, finally finding his voice. "Really."

Max looked away, fighting down a smile. But she was obviously pleased. "I haven't named him yet," she said. "I thought you might want to."

"What do you think, Sam?" Pippa said, bending down to scoop the cat up in her arms. He was as light as a feather, all softness and fur. His nose was mottled and his eyes were two different colors. He was not, she thought, the prettiest cat in the world, but he was perfect for Sam. He was perfect for the museum. "Do you have a name in mind?"

"Easy," Sam said. He reached out and very carefully stroked the cat with a finger, indicating the tiny discolored spots on the very tip of its nose. "He looks just like a Freckles to me."

Pippa smiled so hard she felt like her cheeks might

burst. She buried her nose in the cat's fur, which smelled like fresh milk and new grass.

"Welcome home, Freckles," she said, and they moved as a group downstairs, to show Mr. Dumfrey the newest addition to the family.